The Optimists

ANDREW MILLER

The Optimists

HARCOURT, INC.

Orlando Austin New York San Diego Toronto London

www.HarcourtBooks.com

Extract from *Season of Blood: A Rwandan Journey* by Fergal Keane
reproduced by kind permission of Penguin Books.
Excerpt from "In Plato's Cave" from *On Photography* by Susan Sontag.
Copyright © 1977 by Susan Sontag. Reprinted by permission of Farrar,
Straus and Giroux, LLC. Extract from *The Greek Myths,* by Robert Graves
reproduced by kind permission of Carcanet Press Ltd.
Extract from page 43 of *Tractatus Logico-Philosophicus* by Ludwig
Wittgenstein, published by Routledge, 2000 edition, reproduced
by kind permission of Thomson Publishing Services.
Excerpts from "Dream Song I" ("Huffy Henry") and "Dream Song 29"
("There Sat Down Once") from *Dream Songs* by John Berryman © 1969
by John Berryman, copyright renewed 1997 by Kate Donahue Berryman,
reprinted by Farrar, Straus and Giroux. Reproduced by kind permission
of Farrar, Strauss and Giroux.

First published in Great Britain by Hodder and Stoughton.

Library of Congress Cataloging-in-Publication Data
available upon request
ISBN 0-15-100727-6

Text set in Sabon

Printed in the United States of America

First U.S. edition
A C E G I K J H F D B

For Memuna Mansarah

Part One

It was unlike any other event I have reported on and in different ways it changed everybody – the survivors most of all, but also the doctors, the aid workers, the priests, the journalists. We had learned something about the soul of man that would leave us with nightmares long into the future. This was not death as I had seen it in South Africa, or Eritrea, or Northern Ireland. Nothing could have prepared me for the scale of what I witnessed.

Fergal Keane, *Season of Blood*

I

After the massacre at the church in N— Clem Glass flew home to London. He put his boots and the clothes from his case into a black bin-liner. He carried the bag down to one of the dustbins in the basement courtyard, then came in and scoured the skin of his hands. The next morning he heard the shouting of the dustmen as they worked their way up the street. When he looked out later he saw the empty bins lined up by the railings. He lay on the floor, watching the light shift across the ceiling. He seemed to be lost in the space between two thoughts. A whole day passed. A night. A whole week he could not have begun to account for.

It was May, and already more summer than spring. The leaves on the roadside trees were dustless, vivid, part luminous. Until late into the evening cars crawled in the traffic, windows down, music thudding. Children out of school squabbled in the street, kicked balls against a wall, sang singing games their grandparents must have known – 'Un-der the ap-ple tree, my boy-friend said to me . . .' The people in the house next door were substance abusers. They played tinny radios. In the small hours of the morning they sounded as though they were being dragged down to hell. Occasionally they threw stuff out of the windows. A fortnight after Clem's return they threw a ten-litre tin of purple paint from an upstairs window. The tin split and an inch-deep purple slick spread across two square yards of paving-stones and gutter. The sun put a crust on it but the paint below stayed moist. Soon there were purple footsteps, each print a little fainter than the last. There was even a set of purple dog tracks that circled a lamp-post and disappeared towards the Harrow Road.

The substance abusers were delighted. They gathered on the steps of their house waving bottles and laughing like the troops of some victorious rebel army. A week later they threw out a tin of orange paint, a huge broken egg yolk. Clem's Domke bag was by the door. The Nikon was in there, the Leica, leads, flash units, lenses, twenty or thirty rolls of film. Looking at the egg yolk cooking on the purple pavement he thought of how he would capture it: the response was automatic, a professional reflex, nothing more. The cameras would stay in their bag until he had the energy to decide what to do with them. Vaguely, he imagined taking them back to Kingsley's and selling them. The Leica was worth a lot; the Nikon, his old workhorse, worth something, a month's rent perhaps.

On an afternoon at the turn of the month the substance abusers were evicted. Two police vans arrived, then council workers came with steel screens and began to seal up the building. They covered the wooden door with a steel skin. The bay windows were wound in steel. By the front railings they left a small pile of personal belongings – a sleeping-bag, a hairdryer, some plastic flowers, a crutch. The substance abusers, the women in particular, roared and shook their fists. Clem watched them from his window on the first floor. He admired their passion; he wondered if they knew how futile it was, or if it was that, the pointlessness, that was the root of their passion. When it was over, the council workers left and the police climbed back into their vans. The evicted abusers, still gesticulating frantically, stumped off in twos and threes towards the various shelters and off-licences of the parish. A few of the locals came out and there was some laughter. At dusk, Clem went down to the street. The Grove was almost quiet. He looked at the house, then crouched and ran his fingers over the remains of the paint. Its surface now was smooth and hard as varnish, slightly uneven, mostly smooth. Then, at the edge of the slick, where the paint gave way to the mid-greys of paving-stone, he noticed the faint but very precise skeletal outline of a leaf and, using the flame of his lighter, found others there, scattered around it, thread-delicate prints of dead leaves, half hidden, like drawings under tissue paper. He tried to work out how such images could possibly have been fixed there. Last autumn's rain; last autumn's sun. The weight of thousands of pressing feet. The energy released by decaying matter. The slight absorbency of stone. He examined them until his lighter was too hot to use any more. He remembered Fox Talbot's calotype of a leaf; a world-amazing picture: calotype from the Greek for beauty. He knelt. Ahead of him the metal house glittered in the lamplight. He bowed his head. Would something happen now? Could something be let go of? It was like waiting to be sick. He clenched his teeth, touched the stubborn dryness of his eyes. Behind him, a pair of children spying on him from between two parked cars began to giggle. He struggled to his feet, went up the stairs to his flat, and lay again on the living-room carpet.

At some point after nightfall the phone on his desk started to ring. After five rings the answer-machine came on. His message said he was out of the country. The machine bleeped. There was a pause in which Clem thought he could hear the crying of seabirds, then his father said, 'It's just me. Call when you're back, will you?' Another pause, then: 'Thank you.'

2

In T-shirt, jeans, old brogues, he went on walks that lasted most of the day. The direction was not important. Turn left and he came to the houses of the rich; to the right was the railway bridge, the canal, the council blocks, the supermarket. Under the green girders of the bridge the rails ran like a firebreak through the heart of the city. In the moments when no trains were passing the scene was oddly tranquil. There were young trees at the verges of the track, and tough-looking bushes with gaudy flowers that grew out of the embankment walls or thrust their leaves through the ballast stones. It was not unusual to look down on a half-dozen butterflies, drifting over the tracks like wastepaper.

The canal he learned to avoid. The water was too still, too black: he was afraid of what might appear in it. It would not take much. A plastic bag crumpled into the form of a face. A piece of driftwood mistaken for a hand.

He ate wherever he happened to find himself, whatever was near. A Portuguese place just off the Grove, a Turkish café in Notting Hill, a couscous restaurant on Golborne Road. He ate, paid, spoke to no one other than the waiters. Each afternoon he went to a newsagent to look at the front pages of the papers. In the time before – and this was how he thought of his life before the church at N—, 'the time before' – he had read two, sometimes three newspapers a day, valuing the sense that he knew what was going on in the world and that it was possible to know. Since coming back the news did not convince him as it used to, not because he imagined they were making it up (though he had been around journalists long enough to know that that was not unusual) but because the world they described no longer matched the one he carried in his head, a place it was hard to say anything rational about at all. He looked now only to see if there was a story from Africa, from the aftermath of the killing, from the fall-out. If there was, he scanned for a mention of the Bourgmestre, but was always more re-lieved than disappointed when he found nothing. He wasn't ready yet for Sylvestre Ruzindana. He was a long way from being ready.

He became one of the people who go to the cinema in the middle of the day. He had an ideal film in mind, some-thing with a few songs, an unimportant ending. At the cinema in Shepherd's Bush they were showing *Breakfast at Tiffany's* and he went to see it, sitting among pen-sioners and the unemployed, content until Hepburn, strumming her little guitar, sang 'Moon River' in a voice that was awkward and beautiful and piercing. He stumbled out, blundering past the dreaming usherette and hurrying home, astonished at himself. He had more luck at the Coronet in Notting Hill. An American high-school comedy, like an update of *Happy Days*. He watched it three times on three consecutive afternoons. There was nothing in the film to attend to, nothing that needed to be followed or admired. After each showing the swing-door of the cinema scraped the whole thing from his mind like bones from a dinner plate, leaving only a memory of sitting and the knowledge that for ninety minutes he had been safe.

On fine days he sometimes went to the park and dozed on the grass or sat on a bench observing, without lust, the girls tanning their legs, the young nannies, Scandinavians, Filipinas, playing with the children of their wealthy employers. To be without desire – as he had been now for weeks – was disorientating. He watched women as perhaps he would watch them in his dotage when desire had burned down to a spoonful of warm ashes (if that's how it was for old men. Was it?). But at his age – he had turned forty in January – to live without desire was like the dream he had had throughout his teenage years in which, belonging neither quite to the living nor entirely to the dead, he slowly faded, each moment a little less visible, less able to make himself heard above the world's noise, a kind of drowning in air. It was another symptom, of course, though not one he had been expecting. Was it time he looked for help? Time he spoke to someone? He had not even called Frank Silverman in New York, though they had exchanged home numbers, writing in the back of a careening taxi on the way to the airbase. Silverman was older, more experienced. Different. Tougher? A veteran with a half-inch of grenade casing in his back, a souvenir of the Lebanon. No stranger to chaos then, to human savagery, but a man who had seemed – seemed before they went to the church that night – inured to it by depths of cynicism extraordinary even for a journalist.

And he had a wife, a writer called Shelley-Anne, who,

he said, wrote novels about lonesome women, books that sold by the container load. In the bar of the Bellville Hotel, drinking at a table with Clem, Major Nemo and two Egyptians from UNHCR, Silverman had boasted that her entire career was a rebuke to him for his wandering over the face of the earth, his philandering. Would she help him if he needed it? Would she want to? Despite the picture he had drawn, the marriage had sounded good, worn-in in the right way, and exactly the kind of refuge that he, Clem Glass, had so recklessly failed to provide for himself. His neediness now disgusted him a little. The longing for tenderness, for what had been opened (a view, a wound) to be closed with the stroke of a hand. It was becoming harder and harder to recognise himself, and each twilight as the street-lights came on and the air hung blue and orange between the dirty buildings, he struggled to regain comfortable understandings that he knew in his heart were gone for ever.

3

'Hi! Shelley-Anne and Silverman can't get to the phone right now. Leave your name and a number and we'll get back to you just as soon as we can.' There was a four-second choral burst of 'Canada Oh Canada!' – Silverman's drollery – then the tone. Clem replaced the receiver. The wife had a young voice and the message sounded as if she had recorded it in a hurry between doing interesting things. He didn't think she had sounded lonely or angry.

He tried again an hour later. 'Hi! Shelley-Anne and Silverman can't get to the phone right now . . .'

4

An incident:

Walking on Portobello Road, a Sunday evening around eleven, eleven thirty, he heard a woman in one of the unlit doorways on the far side of the street, a choked lamenting that grew louder as he passed, abruptly ceased, then started again, the sound directed now to the middle of his back. From the instant he became aware of her, his mouth had dried and his heart begun a pounding that made it hard to breathe. But what was he afraid of? Half the streets in London were haunted by the grief-stricken, the chronically lost, yet he found her noise unbearable and quickened his step. She followed him, gaining on him and calling piteously until he stopped. They were outside a kebab and chicken shop. The men inside were wiping down and getting ready to shut. By the glow of a neon sign, a rooster, he saw that she was in her late teens or early twenties. She stood in front of him, trembling, her hands out-held, the mascara in a black web beneath her eyes. She was trying to explain something, what had happened to her. At first, so broken was her speech, he didn't know what language she was using, then realised it was Spanish. Several times he heard her say '*violar*' or '*violada*'. She was holding out her phone to him. He took it from her, called the police and told the operator that a young woman had been attacked. He gave the address of the kebab and chicken shop. When he was asked for his name he finished the call and gave the girl back her phone. She seemed to be sinking. She stood as a child stands when it needs the toilet, or like someone who has been struck hard in the belly. The men from the food shop were watching now, two of them in long grey aprons. Clem tried to think of the Spanish for 'They are coming', but after a few seconds remembered the verb to go. '*Me voy*,' he said, and turned from her. He thought she might come after him again but she didn't. Perhaps she couldn't.

At Faraday Road he stopped and looked back along the track of street-lamps. The place he had left her was beyond the curve of the road and impossible to see. He looked at his watch, looked up at the blank houses around him. How long would the police take to reach her? The nearest station was only a few minutes' drive away. Should he not have heard a siren by now? And what if they didn't come? If he had garbled the address or they thought he was a hoaxer? His blood was calmer now and it struck him clearly for the first time that he had abandoned her, a violated girl. He, who had once assumed himself to be sided with the decent and the brave, what was he to think now? What duty could be plainer than the care of a stranger attacked in the street? He began to run, but when he arrived at the shop the lights were off and the street outside deserted. He went on towards Westbourne Grove, looking carefully down the cross-streets. Several times he heard footsteps or saw someone striding quickly away from him, but no one who resembled the girl. Had the men taken her in? Done what he had failed to do? He went back and pressed his face to the window. A shape – one darkness erupting from another – moved across the floor towards him. He froze, called 'Christ!', then saw it was a dog, squat, black-pelted, watching him through the glass of the door, its eyes flecked blue and yellow as though the sockets were blunt holes down which the creature's electricity were dimly visible.

He went home. There was a moon up: a bright half-moon reflecting off the steel front of the empty house. He stood on the steps of his own house and smoked a cigarette. A night bus went by. An ambulance. He thought about little Odette Semugeshi, a survivor of the massacre whose photograph he had taken at the Red Cross hospital when Silverman interviewed her. Her head had been heavily bandaged, the wound betraying itself in a watery pink line that ran from her forehead to the middle of her skull. She spoke French in a slow, toneless voice. '*Et puis . . . et puis . . .*' The doctor, fearing the child was still concussed, had been reluctant to let them speak to her and stood beside them ready to end the interview should Silverman push too hard. It was a beautiful morning. Through the open door of the office a dozen other children sat quietly in the dust beneath an oleander tree. When the interview was finished Odette went out to join them. 'Doesn't she ever cry?' asked Silverman.

'In time,' said the doctor. He was Swiss and had been in the country for ten days. 'Too much sorrow makes the heart like a stone.'

'It's how the heart survives,' said Silverman.

The doctor agreed, and had looked at them then, at Clem and Silverman, knowing – for Silverman had told him on the walk from his office – that they had been the first journalists at the site. Fleetingly, it seemed he might take an interest in them, go through some questionnaire on trauma, check them over, but he was visibly tired and already, perhaps, doing more than he knew how to properly manage. He shook their hands, raised an arm in wry farewell, and left them to find their own way out.

5

Two days later (he had seen nothing in the local papers about the Spanish girl; no yellow crime-scene signs had appeared on the streets) Clem spent thirty minutes searching for the telephone number of Zara Jones, a freelance publicist he had slept with in March. He remembered her writing it on the back of a receipt that he had put into his wallet then, evidently – for it was no longer in his wallet – put somewhere else. Looking on the kitchen table, a place where many things were put down and forgotten, he found, dispersed among a sediment of old newspapers and magazines, curious fragments from the weeks and months before Africa. Letters, cuttings, invitations. Lists of things to do and buy. A note, scribbled on the corner of an envelope – *Yellow fever, tetanus, malaria. Cholera?* There were contact-sheets from a job in Derry in February. A Christmas card from Clare – Brueghel's hunters – her message: *Dundee under six inches of snow!*

The receipt was in the lockable metal box beside his desk where he kept, in loose order, anything connected to the business side of his life. It was a receipt from a cab company he sometimes used to get to Heathrow. On the back of it she had written her mobile number in purple ink, then her name, followed by a question mark and an exclamation.

He sat at the desk and called her. He did not quite believe he would get through to her, had no clear idea what he would say if he did, but when, after six or seven rings, she answered, he was surprised by how easy it was, how quickly they assumed the necessary manner.

'How are you?' she asked.

'OK. And you?'

'I'm fine,' she said. 'Are you in London?'

'Yes.'

'When did you get back?'

He lied, then asked if she was around in the evening. She said there was an event in the West End, some awards ceremony she had to attend, something dull but unavoidable. 'We could have a drink before,' she said, 'if you want. Do you know the bar at the Soho Theatre?'

'Dean Street?'

'I'll be there at six.'

He had met her at a party for the launch of David Singer's new book of photographs. This was the same Singer who had made his name with pictures of London that made it appear like Calcutta in the rain – sink estates, homelessness, pensioners in high-rise hovels. Images with the formality of Victorian bromide prints, filling a half page in the *Mirror* or the *Guardian*, or in those papers abroad that wanted to remind their readers of how empires ended. Then nothing for years. Then this, *Overworld* (was some pun intended?), a book of subtly coloured abstracts, colour bleeding into colour, the whole thing performed within the walls of his studio in Little Venice. It was art; it would, at least, be sold like art. At the party, Singer was dressed in a chocolate brown Italian suit, a man suddenly glamorous in his mid-sixties, a young wife with him, heavily pregnant, a roomful of people who admired him and wished to be close to him. Prints of his photographs, two yards high, lined the walls like Rothkos. The former work, the former wife, the old ideals were not on view. The story was how he had reinvented himself: now he was the subject of other people's pictures. He shook hands, kissed cheeks, swilled champagne from a flute. To Clem, he had the look of a man who was growing to hate himself.

Zara Jones was good at her job. When she walked up to Clem she knew who he was. She complimented him on his pictures (behind the lines) from Desert Storm. She had also seen a photo-essay on the lives of Sri Lankan fishermen that he had done for a Swedish magazine. '*So* beautiful,' she said, without specifying what it was she had found beautiful – the people or the pictures or both. He thanked her, though declined her invitation to meet Singer. He asked her to stay and talk to him. She said she would try to come back later, smiled, and went off to ask someone else if they would like to spend a few moments with David.

He watched her, spied on her for the rest of the evening, then tagged along to the post-party party where Singer got drunk and his wife told Clem that her nipples seeped continuously. After the restaurant closed there was a complicated game with cabs – who was south of the river, who was north. Zara lived in one of the squares behind Oxford Street and Clem went with her, kissing her in the taxi, her tongue tasting of vodka and seafood and cigarettes. Her flat was several times the size of his own, her father some Croesus in the development world. On the bedside table she cut four lines of cocaine with the edge of her AmEx gold card. When he had undressed her she said she was bleeding a little. He said it didn't matter, and later on stood in the brilliant white bigness of her bathroom wiping blood from his thighs with damp tissues, grinning at himself in the mirror.

The next time was at his place. The central heating had packed up, she didn't like the food he'd cooked, and they argued about politics – her right (her father's right) against his left (his mother's). The sex was perfunctory. After it, they lay awake for hours, each of them disturbed by the other's slightest movement.

The last time was in a hotel on Brighton seafront, a clear evening, blue stars over the sea, the beach dotted with the lamps and little fires of the night anglers. Though Clem was eleven years older than her and had grown up in entirely different circumstances, they bent their histories until their lives assumed a certain likeness. Both had lost their mothers – Clem at twelve, Zara at seventeen. Both had older sisters, both spoke French, both believed the other to be in some way remarkable, if only for the colour and clarity of the eyes. They sat up in the hotel bar getting amorous on drink, and when upstairs they fucked (the headboard clattering the flowered wallpaper) there was an excitement, an urgency that had felt to Clem like the beginning of something good. But the next afternoon, sleep-poor, fogged from the drinking, they parted at the station in London without any firm arrangement to meet again. Three days later she left on a nationwide tour with a snooker player who had written his memoirs. By the time she was back, Clem was packing for Africa. The affair – if that was what it amounted to – already seemed the kind of interlude he had had many times before, an event without much history or consequence. It was then that he must have filed the receipt in the metal box beside his desk, without first bothering to make a copy of her number.

He arrived outside the theatre at a quarter past six. Zara was already there, sitting on a stool at the curve of the bar. He watched her through the plate-glass doors, her image (her back straight as a dancer's) a still point against the reflected flow of the street. She was sipping a clear drink from a tall glass. She shook out a cigarette; the barman lit it for her and she smiled at him. She had pulled her hair back tightly from her face, a style Clem hadn't seen her use before and that made her look thinner, older too, an older woman's chic. She turned, briefly scanned the street, but looked away without having seen him. He wondered how long she would wait for him. Another ten minutes? Another twenty? There were only a half-dozen others in the bar: the playgoers would not start arriving until later. The barman spoke to her again, coming on to her perhaps, or going through the motions out of professional chivalry. A hand plucked at the sleeve of Clem's jacket. There was a man behind him, bearded, his clothes bright with dirt. He excused himself, then explained to Clem that he was gathering the fare for a bus to Farringdon. He had friends in Farringdon and would find some relief there. He asked if Clem knew what he meant. Clem gave him the change from his pockets then started walking back up Dean

Street. He turned into Wardour Street and stopped at the first pub he came to. The air inside was bottle-brown, the customers mostly office workers carrying on their office life in another place. He stayed, drinking steadily at a table on his own. When he came out, two-thirds of the street was draped in shadow, but the tops of the buildings on the eastern side were still brilliantly lit, each detail – the grimed bricks, the blank windows, the uneven lines of moss – vivid and lovely. On Windmill Street he went into another pub. The music there was much louder and the customers did not look like people who ever went to offices. A sign in the toilets read: *Thieves operate on these premises.* In the bar, a screen was showing music videos, which he watched for a long time with great attention before going out to one of the phone boxes by Shaftesbury Avenue. He had some idea of calling Zara's mobile but rang instead a number printed on one of the cards stuck to the inside of the box. The woman who answered put him in mind of an actress (he couldn't recall the name), a comedienne who specialised in old-fashioned Cockney types with fruity voices. She called him 'deary', described the girl she was selling, and gave him the address of a building on the Edgware Road. When she asked for his name he thought he should make one up but his mind was blank, and in the end, after a pause that must have sounded as though he were making one up, he gave his own name, twice.

He took out the money he would need from a cashpoint on Regent Street, then walked slowly along Oxford Street, imagining that some distraction would lead him towards a better hour. He had paid for sex once before, a hotel in Washington DC five years ago, an autumn dusk when, suddenly afraid of his own company, he had looked in the phone book under 'Escorts', and known, at the girl's discreet knocking – known for an appreciable stretch of seconds – an entirely normal happiness, as though the sound announced the half-expected visit of a friend, and not the advent of some utter stranger for whom a car was waiting in the street below.

The building on the Edgware Road was a mansion-block between a coffee bar and an Arab newsagent's. He rang the bell, the catch was released remotely, and he went inside. In the corridor ahead were rows of white doors, all shut. The lift was out of order and he started on the stairs, concrete steps with a metal rail, a fire-door on each floor giving access to another corridor. On the fourth floor he tapped at one of the white doors. It was opened, quickly, and he stepped into a small hall-way, empty except for a single chair with its back against the wall. A woman, whose voice he recognised from the phone call, invited him to sit down. She asked if he wanted a drink of orange juice. He said he didn't. She gave him the laminated card she was carrying. 'The young lady won't be long,' she said (not a comedienne now but a shopkeeper in a failing business). She retreated to her room, to the low-volume bubbling of a television. The card she had given Clem was a menu of services. The cheapest was *hand relief*; the most expensive – though none was particularly expensive – described simply as *Sex*. He placed the card under the chair. A few minutes later the door on his left was opened. A girl, a young woman like any he might have passed in the street half an hour earlier, smiled at him and led him into her place of work, a small, low-ceilinged room with a chest of drawers under the window, and next to the bed a lamp with a pink, tasselled shade. Beside the lamp was a radio, a bottle of baby oil, and the ready-torn foil envelope of a condom.

'I am Irena,' she said.

'Clem.'

'Claim?'

'Clem. After Clement Attlee. My mother was a Fabian.'

She nodded, perfectly used, it seemed, to not understanding what people said, perfectly untroubled by it. She was wearing a tight black dress, and a pair of white slippers of the sort nurses in old-time sanatoria might have worn, and which Clem guessed she had brought with her from whatever country she had recently come from. He gave her the money. She counted it, thanked him, stashed the notes in a drawer.

'I express myself through dance,' she said. She turned on the radio and twisted the dial until she found a tune she could move to. Clem sat on the bed and watched her. She closed her eyes, swung her hips, ran her hands over her little breasts. Her favourite move was a spin with which, having danced a moment with her back to him, she would suddenly turn, as though towards a bank of lights.

When the track finished she switched off the radio and stepped out of her dress. She was wearing panties but no bra. She took off his jacket and undid the buttons of his shirt. When she started trying to undo the belt on his jeans, tugging at it, he said he would do it himself. She reached for the baby oil. Clem lay on the bed in his underpants. She asked if he was shy. He said no and took off his pants. She turned him on to his belly, knelt astride him and rubbed his back with the oil. When his back was coated he turned over and she smeared his shoulders while rocking herself against his crotch. He touched her breasts. She clambered off him, pushed her panties down her skinny thighs, and rolled the condom over his half erect cock. She had shaved her pubic hair to an inch wide strip but had burned the delicate skin there with the razor. She stretched beside him, her legs spread. When he touched the opening of her vagina she was completely dry. He leaned over to kiss her. 'No tongue,' she said quickly, tightening her face as though he might bite her. He sighed and leaned back, then moved down the bed until his head lay between her breasts and he was listening, drowsily, to the patter of her heart. Was this what he had come for? Her skin, despite the trace of some inexpensive body spray, smelt good, and was cool and soft against his cheek. For a minute she let him lie there, even, briefly, stroking his hair with a stray, forgetful strumming of her fingers, but the mood, the posture, was inappropriate, unpaid for, unbuyable, and she pushed free of him, swinging herself to the edge of the bed and scooping her dress from the floor. 'What are you doing?' she demanded, scowling at him and holding the dress up in front of her. 'You are sick? You are sick, or what is it?'

He stopped for more drinks at a place on Baker Street, then hurried towards the West End thinking he might somehow come across Zara 'bored' at her event and persuade her to sit down with him for an hour. He would not try to explain things to her. He would not tell her about the Bourgmestre, or invite her to the flat to see the photographs he had there, pictures he had never sent to the agency because no newspaper could ever publish them. He would suggest a club (she would know one) and perhaps they would even dance. Together, they would perform a trick with time, carrying on as though they had just stepped off the train from Brighton. He would pull the thorn from his eye. *She* would pull the thorn from his eye. He would get free of this thing before he no longer knew how to.

In Leicester Square the pubs were emptying. A crowd, hooting and singing and scuffling, shambled through the brightly lit doors of the Underground station. He had no idea where Zara's event was. He stood at a street corner and looked up and down as if, through an open window somewhere, he might see them all gathered round a table. For the first time it occurred to him how very drunk he was, how addled. He was not going to meet Zara; he would not, he thought, even be able to call her again, and it was almost a relief to realise this, to have for a moment the impression of lucidity. There was nothing for him to do now but find his way to the end of the night, and he carried on towards the river, breaking on to the Embankment just above Waterloo Bridge and turning right, following the curve of the river towards Westminster. He ran at first, then jogged (through Parliament Square, along Old Palace Yard, Millbank), then walked, heavily, as though at each step the pavement descended a little in front of him. Across the river from Battersea he stopped and leaned against the wall. He felt dizzy, hollow. He wondered when he had last eaten anything. He needed a bench, a garden, some little grass square to lie down in. On the road behind him a taxi door thumped shut. A man and a thin, tottering woman went on to the jetty where the houseboats were moored. After a few minutes Clem followed them. He walked to a boat in the darkness at the far end of the jetty and stood there, poised for a challenge. When none came he stepped aboard. He went to the bows and squatted on a hatch cover. He was only some twenty yards from the bank but the air was different here, touched with the chill of the water. And there were sounds, secretive though pin-clear from the middle of the river – birds, the splash of an oar, the tide streaming against the piers of the bridge. As his eyes adjusted he moved around the deck. The cabin doors were padlocked but in the stern of the boat he found the folding cushion from a lounger, a ragged thing that smelt of tanning lotion and diesel fuel. He laid it in the cockpit by the cabin doors, smoked a last cigarette (the ember hidden in the cup of his hands) then lay with his jacket as a blanket, shivered for a while, and slept.

When he woke, a pair of herring gulls were standing on the edge of the cabin roof, large birds on wiry legs, their feathers combed by the dawn breeze. It was high water, slack water, the river lapping against the stone banks, two kinds of grey. He folded the cushion, put on his jacket and stepped over the rail on to the jetty. In the windows of some of the other houseboats orange lights were shining, but no one was out on deck to see him leave.

He was cold. He thrust his hands into his pockets, walked up Beaufort Street, then along the empty paving of the Kings Road until he reached Sloane Square. The station there was still shut. He found a café at the side of it where a man possessing the bearing of a medieval Doge served bacon sandwiches and mugs of tea to taxi drivers and insomniacs. For half an hour he distracted himself with an out-of-date listings magazine, then went back to the station and took a train to Notting Hill.

As it grew lighter it began to rain. He walked down Portobello Road, but not wishing to pass in front of the kebab and chicken shop (might not one of the men already be there, setting up? Might not the *dog* be there?) he turned off and walked up the Grove. He was nearly home when he paused outside St Michael's to pick up the flowers that had fallen from the war-memorial crucifix: hot-house lilies dripping with London rain that he threaded again between the cross and the figure's bowed wooden neck. There were often flowers here, though he had never seen who brought them. One of the local Spanish or Portuguese, someone used to the dressing of images; or the old priest perhaps, a High Church relict who drank most nights in the pub across the road wearing a boot-length coat of ecclesiastical black.

There had been a Christ above the door of the church in N—, Christ the shepherd in white marble, ten, fifteen feet high, the arms outstretched above the murdered congregation. An object of such utter inutility, dumb, wicked in its deceiving, it had begun in Clem an irrational rage (for what did he, Nora's son, expect of stone?), an anger he was no longer properly tracking, and that moved through his blood like a virus. Yet towards this small wooden figure, half grey from years of soot-fall, he felt an ill-defined affection. He could not have cared less what it stood for, was *intended* to stand for. What he liked was the way it looked, the limbs slender and well carved, the buoyancy of it, the way, between the brick wall of the church and the traffic, it possessed some quality of weakness endured, of suffering endured, that was purely human and subtly instructive.

At the flat he showered the scum of baby oil from his skin, dressed in clean clothes, made coffee, and sat at his desk, smoking. The LED on the phone blinked in sequences of three. When he finished the cigarette he pressed the playback button. The first call was from Shelley-Anne. 'Silverman's taken off for a while,' she said (a voice with a sleepless night inside it). 'I think he may have gone up to Toronto. Do you have his cellphone?' She read out the number and asked him to remind Silverman to call home. 'How are *you* doing?' she asked pointedly.

The second caller, who he guessed was Zara, had left no message, just a brief, quizzical silence, abruptly ended.

The last call was from the island. 'Hello again, son. Sorry to keep missing you. The thing is we need to talk about Clare. There's some urgency in fact or I wouldn't keep bothering you like this. I know how busy you are. Anyway, that's all, really. It's just that I'm very worried. Right-oh. I'll go now. It's the old trouble, Clem . . .'

6

As they moved northwards, the carriages, half empty in London, began to fill up. The country flew past them. Hills, hay fields, a motorway, a caravan park; a spire topped with a knot of light where the sun flashed off a weathervane. Then the long deceleration into cities he had passed through a score of times without ever knowing more of them than the view from a train window.

Across the aisle from Clem, four soldiers on leave, their names stencilled on kitbags, drank lager out of cans and played cards (game after stoic game). Clem's bag was on the floor by his feet, a shoulder-bag with a pair of tattered airline tags tied to the strap. He had packed lightly: a clean shirt, a summer sweater, his wash-things, a fold-up waterproof. He did not intend to be away for more than a few days. He would see his father, then, presumably, his sister. A night on the island, a night in Dundee. It was Saturday. By Monday evening, Tuesday at the latest, he would be back in London.

He walked down the train looking for the smoking compartment, finding it a few carriages further back, a helix of blue smoke under the roof. Where he sat someone had left their newspaper behind, a broadsheet, and he scanned the foreign pages, noting a photograph (cars on fire) by Toby Rose, a young photographer he knew in London, a true student of the extreme who, had he been at the Bellville that night as the rumours began, the first talk of a fresh outrage somewhere beyond the limits of the blacked-out capital, would gladly have taken Clem's place beside Silverman in the Land Rover.

He folded the paper and thrust it under the seat. The train was running a little easterly now, towards Newcastle and the coast. The ticket inspector came through, then two Japanese girls with packaged cakes and cups of coffee from the buffet. He lit a cigarette and, as he smoked, distracted himself by trying to work out his father's age. It was years since either had remembered the other's birthday, but after a few minutes of calculation he decided his father must be seventy-seven or seventy-eight. If he had retired at sixty-five then he had lived at the house on the island for more than ten years, during which time Clem reckoned he had visited slightly less than once a year, perhaps eight times in total. To these visits there was a particular routine. Clem would arrive at Berwick on the early train from King's Cross; his father would meet him at the station; they would shake hands and walk together down the hill into the town, going into one of the hotels for lunch. Two hours later, after a conversation consisting mainly of Clem giving polite answers to polite enquiries about his work, they would walk back to the station, shake hands again and say goodbye. Clem had never stayed at the house on the island, though he knew it had guest rooms for the use of male relatives (females had to make their own arrangements). He had never asked to stay, and after the second trip his father had stopped suggesting it, knowing, perhaps, that to raise it a third time would have brought into plain language his son's continuing exasperation at his 'withdrawal' from the world, a retreat that Clem had always considered extravagant, baffling, perverse even. Clare, though capable of heroic intolerances of her own, had argued the other line, reminding Clem (on those occasions when they still bothered to discuss it) that their father, after his own discreet fashion, had been a church-goer all his life; that when Nora died it was his faith that had kept him strong; that without his work – most of his career had been spent at the British Aerospace plant in Filton as an engineer, a specialist in turbines – there was nothing substantial to keep him in Bristol. A few friends and neighbours, the house itself. It was not enough.

'But a monastery!'

'It's not a monastery. It's a community.'

'They're lay monks, Clare.'

'A group of like-minded men, that's all. A brother-hood.'

The brotherhood had a brochure. William Glass sent copies of it to his son and daughter in the week after he moved to the island, a folded photocopied sheet with a sketch of the house on the front, Theophilus House, named, so the text explained, after the Roman lawyer who taunted St Dorothy on her way to martyrdom, asking her to send him the fruits of the garden of heaven. Twenty elderly men there given over to God, widowers mostly, retired men of all backgrounds. A former pub-lican, an ex-policeman, a schoolmaster, a naval officer. They rose at five, a scene Clem had sometimes imagined to himself, the old men like wraiths, rising in the dark and dispersing to chores, devotions. He supposed that he too would have to get up at five, though he had no intention of *sharing in the life of the community*, even for a morning. He had agreed to stay because of how his father had sounded on the phone on Friday: the sighs, the repetitions, the frank admission of helplessness.

He had, he told Clem, received a letter from Clare, a frightening letter, and completely out of the blue. He had had it for weeks and must have read it fifty times without being any nearer to knowing what to do about it. He would, of course, let Clem see it as soon as he came up. He very much wanted Clem's opinion on it.

'So you haven't seen her?' asked Clem. 'You haven't spoken to her?'

But he had not been able to! He had been *expressly* forbidden! The only contact he had had was with a colleague of hers, Finola Fiacc, Irish, something at the university, an administrator, he thought, supposed to be helping, supposed to be a kind of go-between, but apparently intent on obstructing him.

'I have been trying to remember,' he said, at the end of the call, 'everything that happened the last time. Did we let her down in some way? Did I let her down?'

'That was a long time ago, Dad.'

'Yes, I know. But still, I'm trying to remember.'

Some lapse? Some failure of care? What use would it be to remember it now? What could be done about it? Clem that winter – the winter of the 'last time' – had been twenty years old, a student in the humanities department at Sheffield, but already restless, already disenchanted with French philosopher-kings, English Marxists, American feminists (*Wuthering Heights* as a study in menstruation). It was the winter he met Professor Lamb, whose office walls were hung with large board-mounted black-and-white photographs of the Biafran war and Vietnam, the first Don McCullins Clem had seen, certainly the first he had ever *looked* at. Lamb had had a line Clem liked about profundity lying in surfaces and, alert to his student's interest, had introduced Clem to Dorothy Lange's portraits of Depression-era USA, Bill Brandt's work for *Picture Post*, Capa's civil war Spain, Weegee's streets of New York. There, in the big-format books on a table in the library, in the exhausted back of the Jarrow coal-searcher, the flung-out arms of the loyalist soldier dying on a hill outside Córdoba, were truth and beauty, life in the raw, and all that poetry of the actual Clem had not even known himself to possess an appetite for. Almost at once he had been moved to emulation, buying, with money inherited from Nora, a second-hand Nikon – the weighty and indestructible F2. He learned to develop and print in the university darkrooms, grew used to the stink of chemicals, began to talk, breezily and much too often, about Reality, believing then – and how happy it had made him! – that taking photographs was an honest and straightforward way of engaging with it.

Clare was in France doing a postgraduate year at the Louvre. The first Clem knew of her illness (that time as this, a phone-call from his father) she was already in hospital in Paris, though it was another two weeks before he understood that she had not gone down with some infection, some unpleasant but common enough mishap of the organism she was young and strong enough to shake off quickly. She was brought home to Bristol and spent a month at the psychiatric hospital in Barrow Gurney, a second month as an outpatient. Among family and friends the idea took hold that something must have happened in Paris to 'trigger' the illness, and because it was Paris the assumption was made that the trigger was a romantic difficulty. What better cause than love? What more *excusable* one? But Clare had offered nothing to support this theory. To Clem, six or eight months later, she said she had been 'run down', that Paris had 'over-whelmed' her. The vagueness was defensive perhaps, but he had been left with the impression that she herself had no special insight into what had occurred or, if she did, was not prepared to share it with him. As she grew stronger it was easier to forget. Soon, it was hardly spoken of, and never in front of her. She had gone to Paris, she had come back. Even the diagnosis, a language not at all about the flush of young love, was allowed to sink to the bottom of the collective memory. She returned to her studies and thrived, a slightly different Clare, but one whose alteration was visible only to those few who had known her intimately from the beginning. Clare Glass became Dr Glass, an attender of conferences, a giver of papers, a recipient of grants and awards. Every third or fourth year she had a book published by an academic press. Clem had them all in London, though other than the first, *Delacroix and the Economics of Excitement*, and half of the second, *The Fallacies of Hope: J. M. W. Turner in Italy*, he had not read them; nor, he thought, did she particularly expect him to. They were given as a courtesy and he was glad to have them, with their painterly covers, their sober commentaries. Under, he supposed, their mother's influence – though Nora had been impatient of 'ivory towers' and might have preferred Clare to be an ordinary schoolteacher – her writing, what he had seen of it, was strung on a frame of sophisticated left-leaning politics. But beneath the scholarship, the picking over of the bones, the civilised dryness, was an abiding passion for a certain kind of sensual visual luxury. Her public style – her clothes, hair, appetites – had to them all an obvious austerity, yet the paintings she wrote about were soaked in moonlight, drama, in chaos even, a tension Clem had always thought to be a way into her, though he had taken the thought no further.

The last time he had seen her, the previous autumn, she had been guest curator for an exhibition at the Courtauld. They had met at the gallery and gone to dinner at the Chelsea Arts Club. At forty-four, she still drew her share of admiring glances from the men at the other tables, drew them more than before perhaps, an allure that had as much to do with her gravitas, her mid-life swagger, as with the length of her legs, her good skin. After dinner he had walked her to the house of a monied girlfriend of hers in Tite Street, someone she had been at St Anne's with. He had kissed her cheek, then waited at the bottom of the house steps until she was welcomed into the yellow light of the hall and had turned to wave to him.

And now this! 'The old trouble', back after twenty years. Out of the blue? What would people blame this time? What did Dundee suggest?

On a hill to the right he saw the rigid wings of Gormley's giant seraph. They would be in Newcastle soon. Berwick was less than an hour away. What now? He needed a view on all this, a plan of action, but had neither. Reason wasn't helping much. Reason merely told him he was in no condition to help others. It was his heart he needed now and his heart had locked fast the night he had straddled the dead with his lenses. To whom, then, should he explain his unfitness? To his father? To Clare? He could leave the train in Newcastle, of course, make up some story about work, a job he couldn't turn down, but he knew he wouldn't. He watched the city suburbs pass, the track curving towards the river. Then two minutes in the broken shadows of the station, the blast of a whistle, and he was off again, racing north like some foolish doctor with nothing in his bag and not even the will to find kind words.

7

His taxi driver knew Theophilus House, though if he had any opinions on it he kept them to himself. They drove out of the town, travelling back along the coast, then crossed the causeway, a narrow road, pale with salt, which ran between shining mud-flats and banks of marsh grass. On the island they passed by groups of tourists ambling from the coach park, many of them in brightly coloured windproof jackets, for though the sun was on their backs there was a gusting easterly wind that blew the hair around their faces and made them walk with their hands in their pockets. In winter – and winter here would be eight, nine months of the year – the weather would whittle any softness from you. A place for those who were born to it, or for those who could warm themselves with their own thoughts.

Theophilus House was the first big house in the village. It stood at the side of the crossroads, grey, four-square, weathered and undistinguished, a row of low brick outbuildings at the back where a flagstone passage led to an entrance. A man in overalls and welder's goggles leaned his head from one of the sheds. Clem gave his name but the man already seemed to know who he was. Father, he said, examining Clem through the green glass of his goggles, was away in the van collecting feed for the hens. He would not be long now. At this time of the afternoon most of the community were busy. Clem should look for the guest master. He was about in the house somewhere, upstairs perhaps. Tea was at five thirty sharp. 'Egg salad,' said the man, drawing his head back into the shed. 'Listen for the gong!'

Clem went into the house, moving from room to room but finding no one. For a place inhabited by twenty souls there was little to evidence the daily round. No unwashed teacup, no book left casually at the side of a chair. No boots by the door, no whiff of pipe-smoke. It was neat as a barracks.

The walls were whitewashed and mostly unadorned, though beside the half-open door of the office was a painting of an astonished man receiving a basket of apples and roses from a tall *quattrocento* angel. (What was this childish obsession with angels? Did they believe in fairies too? Hobgoblins?) Opposite the painting was a long-case clock with a slow, self-important tick, and next to the clock, a flight of stairs turning at a frosted window and rising to a broad, bare landing. Here, there were four shut doors to choose between. Clem tried the one directly ahead of him, opened it cautiously, and stepped into a small room of butter-coloured light where two men knelt before a simple altar. Candles flickered on the altar cloth. The men's white heads were bowed, their hands clasped beneath their chins. If they had heard Clem they gave no sign of it. There was no discordant modernity. What he saw – the candles, the men's postures, the way they leaned slightly forwards as though pressing into the infinite – he might have seen in identical terms five hundred years ago. On his tongue he tasted the incense they used, a savour of ashes and aromatic wood. The candle flames shivered in a draught from the stairs. One of the men straightened his neck, a dreamer rising to the surface of his sleep. Clem stepped back on to the landing and gently drew the door shut.

The next room he entered was a dormitory, and so like the one he had envisaged he wondered if his father had ever described it to him. Two rows of sternly made-up beds, the old mattresses grooved from the weight of their nightly occupants, each bed with its woollen blanket, its wooden locker. A man was kneeling there too, though he was scrubbing rather than praying. 'Timothy,' he said, looking up at Clem and crinkling his face. 'And you must be William's son.' He was not the guest master: 'Nothing so grand, I'm afraid.' He suggested that Clem look in the gardens or perhaps the laundry, and then, as Clem turned to go, added, 'That's where Father sleeps,' pointing with his brush to one of the middle beds along the left-hand wall, a bed exactly like the others.

Downstairs, the office door was now wide open. Inside, stooping over the desk, William Glass was counting money into a petty-cash tin. There was a moment, three or four unguarded seconds, during which he remained oblivious to Clem, a remote and elderly man in a corduroy suit, his back humped above the shoulder-blades, his long white fingers not quite steady. When he saw Clem he hurried round the desk to greet him. He squeezed his son's arm, appeared briefly at a loss for what to say to him, then asked about the taxi ride – 'How much did he charge you, by the way?' – and when Clem told him, stroked his little grey beard and said it was a high-season fare though not outrageous.

Wheezing a little, he led Clem to a guest room on the top floor of the house. The room was tiny and Spartan. A bed sized like those in the dormitory, a small wash-basin, a dark, varnished wardrobe like an Italian confessional. The window looked over the front garden. Someone was wheeling a barrow with a creaking axle. Above the bed, suspended from the white wall by a nail, was a small reproduction of a medieval icon or screen painting. In a scroll at the bottom of the picture: '*Seigneur, ayez pitié de nous.*'

'St Dorothy?' asked Clem.

'I think that's St Odile,' said his father. 'Founded an order in Alsace. You don't mind her being there, I hope?'

'Of course not.'

'No one's going to push religion down your throat here.'

Clem nodded.

'You're tired,' said his father. 'Shall I leave you to rest?'

'I'm all right,' said Clem. 'I expect you go to bed early.'

'Nine thirty in winter. Ten in the summer. According to the light.'

'Then I'll wait.' He looked around, though there was nothing much to look at. He couldn't think for a moment how it had happened, the precise chain of events that had brought him to this room.

'Well,' said his father. 'Have you lost some weight? I think you have. A little.'

'Maybe.'

'I wasn't sure of your movements work-wise. Whether you were free.'

'No.'

'I imagine you're having a well-earned break.'

'A break?'

'Recharging the batteries.'

'Yes.'

'The agency looking after you?'

'That's not really their job, Dad.'

'Finding you enough work, though?'

'Yes.'

'I like to think I don't miss much of it. You know that when I'm in Berwick I always have a look through the papers. The serious ones, at least.'

'Don't you find that a distraction?'

'Too much of the world, you mean? We're not stylites here, Clem. We don't live on pillars in the desert.'

'I'm sorry.'

'No need to be.' He turned on one of the basin taps, let it run for a few seconds and turned it off. 'Africa was obviously appalling. All that senseless killing.'

'It wasn't senseless. They killed for a reason.'

'Neighbour against neighbour is usually the worst.'

'Only one of the neighbours was armed.'

'You're saying it was slaughter.'

'Yes.'

'And now the others will have their revenge, I suppose.'

Clem looked into the garden again. 'There can be no forgiveness,' he said. 'Be clear about that.' He shut his eyes for a moment. He didn't want this conversation. The words would pull things up by the roots and he didn't know what would happen then. 'What about Clare?' he asked.

'Oh, yes,' said his father. He drew a hand across his brow.

'The letter?'

'I can fetch it for you. Do you want to see it right away? It's just that we'll be called for tea soon.'

Clem nodded. 'Later, then.'

'After tea.'

'Yes.'

His father reached for the door handle. 'I'm so glad you've come, Clem. Glad you made the effort.'

'No great effort.'

'All the same.'

'Have I got time to wash?'

'Another ten minutes before the gong. It's eggs tonight. Egg salad. I don't think you have any trouble with eggs?'

'None.'

'And there's plenty of bread and butter. I can probably break out some jam too, if you wanted it.'

'I'll have what the others are having,' said Clem.

'That's settled, then. Come down when you hear the gong.' With a quick half-wave he left the room. Clem listened to him go, the cautious descent, the creaking of the steps; then he filled the basin with cold water, and several times, with measured, deliberate movements, drew the water to his face and pressed it there.

The brotherhood ate at a long refectory table, bought, along with the beds perhaps, from some extinguished local public school. Space was made for Clem between his father and a man called Simon Truelove, one of the founders, who smiled at Clem from small, pink-lined eyes. After grace, the meal was eaten without any conversation. Tea was poured from large brown pots, each man pouring for his neighbour. Requests for salt or milk

42

were whispered or anticipated. They must have known each other as well as wives, these tidy, conscientious eaters. Their old teeth ground the lettuce leaves. They dabbed their moistened lips with handkerchiefs. There was a mood of forgiving each other for the embarrassment of their bodies, the occasional gurgle, the stubborn clicking of a mandible. Then, with the teapots drained, the cutlery neatly paired on the heavy china plates, the last of them, Simon Truelove, rattled his cup onto his saucer and the meal was over.

William Glass was on the rota to wash up. Clem offered to help but his father suggested that he wait for him in the library, a room at the front of the house on the far side of the stairs. Here at least were some of the home comforts conspicuously absent from the rest of the building – armchairs, lamps, a tiled fireplace, some rugs. Shelving ran the length of the back wall and he browsed the spines of the books there hoping to find something that had nothing to do with religion.

After ten minutes he pulled out a small rose-coloured volume, a 1926 illustrated guide to the counties of Somerset and Gloucestershire, a vestige of someone's remotest youth that now shared a shelf with *The Five Glorious Mysteries*, *We Preach Christ Crucified*, *Lives of the Bartholomites*. Glued between the book's middle pages (next to a puff for the Channel View Hotel, 'separate tables and electric lights throughout') was a fragile, intricately folded map that Clem opened out at the table by the window. The counties were shown as nets of fine grey lines with faded blue-green dots depicting bodies of water. Some of the place names, those nearest to Bristol, were well known to him. Others he had driven through or heard spoken of. A surprising number he had never heard of at all, as though, some time in the last sixty years, they had sunk into the ground. He crossed Somerset with his fingertip until he found Frome and Radstock and Shepton Mallet. Old market towns – old mining towns too, for the whole county was humped with the sealed and grassed-over workings of former industry. He was looking for Colcombe, the village where Nora's sister, Laura Harwood, had a house, a place where he and Clare had spent a dozen holiday weeks and weekends while Nora busied herself with those meetings and marches, the endless talking that in the end had worn her to nothing. Leaving the children at Colcombe had been a convenience for her, but not one that Clem had ever resented. He had liked the house, its lawns, the tarmacked tennis court (sticky in summer), the kitchen with its muddy dogs sprawled by the side of the Aga. Oddly important things had happened there. He had ridden a horse for the first time, drunk gin for the first time, swum in the eerie chill of a flooded quarry. And in the attic one afternoon he had touched, as part of a dare or game, the secret whiteness of his cousin Frankie's thirteen-year-old breasts while she lay, a little Maja undressed, among the bound piles of *Punch* and *Country Life*, the enormous ribbed packing cases.

He found the village, a dot in a wrinkled labyrinth of B roads, the abbey marked to the side of it, another cross showing the old Colcombe church, the 'plague' church that stood on its own a mile from the village in a field of yews. Strange that a map – a thing so utterly abstract – should return to him, in such bright sequences, a time he had not thought about in years! It made him suspicious (he was a practised distruster of woolly-minded reverie) but he let himself enjoy it for a minute, his own childhood almost persuasive as a term in the argument opposed to the new understanding he had, the new certainty.

But how was Laura now? He had seen her only once since Uncle Ron's funeral, tea and fancy cakes at Harvey Nichols when she was up in Town two years ago, an appointment in Harley Street. And Frankie? And what about her brother Kenneth? Did he still plod behind Laura, wide-eyed, dumb as a flower? As far as Clem knew, the pair of them still lived together.

He was returning the book back to its slot on the shelf when his father, hands pink from the hot water, called for him and led the way to the garden. They sat on a bench. Fifteen yards away two of the old men, in gum-boots and shirtsleeves, were bent over a bed of freshly turned earth.

'Sowing beans,' said his father. 'Carrots, lettuces, onions, peas, rhubarb.' He grinned. 'We've even been planting trees.'

'Where do you keep the chickens?'

'On the other side. You'll hear them in the morning. Rhode Island Reds mostly. A few white Leghorns. Did you want to see them?'

'Another time.'

'As you like.' He reached into one of the side pockets of his corduroy jacket and took out an envelope, the lip ragged where he had used his finger as a letter knife. 'You might as well have this now,' he said.

'You want me to read it here?'

'It's only a few lines.'

Clem took the letter from the envelope. It was a single

sheet written over with hurried pencil strokes. Each full stop had pierced the paper.

Daddy

I am writing to tell you I have become ill again. Why it should have happened now after so many years I have no idea. You believe in sin and the devil and judgment. Am I being punished for something? For weeks I have tried with all my strength to continue a normal life but that is no longer possible. Tomorrow, to forestall the inevitable, I will admit myself to a private clinic. I cannot go on a public ward like the one at Barrow. I am not 24. I would not survive it. Let people call me a hypocrite if they want to – I am beyond caring what others think. YOU MUST NOT TRY TO SEE ME. There is NOTHING you can do and seeing you would only make this INFINITELY harder than it already is. My friend Finola Fiacc will communicate whatever is necessary. You can speak to her at the department. I have put her home number at the bottom of this page. I don't want anyone's pity, certainly not yours. If I could make people forget me I would.

   Please RESPECT my wishes!
   Clare

Beneath her name was a drawn heart struck out by a single line. No love? I cannot be loved? My heart is broken?

Clem folded the paper and slipped it back into the envelope. When he turned to his father he saw that there were tears in his eyes. 'You'll go to her, won't you, Clem?'

'I'll go tomorrow.'

'Thank you.'

'I'll phone this colleague of hers. Arrange something. Do you want the letter?'

'You keep it.'

They sat a minute, watching the old gardeners press the seeds into the soil and water them.

'Has she been overworking?' asked his father, speculating aloud. 'I don't think she eats properly. Do you?'

'She never had much of an appetite.'

'More of an appetite for books than food. For paintings! And where do you think this clinic is? In Dundee? Edinburgh? You'd be amazed at the number of private clinics there are in Scotland. I've done some research at the library in town. Most of them are for drinkers, I suppose.'

'I'll find it,' said Clem.

'She's too far north. There's not enough light for her. Not enough warmth.'

'The first time was in Paris.'

'I know, I know. I'm talking nonsense.' He smiled miserably. 'Shall we walk a little? A walk might do us good.'

In the village, most of the tourists, other than the few staying the night in bed-and-breakfasts, had left. The tide was in, the causeway sunk under the waves, the island an island again. They walked out along a promontory towards the castle, then came back and crossed a shingle beach where the weathered hulls of upturned fishing-boats had been made into sheds and workshops. At the end of the beach the path led steeply upwards to the lighthouse. They climbed and stood at the base of it, the wind on their faces. They were quite alone.

'Travelling from here,' said his father, pointing along a

line of latitude, 'you'd come eventually to the coast of Denmark. And beyond that to Moscow, the Aleutian Islands, Canada.'

'And back here again.'

'Yes, eventually. But I'm not like you, Clem. My travels are all in my head. Unless you count going to Berwick once a week. Do you know I've never even been to the Americas? A whole continent I've never set foot in!'

'Is that where you'd like to go?'

'I think I'd prefer to go to India.'

'You could still make it happen.'

'Well, in dreams, perhaps.'

Far out, where the blue was darkest, some vessel in the shipping lanes had switched on her navigation lights. They watched her glinting on the horizon until the wind made their eyes water. 'I always have the oddest temptation to wave to them,' said his father. 'As though they could possibly see me.'

'Shall we go back?' said Clem. 'It's getting chilly.'

The path down the bank was all in shadow; the old man took hold of Clem's elbow, letting go of him once they were on the beach again.

'I went into the little chapel,' said Clem. 'There were two of your friends there. I'm not sure if they heard me.'

His father told him not to worry. 'There are always two of us in there. We do a two-hour shift and swap over.'

'All through the night?'

'Day and night. You get used to it. It's the heart of the house.'

'What do people pray for?'

'There are no rules on that. You can pray for whatever you wish.'

'Can I ask what you pray for?'

'Me? Oh, for understanding.'

'Always that?'

'Yes,' he said, smiling to himself and slipping his hand again under his son's arm as they came on to the road. 'Always.'

8

The next morning – Sunday – Clem caught the eleven thirty-three from Berwick, changed at Edinburgh, and crossed the Tay at a quarter to two, the train skimming above the water towards roofs that gleamed and grew dull again in broken sunlight.

He had called Finola Fiacc from the telephone in the office of Theophilus House. She had sounded flustered at first, caught off guard, but having no real objection to make and no time to think of one, she had agreed at last to meet him. She would know him, she said, from photographs Clare had shown her (this detail was interesting: his sister showed people photographs of him!) but it was Clem, coming out of the station ticket hall, who identified her – no one else there looked likely to own such a name – a tall, middle-aged woman in a tracksuit and vulcanised raincoat, scanning, through horn-rimmed lenses, the faces of the twenty or so passengers who had left the train at Dundee.

'Fiacc,' she said, as Clem appeared in front of her. 'I am Finola Fiacc, and you might as well know from the start that I am a recovering alcoholic. I have not taken a drink in four years and four months, thanks, in great part, to the kindness of your sister.' She paused as though offering Clem the opportunity to make a confession of his own, then added: 'I have taken in her cats. My van is over there.'

They crossed the car park towards a camper van, a green Volkswagen streaked with rust, an old sticker – 'A Dog is for Life' – hanging, half peeled, from the glass of the sliding door. In the windscreen was her Dundee University car-park badge.

'You called her?' asked Clem, as Fiacc strong-armed the van into reverse gear.

'She has decided to see you.'

'And we're going there now?'

'Where else?'

'You haven't told me what this place is called.'

'You haven't asked.'

'What's it called?'

'Ithaca.'

'Ithaca?'

'On the Arbroath road.'

She drove in attitudes of rage, gunning the van down the hills, then leaning forwards and pressing the wheel as they crept up the slope of the next. Clem made no attempt to talk with her and this seemed to suit them both. He was bemused to be travelling between these oddly titled communities, and found it hard to imagine his sister as the friend of this ungainly woman whose eyes flickered behind the lenses of her glasses. The weather turned to squalls, rain rattling off the side of the van; then the clouds swept past leaving a fine washed blue, until more clouds turned the world dark again.

'You mind if I smoke?' asked Clem. She bared her teeth then said that she would smoke too, though not one of his machine-made cigarettes. 'They're full of poison,' she said. 'Ammonia. Gunpowder.' She had a tin of tobacco in the glove compartment, untreated stuff, which also happened to be cheaper. Clem passed it to her, watching from the corner of his eye as she rolled a cigarette while steering the van with her elbows. Strands of tobacco dangled from the end of the finished cigarette. When she lit up, the strands fell in fiery curls to her thighs where she beat them out with a free hand, though not before two or three tiny burns joined the dozen others that speckled the nap of her tracksuit trousers.

'A rainbow,' she said bluntly, gesturing with her cigarette to where a half-arch stood out over glistening hills. 'Not that they mean anything.'

They turned off the main road, accelerated through a huddled village, climbed past soaking fields, glimpsed the sea, then descended into a valley, Fiacc pumping the brake with her plimsolled foot before swerving on to the gravelled forecourt of a large white house.

'Ithaca,' she said, switching off the engine and slumping back in her seat, apparently exhausted. Clem climbed out of the van. The air was cold, a day like the beginning of March, or the beginning of March in London. Ahead of him was a blue front door, a pair of bay windows on either side of it, their lower panes hung with netting. A new two-storey wing had been added at one end of the house. Everything was in good order, smartly painted. A line of old trees, their tops bowed by the prevailing wind, screened the house from the road.

'Four hundred a week,' said Fiacc, joining Clem on the gravel, 'and that without extras.' He saw she had put on some lipstick, a bright red that made the rest of her face look bled out, like French veal.

'What kind of extras?'

'Hydrotherapy, physiotherapy, yoga. Sure they've got it all in there.'

She rang the bell. After half a minute the door was opened. A man in a green Paisley dressing-gown blocked their way, a balding, sack-like figure who widened his bloodshot eyes like the villain in an operetta. 'If you're the bloody press,' he hissed, 'I'll set the bloody dogs on you.' He scowled at Fiacc. 'I know *you*,' he said.

'And I know you,' she answered, pushing past him.

'Room for two more inside!' bawled the man, swinging the door shut. 'Ding ding! Ding ding!'

They were in a type of lounge, a day-room with armchairs, mint-coloured walls, large ashtrays, pot plants, a fire extinguisher. A young woman with wavy grey-blonde hair appeared through a doorway at the rear of the room, her ID clipped to the waistband of her jeans. 'Oh, Raymond,' she said, 'Raymond, dear. Are we getting a wee bit loud again?'

'I, am, dying, of, fucking, boredom,' said the man, though in a quieter voice. He sat down.

The young woman turned to Fiacc. 'You're come to see Clare?'

'This is her brother,' said Fiacc. 'Clement Glass.'

'Pauline Diamond,' said the woman, shaking Clem's hand. 'One of the care team. When you've seen Clare you might like a chat with Dr Boswell. That's his office there. He's on all afternoon. We're great believers here in the family input.'

Clem signed the visitors' book, then followed Fiacc to the end of the new wing and up a flight of carpeted stairs. Clare's room was at the back of the house. Her name – first name only – was written on a piece of card slotted

53

into a Perspex holder on the door. Fiacc knocked but, getting no response, nor, it seemed, expecting one, she opened the door and leaned inside. 'Just me,' she cooed, a voice quite distinct from the one she had used on Clem. 'And I have your brother here. If you're feeling up to it.'

Clare was sitting on a straight-backed chair between a table and the window. Fiacc put an arm round her shoulders and drew her into a quick, one-sided hug.

'Hello,' said Clem. He bent to kiss his sister's cheek. Their eyes met for a moment, then she looked towards the window. Fiacc took off her raincoat, wiped away some marks from the mirror over the wash-basin with the corner of a piece of tissue, then sat on the end of the bed. For ten minutes she kept up a flow of talk about the comings and goings at the university. Clem leaned against the wall by the window-sill. He did not know if Clare was listening to anything; she gave no sign of it. He tried not to stare at her. He had of course expected her to look poorly, to be thinner and paler, but this listless woman with her drab hair limp over the bones of her shoulders, shadows like bruises under her eyes, flakes of dry skin on her brow, was more than he had prepared himself for. She was dressed as though for mourning – black woollen tights, a black dress, black cardigan. In her lap her fingers, ringless, plucked at each other, the pulse of some continuous, unassuageable disquiet.

'I saw Dad,' he said, when Fiacc paused. 'He sends you his love.'

She nodded and drank the last of the water in the glass on the table.

'Would you like some more?' he asked. He carried the

glass to the basin and refilled it. When he set it beside her she mumbled something; he bent closer.

'Door key?' He looked across at Fiacc.

'Now didn't we talk about that before?' said Fiacc, addressing the side of Clare's face in tones of mock-admonishment. 'There is no key, dear. The door has no lock at all.' To Clem she said: 'It's the fire regulations.'

Clem went back to the window. 'Have you been out today?' he asked. He had no idea what to say to her. 'We saw a rainbow on the drive over.'

'The people in the next room,' said Clare, 'are at it all the time.'

'At it?'

'And at night someone runs up and down in the corridor. Up and down, up and down, up and down. All night.'

'I met someone downstairs,' said Clem. 'Pauline? She seemed nice.'

'The medicine makes me thirsty,' said Clare.

'But it's making you better,' said Fiacc, loudly. 'Are you not having fewer frights now?'

Clare looked up at Clem again, frowning slightly as though she could not yet make sense of his being there, could not yet decide how she felt about it. 'I couldn't stop,' she said, shifting her gaze again to the floor by her feet. 'First one thing. Then another. You lie to yourself. Then everything goes.'

'I'm sorry,' said Clem. He watched her face crease up but there were no tears. After a moment her expression settled.

'Shall I have a go at that hair of yours?' asked Fiacc, standing and bustling over to the little dressing-table where

Clare's toiletries were laid out. 'You'll be having birds in it if you're not careful, like your man in the poem.'

Clem looked down into the garden. There was a *t'ai chi* class in progress, a half-dozen men and women in a slow-motion struggle with the air.

'No need for you to wait,' said Fiacc, starting to jerk the brush through Clare's hair. 'We're just going to do girls' things. You could take a look about the house, why don't you.'

He nodded, then stepped forward and crouched by his sister's knees. 'You got better before,' he said. 'You'll get better again.'

'You're coming tomorrow?' she asked, a simple question, neither anxious nor expectant.

He held her hands and briefly pressed them between his own. 'If I can,' he said. 'Is that all right?'

He went down the stairs and out of a door at the end of the new wing. There was a pathway there, leading from the forecourt to the back garden, and he squatted by the wall and started smoking. The man in the dressing-gown came out and asked for a cigarette. Clem gave him one and the man hunkered down beside him, emitting little 'ahh's of pleasure each time he exhaled.

'A word to the wise,' he said. 'The eating disorders and the depressives are all right. It's the bi-polars and the drunks you have to watch for.'

'Which are you?' asked Clem.

'A drunk,' said the man. 'And you?'

'Just visiting.'

They finished their cigarettes. Clem went back to the day-room and knocked on the doctor's door.

'Come in, come in,' sang the doctor. 'Pull up a pew.' He had Clare's file ready on his desk. He wanted to check the address of her next of kin. He had Fiacc's address – 'but she's more kith than kin, isn't she?' Clem gave his father's address. 'A lovely part of the world,' said the doctor, writing with an old-fashioned fountain pen. 'No way, I suppose, of getting hold of you?'

'Not at the moment.'

'Busy busy, eh?'

'Work,' said Clem.

'Thriving?'

'Not bad.'

'Excellent!' The doctor jotted something down then sat back and dragged off his glasses. 'I think,' he began, 'that we've got Clare through what might be called the acute phase. She's not, for example, hallucinating any more. Far less confusion than when we first saw her, less obvious distress. Typically, however, it's more of a challenge to treat the negative symptoms. Apathy, emotional blunting, et cetera. Still lots of things for us to try. New drugs coming on line all the time, and much better than what she would have had before. As you probably know, the old neuroleptics could have pretty nasty side-effects.'

'And the new ones?'

'Dry mouth, blurry vision. Some people get spasms. And of course with the newer drugs we don't always have the long-term story. But this is looking on the dark side . . .' – he squinted down at the file – '. . . Clement. We're learning more all the time. Social influences, brain chemistry, genetics. There's a real explosion of new knowledge in the neurosciences. I'm very optimistic.'

'Why did it happen?'

'Why?'

'Why now?'

'The short answer is I don't know. Some patients have one attack, a single episode, and that's the end of it. Others suffer chronically. Clare seems somewhere between the two. The fact is, if someone has a predisposition to these symptoms there is always a risk, however slight, of a relapse. Even after years of being perfectly well. Very unfair, of course.'

'How long will she have to be here?'

'Tricky,' said the doctor, grimacing. 'The only real answer I can give is that Clare can stay for as long as she needs us. Some weeks certainly. A month or two.'

'She seems worried about her door. There's no lock on it.'

'Pauline said she had been expressing a concern. I think that has to be seen as part of a general pattern of paranoid behaviour.'

'She's always been a very private person.'

'Everyone here is going to respect that a hundred and ten per cent.'

Clem nodded. The doctor's room was hung with expensive-looking paintings. Country views. Portraits. A nude. A beautiful acrylic of a red-haired girl on a mule, the pair seeming to have surfaced from a dense fog that might, at any moment, reclaim them.

'Father's alive and well but mother passed on . . .?'

'Twenty-seven years ago.'

'Anyone in the family with a history comparable to Clare's?'

'No one I know of.'

58

'And the last time she was ill was when she was in Paris?'

'Yes.'

'Did you see her then?'

'Not until she was home.'

'Boyfriends?'

'I suppose.'

'But you haven't met any?'

'One or two.'

'And girlfriends?'

'I don't think she'd advertise it. Not to me.'

'Would you describe your relationship with Clare as close?'

'She's my sister.'

'The two don't necessarily follow.'

'We grew up together.'

'What's the difference in age?'

'Five years.'

'Your big sister then.'

'Yes.'

'And what did Mother die of?'

'A cerebral haemorrhage.'

'Must have been quite a shock for you all. How did Clare react?'

'She got on with things.'

'What sort of things?'

'She ran the house. She was studying for her A levels. She kept herself busy.'

'Tears? Tantrums?'

'We're not that kind of family.'

'Not demonstrative.'

'No.'

'But Clare looked after you?'

'Yes.'

'A lot of responsibility for a very young woman.'

'I suppose we thought of her being like Nora.'

'Your mother?'

'Yes.'

'Capable and strong?'

'Yes.'

'And yet it's the women who have succumbed, if I can put it like that. It's the men – you and your father – who have turned out to be the survivors.'

'We had an easier ride.'

'Perhaps, perhaps. I understand Mother had a visual impairment?'

'Glaucoma.'

'Glaucoma?'

'She never stopped long enough to have it properly treated. When she did it was too late.'

'An active woman?'

'Always.'

'In the house?'

'She was a lawyer. A campaigner. Her life was politics.'

'Making a better world.'

'Trying.'

'And Father was . . . different?'

'Yes.'

'Less of a force?'

'Yes.'

'Ineffectual?'

'He's who he is.'

'And why wouldn't he be, indeed? Sorry about the third degree, Clement.'

'Is there more?' He could hear Fiacc's voice from the day-room loudly asking someone if he was still in with the doctor. 'We have to get back,' he said.

'Of course you do.' The doctor stood and shook Clem's hand. 'Very good to meet you, sir. You know where we are now.'

'Yes. Thank you.'

'Any questions, just pick up the phone.' He came round the side of the desk and walked Clem to the door. 'Like art?'

'You mean the paintings?'

The doctor nodded. 'It's a mystery to me. I mean, quite genuinely a mystery. A power beyond reason.' He patted Clem's arm and smiled at him. 'Until next time,' he said.

9

Clare's flat was on the hill above the station. Clem followed Fiacc up four flights of stone steps and stood behind her as she took the keys from her raincoat pocket, a long key for the mortise, a small brass key for the latch. Inside there was a warm, sweetish smell of dust and carpets, and something untraceably organic, like fruit peel or dead flowers. Though he had not been to the flat before – for years now all their meetings had been in the south – he immediately recognised some of her old possessions: the picture over the telephone, the art-deco lamp, the bureau in the alcove at the end of the hall. More than this, he recognised her way of setting things out, the orderliness, the few good pieces, the expression of a taste more refined, more artistic, than his own.

He dropped his bag in the hall and went into the kitchen. Here there was a tall window that looked over the station roof and out across the river. Fiacc was watering the plants on the window-sill. Clem sat at the kitchen table.

'What happens to her mail?' he asked.

'I take it to her.'

'What does she do with it?'

'She gives it back to me. I deal with whatever I am competent to deal with. The rest can wait.'

'It's warm in here,' he said. She didn't answer. He looked at the stuff on the table. A pair of chemist's reading glasses, a travelling alarm clock, a pack of electric bulbs in a torn polythene wrapper. Also a Sunday supplement that he knew contained some of the photographs he had taken in the spring. He turned back a corner of the magazine, flicked through, saw a corner of one of his pictures, flicked past.

'Will they catch him?' asked Fiacc, pointing to the magazine with the spout of the watering-can.

'Catch who?'

'The man responsible.'

'Ruzindana? I don't know. We looked for him. He'd fled. Half the country's fled.'

'Did you give up on him too quickly?'

'You would have gone on?'

'To confront a man like that. You must have wanted to?'

'Of course.'

'Put his crimes to his face.'

'Did Clare see these pictures?'

'The magazine is hers.'

He nodded.

'I'll make up your bed,' said Fiacc, putting down the watering-can.

'There's no need,' said Clem. 'If you show me where things are . . .'

'It's what she asked me to do.'

'Really?'

'Really.'

He followed her across the hall. He would not have minded a row with her, a spat to put her in her place, make clear to her that there were limits to what the family would tolerate. He leaned against the door of his sister's room – the only bedroom in the flat – watching Fiacc bending over the tin trunk at the foot of Clare's bed, rummaging through the linen there. What was it Clare liked about her, this big, mannish woman? Her loyalty? Or the knowledge that she too, in her way, was a casualty, and thus lived, as Clare lived, as Odette Semugeshi lived, as the Spanish girl would live, in some interminable aftermath?

'I can make my own bed,' he said.

'One would hope so,' she answered, 'at your age.' She straightened up, the sheets in her arms, and walked past him into the living room. Clearly, then, he was not invited to sleep where his sister slept, but he hung back a while, stepping into the middle of the room, curious to try to read the place. It was on the far side of the house from the kitchen and so faced north-east, the narrow window letting in a sober light like the white-grey of clear, still water. Twelve or fifteen dresses dangled from the chromed bar of a Habitat wardrobe, six pairs of shoes on the boards below, toes to the wall. On the mantelpiece, under a silvery watercolour of morning or dusk, there was a line of sea-shells. The dressing-table was uneventful: hairgrips, a bottle of perfume, a tub of hand lotion, a blister pack of evening primrose oil. He slid open one of the side drawers and found an old white-bordered photo of Nora in her Chiang Kai-shek glasses. But nothing in the room was more interesting, more suggestive, than the robe of lined scarlet silk that hung in dense pleats from a hook on the back of the door. He touched it; the material had a coolness entirely its own.

Half a month's salary there for sure. Or a gift? Not, he thought, a garment for a woman who had given up on the sensual world.

'Have you finished in here?' asked Fiacc.

He wondered if the reason he was not permitted to use the bed was because Fiacc herself had used it. Was that what Dr Boswell had guessed? What he was hinting at?

'Why all the bulbs?' he asked. There were four more in cardboard jackets next to the lamp on the bedside table.

'Against the darkness,' said Fiacc. 'She couldn't have it at all by the time she left.'

'Couldn't?'

'Was afraid to.'

'Afraid of the dark?'

'Of what might come out of it.'

'And what might?'

'That's for her to say.'

'So you don't know.'

She snorted. 'There are no secrets between us.'

'You don't think it's information her family should have?'

'You mean you and your father?'

'And why are the windows sealed?'

'For the same reason.'

'Because she was afraid?'

'Because of the illness! Have you understood so little?'

They glowered at each other. In a fight, he thought, a physical fight, she would give a good account of herself, swinging those heavy arms. He could also imagine himself rushing her, kneeling across her, pressing his knuckles into her neck and choking the life out of her.

'Let's go,' he said. He didn't trust himself to stand so

close to her. In the living room he saw that she had made up a sofa-bed for him. He thanked her.

'Will you want collecting tomorrow?' she asked.

'I'll call you,' he said. 'You'll be at the university?'

'Until four. I like to be at Ithaca by five thirty at the latest. I've left a set of keys on the kitchen table.'

'Right.'

'And there are tins in there. Some rice and pasta in the big jars. Or you can walk into the town. You won't starve.'

'I'll be fine.'

'I dare say.'

He felt suddenly ashamed at how effortlessly they had made enemies of each other: a pair of children squabbling over a bag of sweets. 'Would you like some tea?' he asked, a conciliatory voice. 'A drink of something?'

She shook her head. 'I have to go. I have her cats to feed.'

They went into the hall together. She pulled fast the bedroom door and glanced around as if to see where else he might snoop. 'And when you go out you'll please remember to lock up properly. It takes two turns of the key.'

'I'll remember.'

Vigorously, she drew the flaps of her coat together. 'Clare will talk to you when she's ready,' she said.

'Then I'll have to wait.'

'You can't expect just to come back . . .'

'I realise that.'

She lingered in the doorway a moment, as though considering saying something definitive. Her mouth half opened, but she shut it again, nodded her farewell, and left.

When she had gone he unsealed the kitchen window, stripping away yards of black insulating tape and forcing up the sashes until the sound of the evening traffic flowed into the room on a curl of cool, damp air. He closed his eyes and breathed in deeply. He was glad to be alone again, hidden up here in his sister's flat. The place carried, of course, the memory of a descent, but carried it only faintly. The misery of it had gone with her to Ithaca; what remained were a few souvenirs of ingenuity and panic – the tape, the bulbs, the new steel bolt on the front door. Mounting the bolt would have needed the use of an electric drill. Did she have one? Or had she knocked at a neighbour's door, some comfortable older man who, carrying up his tool-box, talked about a time when folk went out and left their latches off, a time with less fear? And had that same neighbour then returned to tell his wife there was something wrong with the woman upstairs, the university woman they had so approved of when she first moved in? It was not an unlikely scene. Unless it had been Fiacc who helped, Fiacc's big fist turning the screws while Clare gazed on, half grateful, half appalled.

He looked for something to drink and found in a cupboard next to the fridge a half-empty bottle of grappa, a price tag in lire on the side of it. He poured a couple of inches into a tumbler and carried the glass out to the bureau. The front of the bureau was folded down to make a writing board and at the back there was a network of little drawers and slots for envelopes and paper, ink, spare pens. The work she had been doing before she left was still there, a sheaf of annotated typescript, a finely sharpened pencil at the side of it.

He began to read. It was an essay on Théodore Géricault, a painter she had talked to him about when they last met in London, a young Frenchman, a Romantic, but a Romantic obsessed with giving to his work a shocking new realism. For the painting of a disaster at sea, a notorious shipwreck off the West African coast, he had sketched in hospitals, visited morgues, even smuggled body parts into his studio in the hope that this butcher's haul would infuse his painting with that quality of the authentic the first photographers, setting up their tripods in the Crimea and Gettysburg, would soon claim for their own. On first being exhibited – the Théâtre Français, 25 August 1819 – the painting was considered a failure. Later it was admired. First title: *Scene of a Shipwreck*. Second title: *The Raft of the Medusa*. Clem looked for it among the photocopies clipped to the back of the essay. There were horses and wounded soldiers, a drawing of a sick old man on a bed, a pair of decapitated heads, a portrait entitled *The Monomaniac of Stealing*, but no shipwreck. Had Clare taken *The Raft* with her? He did not remember seeing it, but it might have been up in her room at Ithaca, something to remind her of work, the sanity of work.

He slid the pages to one side, took a sheet of writing-paper and one of Clare's pens and wrote a short letter to their father. He could have used the telephone, of course, it was just behind him, but a letter would arrive in a day or two, and on the phone his reassurances might sound too hollow, too easily chased down. He mentioned the clinic's setting, the good facilities, the doctor's optimism. Of Clare herself he said she had looked 'sleepy' but otherwise not too bad. She was in good hands, had a view over the garden and would, in time, be her old self. He did not write of his own plans; he did not have any. He signed, *With love, Clem*, found an envelope and a book of first-class stamps, put the envelope in his pocket and left the flat, turning the key twice.

He posted the letter in a pillar-box at the corner of the road, then walked towards the town centre. In a small shop where a pair of young Chinese worked at bins of smoking oil, he bought a piece of fish, had it wrapped in a sheet of newspaper, and carried it back to the flat. He ate at the kitchen table, swilling the grease from his tongue with another mouthful of grappa, then took a shower. He did not intend to go out again. He left his clothes in a pile on the bathroom floor and crossed the hall to Clare's bedroom. From its hook behind the door he took the robe and put it on, glimpsing himself – a flash of red and white – in the dressing-table mirror. The robe was tight across his shoulders but otherwise fitted him well. He went through to the living room and sat in the armchair, the grappa bottle and his cigarettes on the little table beside him.

There was a television, an old bubble-screen portable. Finishing the drink, he watched a documentary about underwater volcanoes, an American comedy show, the last part of a detective drama. He smoked carefully, holding his hand under the tip of his cigarette to keep any sparks from burning the robe. He yawned: he had been awake since before five and had seen from the window of the guest room the island's first hour of light. At breakfast, the old men with their diabetic jams and bowls of All-Bran had smiled at him, encouragingly. What was it they imagined him doing? Did they hope he would come to share their impossible religion? Or was something more general intended: live well, do what was right, be a force for the good? Having thought he would find them ludicrous he had ended up by liking them, their seriousness and their awkward domesticity. If they wished him well then he accepted their wishes – even their prayers.

The detective drama ended with a confrontation, a lucky shot. When the credits ran he decided to move to the sofa-bed but when he woke, full of confusion, hours later, he was still in the armchair, the room spectral with the blue of the television. He had been dreaming that he was going into Clare's room. There was no door, just a curtain which he drew back slowly with the point of a long-bladed knife he was carrying. Was it a scene from the film? He couldn't remember. He climbed from the chair, switched off the television, and shuffled into the kitchen. The travelling clock read four forty-five. He drank a glass of tap water looking out of the open window at the street-lamps, the lights of a small boat curving over the firth. Then he fetched his wallet from his trousers in the bathroom and stood under the hall light searching for the piece of paper on which he had written Silverman's number. The phone was on a low three-legged table. He squatted beside it and dialled. There were several seconds of silence, then a ring tone, a burst of static, and finally a voice, friable, imperfect, remote as the Arctic, but distinctly Silverman.

'Who is this?'

'Clem. Clem Glass.'

'Clem? Jesus! You tracked me down.'

'Shelley-Anne said you were in Toronto.'

'Who?'

'Shelley-Anne!'

'She's fine. Well, she's pretty mad at me, in fact. Thinks I'm going to stay up here.'

'What are you doing?'

'I'm driving.'

'But what are you doing in Toronto?'

'Starting again at the beginning.'

'The what?'

'The beginning. Christ, Clem. It's taken me until fifty-two to discover the meaning of a word like "hope".'

' "Hope"?'

'Maybe that's not the word. Where are you?'

'Dundee.'

'Dundee, Scotland?'

'Yeah.'

'You sound like shit.'

'It's the line.'

'You should be here. Don't they have planes in Dundee?'

'Not to Canada.'

'I know how you feel, Clem.'

'I know.'

'I said I know how you feel. We made ourselves sick out there. When I got back I was afraid to sleep. I was dying.'

'Dying?'

'Trying nothing. Are you there?'

'Yeah.'

'We made ourselves sick, Clem.'

'I think about the little girl.'

'Odette.'

71

'The girl at the orphanage.'

'I know, I know. And still they haven't caught the bastard.'

'Do you know anything?'

'It won't make any difference, Clem. We have to let go of all that.'

'You're wrong.'

'We hang on to it and it'll kill us.'

'You've heard something?'

'I'm not even looking. I'm out of it.'

'What are you doing there?'

'I'm working, but not what you think. I can't even talk about it without sounding like Mother Teresa. One night you'll come with me and I'll show you.'

'In Toronto?'

'Huxley called it a sanctimonious ice-box but it's not so bad. OK, listen, listen. I'm going into the underpass. Can you hear me?'

'Just.'

'To hell with history, Clem. To hell with politics. To hell with religion. To hell with newspapers. To hell . . .'

The voice faded. Clem waited, straining towards a distant roaring of air; then the signal broke and he was returned to his surroundings, the hall, the rug under his feet, the first cries of the gulls. He dialled again and got the answer service. He left a short message then put a five-pound note on the table next to the telephone. He lay on the sofa-bed. The light grew stronger at the edges of the window. He drifted either side of sleep, thought of Silverman, then had a morning dream of him driving furiously through an orange-lit tunnel and out into a schoolbook Canada, the night sky blind with snow.

It was broad daylight when he came to again. He dressed quickly, hung the robe behind the bedroom door, smoothing his shape out of the silk. He washed the glass, shut the kitchen window and left the flat, his bag over his shoulder. He reached the station a few minutes before ten. He waited there, sipping black coffee from a polystyrene cup, then caught the first train south.

Part Two

Photography implies that we know about the world if we accept it as the camera records it. But this is the opposite of understanding, which starts from not accepting the world as it looks. All possibility of understanding is rooted in the ability to say no. Strictly speaking, one never understands anything from a photograph.

Susan Sontag, *On Photography*

10

His food, some manner of pizza, had a bitter taste of burnt herbs, and he pushed it away. An Asian woman in a blue overall, '*Food Village*' sewn over her breast, took his plate and tipped its contents into the bucket on her trolley. Her eyes, too, seemed to rebuke him. He turned to the windows. In the pearly light of mid-afternoon the planes stood gleaming at their gates. The PA announced flights to Islamabad, Chicago, Tokyo. Late passengers were sternly summoned; families reunited at the information desk. Again, Clem imagined making phone-calls, and again failed to imagine what he might say to anyone. Those who trusted him would need to trust him a little further. Wasn't that part of it? Suspending judgement? Lending respectable motive to behaviour you could not understand at first, or perhaps ever? Somewhere in her poor abused head Clare would accept there was a reason he had not returned to her. But what had Fiacc said? Certainly she would have had no interest in defending him, and it was easy to picture her patting Clare's hand, explaining how she had waited for his call then gone to the flat and found it empty, his bag gone, no note, nothing at all. She would be glad, of course. She had not wanted a rival, some never-before-seen brother who brought with him the claims of family. She had seen him off. Now Clare was hers again.

Pitiful, though, to think of Clare listening to such stuff; pitiful to think of her face, the play of confusion there as she sought to make sense of Fiacc's news. Could he send her a card? The idea was comically inadequate but he snatched at it as a course of action that fell within the narrowing range of what he still felt capable of, and immediately he went on to the concourse and found a carousel of postcards, buying one with a strange over-coloured aerial shot of the airport she might even find funny, or would have done in better times. He rested the card on a pile of magazines. He could write to her how he caught from his own skin still the sweet, continuous stink of decay. That she would smell it too in time. That he couldn't help her. That he wanted to but couldn't. That he was exactly the wrong person to try to help her. Instead, he wrote: *Called away! In touch soon. Hi to Finola*. He didn't have a postal address but decided that 'The Ithaca Clinic, Nr Dundee, Scotland' would get there in the end.

He flew Air Canada, the flight almost full, the man in the seat beside him passing the hours with little books of word-search puzzles. Clem watched the film, then ordered his fifth quarter of wine from a blonde stewardess whose youth and nervy attentiveness to the details of her work suggested it might be her first week in the job. The day extended. Below them, clouds darkening through a range of blues stretched away to perfect horizons. A moon rose, red with the light of the slowly setting sun, and for a while the world beyond the chill double-skin of his window was dreamlike, ideal, casually superb. He remembered Fiacc's comment on the rainbow – 'It means nothing, of course.' Strange, then, how persuasive it remained, how powerfully such beauty offered itself as the world's deep character, the evidence of a moral order, profound, and profoundly good. He sat back. His neighbour went on with his puzzles, shaping lines with a biro around the words he found concealed in fields of letters. He exuded a sort of lunatic serenity. He had no interest in what the sky was doing.

Clem read the in-flight magazine, cover to cover. Celebrity restaurants, socially minded businessmen, the continents bound in a cat's cradle of flight lines: the heady conceit that Air Canada would ferry them between one shining culture and another. When he looked up again at the film screen a little schematic plane showed them poised at thirty-six thousand feet over the eastern seaboard of Canada. The first officer – a voice that might have done well selling bourbon or good cigars – invited them to alter their watches. It would be a fine evening in Toronto, clear skies, eighteen degrees, a breeze from the west. Clem pillowed his head against the wing of his seat. The night at Clare's had been followed by two more, equally disturbed, at the flat in London, and fatigue had him on the edge of a longer and longer drop. He had become fearful, panicky almost, that the rest he craved was lost to him for ever, but now, when there was no real time for it, the wine, the hum of the engines, the cabin's twilight, drew him down, and he slept like a creature in its burrow until startled awake by the young stewardess tapping his shoulder and asking him to fasten his seatbelt.

Fifteen minutes later they banked over grids of light. The man put away his books and biro. On the screen the plane stood over the city. The altitude dropped to five thousand, three thousand, fifteen hundred. Clem gazed down at the headlights of cars moving along a strip of road bounded by a darkness he took to be the darkness of water. He thought of the dead, how they crowded in among the living, thin as leaves. Was it they who had led him here? A host reciting their cause from broken mouths? Voice was all they had left to them. Stories, complaints sharpened on repetition. Pushing against stone or skin they could move nothing, but with their voices, their crooning, they recruited the living, though hid from them perhaps, as long as they were able, the nature of the justice they craved, the form, the sacrifice, the appetites that murder breeds.

11

He left a message on Silverman's cellphone, giving the name and telephone number of the hotel he was staying at, an inexpensive thirty-room place on the edge of Chinatown called the Trillium Inn. The manager was a tall, lame man who looked like John Steinbeck in the Capa photograph taken in Russia in the 1940s. He gave Clem a complimentary map of the city and explained that the hotel's air-conditioning had failed, for which he was offering a five-dollar-per-night reduction in the bill.

In the morning Clem called Silverman again, though this time a recorded female voice informed him that the phone he wanted was switched off. (This, Clem understood, was the phone as a powerful means of not speaking to people, just as the camera was often a device for not looking at the world, a box to hide behind.)

He went out and walked around Chinatown. At ten he found a place for coffee and sat next to a table of students who sucked at soya milkshakes discussing, in nasal accents, some event of the night before that had kicked their asses. Walking again, he pocketed his map and took streets at random. It was much hotter, much more humid than he had expected. Twice more he tried Silverman, calling from public phones; twice more the voice told him the phone was off. The heat made him despondent. As he trudged between the high-rises of the financial district –

huge clichéd buildings, monuments to the erotics of money – he rebuked himself for having come so far with nothing more than a number pencilled on a scrap of paper. Even for someone accustomed to long-haul, to the feebly disguised indignities of budget travel, this was extravagant. He could not have stayed in Dundee; he had not dared to remain in London. But what did he want from Frank Silverman, this man who he now began to suspect might be hiding from him? He had come more than three thousand miles on a whim. He had no business at all in this sticky, well-mannered city.

It took another hour of walking to get back to the Trillium. He cooled off under the shower, then lay on the bedcovers letting the water dry over his skin. The curtains were part drawn, the room nicely shadowed. Half asleep, half awake, he suddenly wanted the reassurance of an erection, the distraction of pleasure (a pleasure he had hardly known in months). He thought of Zara, of the lovely sexual blush on her neck and cheeks when she started to come. His cock began to stiffen in his hand, but his imaginings became confused. There were other faces, other sounds, other intentions: images thrown by some feverish inward cinema, the sort of flickering, locked-booth pornography he wanted no part of, or had not, before the spring, suspected himself of wanting. And now? What had those hours on the hill unearthed in him? Was this self-knowledge? *This?*

He climbed from the bed, dressed, then shaved with excessive care, elaborate thoroughness, as though he were removing the evidence of something, scraping back to the smoothness of skin the emergent animal. Back in the bedroom, to work off the sour energy of unexpended lust, he did press-ups, squat thrusts, thirty sit-ups. He had to stay connected; to pretend, if only to himself, that he was a man of good habits, confessable ambitions, moderate appetites. A man who would not be automatically followed by a store detective or found suspect by the infra-red gaze of women and children. Dress, shave, exercise. Observe the common courtesies. Do not spit on the pavement or put your feet on the seats or get drunk in the morning. Do not clutch the arm of a stranger and ask him to pray with you. Do not tell what you know. Do not show your fear.

He was on the floor still, laid out and staring vacantly at the light fitting, when a note from the hotel reception was slipped beneath his door, a message on headed paper (the three-petalled Trillium flower) explaining that a Mr Silversham had called at 11.05 and would be lunching today at the Café Cavour on College Street at around four o'clock. Would Mr Glass like to join him?

According to his map, College was a cross-street seven or eight blocks north of the hotel. He had thirty minutes and the distance looked walkable. Coming out of the hotel, and then out of the hotel side-street, he turned on to a broad north–south avenue, passing bars with their shutters up, old-fashioned retoucheries, a half-dozen Chinese stores with boxes of kung-fu slippers and dried mushrooms in the deep shade of their awnings. At the intersection, unsure which way to turn, he guessed left, walking into the old Italian part of town and finding the Cavour ten minutes later on the corner of a small junction, a dozen tables outside, the music of some mournful, flippant love song coming from a speaker suspended among the trailing plants. Inside, the walls were hung with photographs of Italian ice-hockey stars. A bar, black and heavy as a catafalque, stood at the right-hand side of the room. Opposite the entrance, a second door spilled feathers of cooking steam whenever one of the waitresses swung through.

Though the lunchtime rush must have been over, there were still plenty of customers dawdling at the tables. Clem found a seat by the window, took off his sunglasses and ordered a double espresso. When it came he drank the water immediately, then sipped at his coffee. A few minutes before four Silverman arrived, coming through the door already looking for Clem, and waving brightly when he saw him. On his way over he was stopped by the café proprietress, a powerfully compact woman in a tight red dress and red high-heeled shoes. She was about Silverman's age and played coquettishly with her expensive, tawny hair while she spoke with him. Clem was surprised to hear them talking Italian, surprised how different it made Silverman seem, like someone he didn't know at all.

'It's my old man,' said Silverman, shaking Clem's hand between both of his own, then sitting sitting down opposite him. 'They remember him here. Carlo Argento from Crotone. A real southerner.' He chortled. 'He's creeping into my skin or I'm creeping into his. I make the same face as him when I pull the hairs out of my nose.'

'Everyone makes that face,' said Clem. 'You can't help it.'

Silverman nodded. 'My mother was Irish Canadian. I'd rather see her face in the mirror.'

'I had the opposite problem,' said Clem, remembering

how, throughout his teens, dead Nora appeared at the periphery of crowds at dusk, or stood at the top of the stairs in the house in Bristol, a presence composed of half-lights, the sound of rain on the window.

'You've eaten?' asked Silverman.

Clem said he hadn't but that the heat had taken his appetite. Silverman ordered two servings of spaghetti and clams. 'You need something on those bones,' he said. 'And you'll be working late tonight.'

'Working?'

'Relax. You won't need cameras.'

He was dressed in jeans and a black cotton shirt, the sleeves rolled. His hair was cropped, the skin tight and tanned over the angles of his skull. He looked like a three-star general in mufti. Eating, they talked about the people they had in common – newspaper people, television people, people whose careers circled their own – but before the food was finished it became apparent that neither of them had the latest on anybody, and that both, in their way, had dropped out of that world.

'I'm delighted you're here,' said Silverman. 'Delighted and a little amazed. What would you have done if I was out of town?'

'Gone home, I suppose.'

'And what would you have done there?'

Clem shrugged. 'Do you miss New York?'

'Not a whole lot. It became a troubled and troubling place for me.'

'And Shelley-Anne?'

'She's on page five hundred of something. A determined woman. I'll go back one day, if she'll take me. Right now I'm not in a fit state to live with anyone. Are you?'

'Who would I live with?'

'Are you drinking?'

'It doesn't seem to help me.'

'It doesn't help anyone. The reason I came up here, Clem, the straw that broke this camel's back, was waking with a bloody head down by the Staten Island ferry terminal, seven in the morning, stinking of Four Roses, commuters streaming past. No memory whatsoever of how I got there. I thought I was hardened against it all, this stuff we look at. Thought I could keep it tidied away in a box called work. Not this time.' He fell silent.

'You have family here still?' asked Clem.

'A brother on the west coast I haven't seen in years. A cousin in Moose Jaw. When I came up I stayed with an old couple my mother used to know along the lake shore by Hamilton. The Petersons. He's a retired ophthalmologist, eighty-something. A wife called Maggie. They're both pretty gnarled, these days, but Maggie goes out three times a week with hot soup for the street sleepers. Rides around in this big Japanese SUV she can hardly see over the dash of. No one's ever asked her to do it. They're not churchgoers. No idea what their politics are. One evening when the joints in her legs were swollen she asked me to drive her. Went out with her again the next week. Then regularly until I moved into the city.'

'Hot soup?'

'Feel free to laugh.'

'I'm not laughing.'

Silverman tucked some dollar bills under the edge of his water glass and stood up. Clem followed him through the swing door to the kitchen, a space only a half-size bigger than his own small kitchen in London, every corner and surface piled with plastic containers, chopping-boards, bags of peppers and onions, thick brown bags of bread. The cook was a stick-thin Cambodian whose apron wrapped around him almost twice. Silverman squeezed the man's shoulders and winked at Clem. 'The Café Cavour's greatest secret,' he whispered.

The cook called to his assistant, a big creamy-skinned girl slowly peeling a potato. She fetched two carrier-bags from the chiller. 'Some good minestrone,' said the cook, his voice split somehow between Phnom Penh, Toronto and Naples. '*Polpettone. Torta di patate. Tiramisu.* All good. All fresh.'

'May your ancestors see to it you get blown tonight,' said Silverman. The cook grinned. A fly hit the light trap, died, and fell to the floor. They cheered. Silverman took one of the bags, gave the other to Clem and led the way out. They walked for a few minutes along a street of neat red and brown brick houses, an over-sweet scent of summer jasmine in the air. At points along the way they passed little groups of men, languid, patrician, their hands in their pockets, watching the road as if nothing would ever quite interest them again: some stubborn sense of exile, perhaps, or simply the Old World melancholy of the Mediterranean taken root among the grids of the New.

'Prepare to suffer envy,' said Silverman, calling to Clem over his shoulder. He put down his bag beside a blue van, a gleaming, bull-like vehicle with tinted glass and racing tyres, the twin exhausts, chromed, fat as organ pipes.

'Bought it from a young fellow who was about to get married and start a responsible life,' he said, laughing at himself or the young fellow. 'Pitiful and he knew it. Gave me the keys as if handing over his own bleeding balls. Had no idea what a derelict like me would want with it.'

He unlocked the rear doors. 'The boy had everything you'd need for a party *à deux*. I stripped out the fur and the fairground lights but kept the music system. Speakers in the head-rests. Speakers everywhere. Johnny Cash never sounded like this before.'

There were fifteen primary-coloured plastic cool-boxes in the back. They put the bags into one of them and Silverman drove on to College Street, the van's engine throbbing like a boat's.

'Power steering!' shouted Silverman, over the noise of the music. 'Electric windows! Air-con!'

They stopped at two more Italian places – more fulsome greetings, more busy chefs, more bags for the cool-boxes – then drove to a wholefood restaurant and picked up fifty gluten-free rolls, a tub of green curry, four of last week's blueberry pies. Across town they called at a place called Chez-Soi, another called Eden. The last stop was a hotel by the lake, thirty people in the kitchens starting to prepare for the evening's sitting amid a row of clashing metal and military-style confusion. The cool-boxes were almost full. On the tape deck Silverman exchanged country for rap – 'I love these angry boys!' – and slotted the van into the chain of home-time traffic, beating rhythm on the ridged leather wrapping of the steering-wheel. They made slow progress but after forty minutes they pulled on to a narrow street of English-style A-frame houses, a street Clem thought he remembered walking down that morning. Silverman backed the van into a little forecourt.

'Home?'

'For now. A couple of others here too. Art-installation types. Like to video each other using the john.'

They went up a flight of wooden steps to the first floor. The room Silverman rented was spacious but almost bare. The window overlooked the road. Silverman sat on the single bed. 'A dream of discipline,' he said, smiling ruefully. He hugged himself and briefly shivered, though the room was warm. Clem sat on the only chair. Behind him on the table was an electric typewriter, and a sheaf of papers face down on a large brown envelope, a Mickey Mouse bottle opener for a paper weight.

'My piece for the *New York Times*,' said Silverman, pointing to the papers. 'Though I guess they've given up on me by now.'

'You don't want to do it?'

'I seem unable to.'

'You've made a start.'

'Notes, sketches, try-outs. Little that's coherent. And a piece like this must lead somewhere, must have a conclusion. Write about horrors and you're expected to make some sense of them. But what's it to be? The pity of it all? Exterminate the brutes?'

'The brutes?'

'Last time I wound a sheet into the machine I couldn't even lift my hands to the keys. A head-doctor would call it hysterical paralysis. Prescribe a course of electric-shock therapy.'

'Have you seen anyone?'

'Head-doctors? Christ, no.'

On the floor beside the bed was a leather holdall, unzipped. Next to it was a radio, and two books: a collected Berryman and one of Shelley-Anne's novels, *A Stitch in Time*. Clem asked Silverman if he was reading her.

'I keep it for the picture,' said Silverman. 'It's an odd thing but I can get a picture of my wife in any good bookstore.'

'And Berryman?'

'"Huffy Henry hid the day/unappeasable Henry sulked. . ." I don't read him any more but he's an old friend.'

Clem nodded. He asked what happened now.

'This is a time I don't care for,' said Silverman. 'There's a liquor store at the corner and I think about it a lot. It's good you're here. Can you play chess?'

'A little.'

'A little will do fine.'

From the holdall Silverman took out a hinged chess set. They played for an hour, the set between them on the bedclothes. When the game was over, Silverman made coffee. They listened to a baseball commentary on the radio. Clem read the first chapter of Shelley-Anne's book and looked at her photograph on the inside cover, a studio shot, clumsily retouched. The artists came home, fought in the kitchen and made up noisily in the room beside Silverman's. Night fell. Clem smoked at the window. Silverman made more coffee, then lay on the bed with his hands behind his head. At ten thirty he insisted on another game of chess. Clem won again. Silverman shaved and changed his shirt. 'Soon now,' he said. 'Almost there.' Clem drowsed and, half-asleep, bit his tongue and tasted blood. At a quarter to one, Silverman called his name and they went down through the hushed house to the van. The last time they had set out at night together they had travelled in UN Land Rovers with a patrol of frightened blue-helmets. That, too, had been Silverman's plan, for Clem had not wanted to go out in the curfew. After two weeks in the capital he had plenty of material. The agency was sated; the story was off the front pages; it was time to think about flights out. But Silverman, the older man, the man of reputation, of charm, had worked him round, talking, half seriously, half teasingly, about a money-shot, a picture to excite a prize jury. In the end, Clem had gone because he liked him, this rangy North American with his over-experienced face. In the end he'd gone because he didn't want to miss anything.

They checked the cool-boxes and climbed into the van.

'A short drive,' said Silverman, turning on the ignition.

'And then?'

'Aha.'

'You're full of mysteries,' said Clem.

Silverman smiled. 'That sounds OK. Does it bother you?'

The roads were almost empty now. A few taxis, a prowl car, a last street-car, brightly lit, a couple in the very back the only passengers.

'You know,' began Silverman, 'when I regained my senses down by the ferry terminal I didn't have a nickel left on me. Cleaned out. I had to walk home. It took an hour. All the way I saw myself in store windows. A madman. A ghost.' He paused. 'The human nervous system can handle a great deal of insult, but it's not endless. I came up here to save my life.'

'I need a Canada of my own,' said Clem, softly.

Silverman gestured in the dial-green gloom of the cab. 'Canada is bleak. Physically and spiritually bleak. But coming back here I found something. A truth about people I didn't have before.'

'A truth?' Clem twisted in his seat. 'What are you talking about?'

'Just that. A truth I didn't have before.'

'And the church? Haven't we already seen the truth about people? Haven't we *smelt* it?'

'I'm talking about something else, Clem.'

'Obviously.'

'Truer, perhaps.'

'A truer truth?'

'OK. A better one.'

'What makes you think we can choose?'

'What makes you think I can't? Anyway . . .'

'Anyway what?'

'Do we really know what we saw out there?'

'Don't fucking do this.'

'I mean it. What did we really see?'

'I'll send you the pictures.'

'I don't need the damn pictures.'

'Then what the hell do you need?'

'What I *need*,' said Silverman, raising his voice to match Clem's, 'is something that lets me sleep at night. What you're talking about is . . . nihilism. An impossibility.'

'I'm talking about what we saw. You and me.'

'And you can live with that?'

'What I can live with is irrelevant! It changes nothing!'

'You blame me.'

'Blame you?'

'You blame me for getting you into it.'

'No.'

'You blame me.'

'No.'

'Why not say it?'

'I don't blame you, Silverman!'

'Yeah, but I know you do.'

They stopped at a red light. Clem found the rocker switch for his window, let the window down and lit a cigarette. He would have liked to get out of the van now and walk until he was exhausted. Where was the city boundary? How far from here? He wanted to find himself beyond the range of street-lamps, walking on a prairie as big as a sea, as black as the sea. Poor Silverman! Whatever he was into now, this mystery tour, this 'truer truth' he held up as a shield, he was not the guide Clem needed. Unfair, of course, utterly unfair to have expected it. Unfair, cowardly and lazy. Had he, for a single moment, considered what he might do for Silverman? What Silverman might have hoped to get from *him*? He flicked the end of his cigarette away and put up the window. Between them the silence grew pointlessly tense. To break it, Clem said, 'My neighbours in London used to throw paint from their windows.'

'Protesting?'

'Maybe.'

'Good for them.'

'Yeah.'

They drove past the doors of a big hotel; Silverman U-turned and brought them up to the kerb on the other side of the road. 'Union Station,' he said, pointing to the row of green railings and solid grey pillars that faced the hotel. 'Nineteen thirty. Classical revival. The railroad built the hotel too.'

On the pavement in front of the station were two hot-dog stands (*Great-tasting Sausage in Toronto!*), make-shift affairs with coloured canvas covers. To one of these they started to carry the cool-boxes.

'I have an arrangement with the man whose pitch this is,' said Silverman, fitting a key into the padlock that secured the lashing at the back of the stall. He ducked under the canvas. A minute later he let down a board at the front. Clem brought the last of the boxes over. Silverman hung a pair of electric storm-lamps from the roof of the stall, then opened the valve of the gas bottle and lit the rings.

Since getting down from the van, Clem had been aware of movement, a flickering of shadows around the bases of the station pillars. Now he heard voices and, turning, found himself in the company of a half-dozen ragged, bright-eyed men. 'We too early?' asked one, peering at Clem from under the brim of his slouch hat.

'Give me fifteen!' called Silverman, rattling pans on to the burners. The men withdrew a few steps; others began to join them, men and women of all ages, many of them carrying bags or little packs, a blanket over the shoulder, a sleeping-bag rolled under an arm. They were patient, orderly, now and then sniffing the air as it became savoury.

'Hey, Clem! You know which box the *fettunata*'s in?'

Clem said that he thought he did.

They served for an hour. The soup went into plastic beakers, everything else on to disposable party plates.

With the two of them inside the stall, both long-limbed men, they had to move with due regard. Many of those they served Silverman knew by name. 'You back for seconds, Mac? How are the feet today, Patrick? Is Debbie coming down tonight?' By two twenty they were serving the stragglers and by two forty the last had tottered away to whatever nook of the city sheltered him. The range went off, the pans were stacked, the empty cool-boxes returned to the back of the van. Silverman poured the remaining soup into a pair of flasks. There was also half a bag of rolls left, some rice salad, two of the blueberry pies.

'Phase one,' said Silverman, padlocking the stall.

'There's more?'

Silverman put his hand on Clem's shoulder and, with a quick look round at the street, guided him towards the station. '*This* is what I wanted you to see. What I was trying to tell you about.' He tapped at a tall green door.

'Silverman?' challenged a muffled voice.

'Yeah, it's me,' said Silverman.

The door opened; they slid inside. 'This is Defoe,' said Silverman, nodding to the young security guard. 'Defoe, this is Clem. A *compadre* from the mother country.'

'Getting worried you weren't coming,' said Defoe, locking the door.

'You should know me better than that,' said Silverman, soothingly.

They were standing in the station ticket hall – archways, arched windows, high walls of hewn stone, a vaulted roof. For these night hours the lighting was minimal. The hall, eerie as any public space deserted, seemed set for the arrival of a troupe of actors. Clem found himself suddenly remembering the painting in the doctor's office at Ithaca, the red-haired girl on the mule. It would not be so strange to see her here, ambiguous sprite, observing them from the watery shadows beneath an archway.

'Defoe and his uncle Edward do alternate nights,' explained Silverman. 'It was Defoe who told me about the people we're going to now. Right, Defoe?'

'Right,' said Defoe, touching the red line where his collar scratched the skin of his neck.

'But we tread with care,' said Silverman. 'There are parties who would not be sympathetic to this. Not at all.'

They went down a flight of steps to a small arcade. A juice bar, a bakery, a place to buy souvenirs, newspapers. Between a florist's and an ATM was a painted door, the top of it about the height of Clem's lowest ribs. After a glance at Silverman, Defoe knocked with his keys. They waited. Defoe knocked again. From the other side of the door came the sound of some obstruction being dragged free of the way.

'We still don't know how any of them got in here,' said Silverman. 'There may be a way in from the tracks. The whole place is a maze. Watch your head now.'

Clem crouched low and moved, an awkward shuffling, into the dim space ahead of him. Silverman came next; Defoe remained outside, to keep watch perhaps, or for fear that his uniform, not unlike a policeman's, might spread alarm. The ceiling of the room – it must once have served as storage space – was not quite high enough to stand under. Along one side, four men and three women sat with their knees drawn up, their backs against the wall.

Silverman shook their hands. One of the women, her hair under a red or brown scarf, tried to press his fingers to her lips but he withdrew them, gently. 'No, no,' he said. 'I'm not the bishop.'

He began to unpack the food.

'Where are they from?' whispered Clem, helping to set up.

'As best as I can make out they're Moldovans. Or Romanians. Maybe gypsies. About three words of English between them. No papers, of course. No money.'

'Couldn't they just claim asylum?'

'My guess is they tried that last time and found themselves on a flight back to Chişinău. Picked up pan-handling. Fell foul of some cop or city bylaw. Who knows?'

'A better chance here than in the States?'

'Actually,' said Silverman, 'I suspect that's where they think they are.'

The men were thin, delicately made, dressed in white shirts and cheap suits. The women wore the kind of traditional outfits peasants in Dracula films wore. Clem doled out the rolls and cups of soup. They muttered their thanks. He pitied them.

'They get to stretch their legs at night for an hour,' said Silverman, tapping softly at an even smaller door at the rear of the room. 'Use the station restrooms. I'm sorting some legal rep. When the time's right we'll move them out. Make them all Canadians.'

The smaller door swung open. A long, sallow face peered out and blinked at them.

'*Buenas tardes*,' said Silverman.

'*Buenas tardes*, Señor,' said the man.

'Previously of Guatemala City,' said Silverman to Clem. 'They arrived with even less if you can imagine it. The good people here let them share the place.'

As if on cue, one of the men from Moldova or Romania waved a neighbourly greeting to the Guatemalan and, shifting stiffly from the wall, began to pass through the remaining food. Clem knelt by the door – more hatch than door – and looked inside. Around a single source of light, chiaroscuro fashion, the man and two solemn women nodded to him as they began their supper. Beyond them, laid in a crib of carboard boxes, a child, four or five years old, sucked at a piece of bread and stared at Clem from satin, unamazed eyes.

'He's not theirs,' said Silverman, his voice thickening with emotion.

'No?'

'Little mite must have become separated from his parents on the way through. Anyway, these folks care for him. Treat him like their own.'

The child stirred, and from under his blanket produced a tin, an old milk-powder or coffee tin perhaps, harvested from trackside jetsam. The lid had been punctured with some kind of spike. The boy waved to Clem: an odd, languorous gesture.

'Go on,' said Silverman. 'This is priceless . . .'

Clem went in on hands and knees. The adults moved aside to let him pass. The women smiled. '*Hola*,' said Clem to the child.

'*Mira*,' whispered the boy. With the points of frail fingers he struggled to dislodge the lid from the tin. Clem slid a coin from his pocket, a Canadian dollar, and prised the lid loose; the boy lifted it away. It was, at first, too dark to see what was inside (what moved in the can's black air) but behind Clem someone raised the lamp until the light fell on the raw snouts of a pair of nude-looking mice, the kind of vermin Clem had often seen scurrying beneath the rails of the London Underground, intent, semi-blind creatures that fed off dust and ashes.

'*Son míos*,' said the boy, gazing at them, his expression split between ruthlessness and love, like a little dictator smiling on the crowd from a palace balcony. He dropped a scrap of bread inside, then quickly sealed the tin, stealing it back into the gloom beneath his blanket.

There was no room for Clem to turn round without inconveniencing the others. He thanked the boy, and for a second or two locked eyes with him, then he lowered his head and began, very slowly, crawling backwards towards the door.

12

He slept for only a few hours, waking still dressed, lying on the bed covers, cut in two by sunlight. He had been dreaming but the dream was in fragments. An image of himself scrabbling among rubbish. A room. The room at the station. And Silverman? Yes. Silverman, the Guatemalans, the boy (possessed now of the enormous liquid gaze of a doomed cartoon fawn) looking back at him from the door. Silverman pushing the door shut with his bishop's crook, shouting, 'We have orders,' or 'Our orders are clear'. Unnerving, senseless stuff.

He sat up. The hotel was quiet, the road too. He left the bed and went to the window, squinted against the light, remembered, looking on to the angles and morning shadows of an empty street, that the day was Sunday.

In the bathroom he swilled his mouth with water from the tap. There was some discomfort in his head, a point above his right eye, like the hot tip of a wire, an ache running back along the wire an inch or two into the interior of his skull. He leaned and examined his eye in the mirror. His right eye, his view-finder eye. He had a certain professional knowledge of eyes – the sclera, the choroid, the myriad cells in the cup of the retina where the light converges. With his left hand he covered his left eye. The right, singled out, looked back at him like a small cowed animal. Leaning closer he noticed a hint of inflammation, a redness around the inner rim of the lid that was perhaps the beginning of something, something he had been expecting for a long time. Could an eye be damaged by what it looked at? Too fierce a light will burn it. What else? Though he had studied it as the camera's conjunct, a metaphor for what the camera will do with metal and glass, the eye was not a machine. It lived, glittered in the face, was washed by tears. Could it look on a living child the way it looked on a child's two-day corpse? Hard to believe something so delicate would not be altered. Hard to believe it. He could not, in truth, believe it.

In the bedroom he picked up the remote control, turned on the television and scrolled through the channels until he reached the US Weather Channel ('Well, Diane, we're looking at highs in the high eighties outside of Lawton today . . .') The sun in the room made the picture hard to see but he didn't want to see it, he wanted to listen. He had had a certain fascination with this channel ever since he came across it in a motel in Texas, years ago; was amused by it at first, surprised that an entire channel should be devoted to weather, then found the seamless detailing of ephemeral conditions in places he knew little or nothing about soothing, like hearing in childhood the lullaby voices of adults talking round the table late into the night.

He had told Silverman, when Silverman, after a short, wordless trip from Union Station, dropped him off outside the Inn at a quarter to four in the morning, that he intended to spend the day sightseeing, a trip to Niagara perhaps. Silverman had approved. The Falls, though heavily exploited, were, he said, worth seeing. There was a cable-car ride over the water, and it was always fun to see the honeymooners. Then Clem had reached through the van's window and they had clasped hands, the pair of them grave as generals at a surrender, or as though their leavetaking were not for a night but final and for ever.

Clem had seen cards for the tour companies in boxes on the curve of the reception desk. If asked, the manager would surely arrange something. He could take a coach, eat lunch out there, see the Falls, and be back by early evening, not having spent the entire day in his hotel room. He thought – aware he was not thinking well and that soon he would have to do much better – going to the Falls would make some sense of his coming over. What did he do? He went to see the Falls, one of the wonders of the world. And how were they? They were impressive. They were very impressive.

From the fridge with its mock-wood door he took a bottle of beer, a bag of salted nuts, and propped himself against the headboard of his bed. Later, if he was hungry, he could send out for something from Chinatown. Everything else – painkillers, drink, cigarettes – he had there with him. On the screen, shades in human form loomed against the landscape. Deserts, cities. There were updates from the Mississippi Delta, the Virginia Highlands, from Flathead Lake. The news from Calvert County was that a freak storm had blown a child through a store window, but the storm was over, people were sweeping up, and the child was doing well, considering.

Monday was departure day. He woke after thirteen hours' dead sleep to find another message on the carpet by the door. It informed him that a Mr Silverton had called (apparently Clem had slept right through it). He was sorry not to be able to see Mr Glass today but there were errands, an unexpected weight of work. He wished Mr Glass a *bon voyage*. He looked forward to seeing him at some other time.

Clem showered, then walked to the café where he had sat beside the students on his first day in the city. It was a cooler morning with rafts of low, moist cloud. At the café he ordered an espresso and a bagel with cream cheese. He ate half the bagel then swallowed a pair of ibuprofen. Overnight, the wire-tip had become the complicated head of a small flower, a circle of overlapping petals pressing against the skin beneath his eyebrow. He thought, lugubriously, of Nora falling stone-dead into the front row of the South Bristol Women's Low Pay Action Group; then briefly of Silverman's delicacy (or rank cowardice) in sparing them both any fresh embarrassments. He lit his first cigarette of the day, sputtered, ground it out, and left the café – 'Have a good one!' called the boy from behind the counter – to spend an hour or two on foot, a hike to shake off this sluggishness. His blood was thick as syrup. He walked fast, almost running. It rained for a while; he kept going; the rain was helpful. At two, he ate a bowl of udon in a noodle bar on Dundas Street. At three, he returned to the Trillium Inn and packed. When he tried to pay the bill his Visa card was rejected, twice. 'Maybe the system,' said the manager, doubtfully. Clem dug in his pockets, found dollars he didn't know he had, paid cash.

Down to his last twenty-five, he took the subway to a station called Yorkdale, then caught a transit bus to the airport for less than three dollars. He was late for his check-in but the queues were short and he had no luggage for the hold. He bought a pack of painkillers at the airport pharmacy, then used the change to buy a word-search puzzle book and a biro. He was in the line for security, almost at its head, when he heard his name called and looked back to see Frank Silverman jogging towards him, a rolled newspaper in one hand, a large brown envelope in the other.

'Jesus, Clem! Almost missed you.' He bent slightly to catch his breath. 'Expressway's fender to fender. What time's the flight?'

'Seven.'

'That's what I thought. Let's get ourselves a quick drink. There's a place right here. Damned convenient.'

They went in and leaned at the bar. Silverman ordered a double tonic water; Clem had beer.

'If I'd known you were coming,' said Clem.

'Didn't know myself until a couple of hours ago. Thought you'd go home with a poor impression of Canadian hospitality.' He grinned. 'How were the Falls?'

'I didn't go.'

'No, well, I didn't think you were going. Here's mud in your eye.' They tapped glasses. Silverman said, 'I'm sorry we haven't had more chance to talk.'

'We'll talk some time,' said Clem.

'It's knowing what to say.'

'Yeah.'

'I don't know what to say, Clem.'

'It's OK.'

'You're not exactly effusive yourself.'

'I'm glad I saw you.'

'I'm glad too.'

Distracted, they turned to look along the bar to where a man in a white linen jacket was talking at high volume to an embarrassed-looking woman. They watched a moment.

'Ass,' said Silverman. He turned back to Clem. 'You'll stay in touch?'

'Of course.'

'Of course! Is that Brit-speak for no?'

'It's Brit-speak for of course.'

'We need to get past this, Clem. If we can't get past this then Ruzindana wins.'

'And if they find him,' asked Clem, 'what will you do?'

'Other than hope they make him swing? Nothing.' He paused. 'What *is* there to do?'

Clem shook his head.

'Anyway,' said Silverman, fishing the lemon slice from his glass, 'don't hold your breath. It's a big world. He could be anywhere.'

'But you think he's alive?'

'In one of the camps maybe. Or someone's protecting him. Europe. The States, even. The Devil takes care of his own.'

'Agree on one thing,' said Clem.

'Sure.'

'That nothing can be forgiven.'

'Agreed.'

'Nothing.'

'Agreed.'

'No amends. No forgiveness.'

'Agreed, agreed. But you can't stop the grass growing, Clem.'

'I've no idea what that means.'

'It means the grass is growing over their bones. It will grow over ours one day.'

'You suggest we forget about it?'

'Of course not! That's not humanly possible. But we should be ready to move on.'

Clem bit back his reply. For a moment, neither wished to catch the other's eye. Silverman rubbed at his wedding band. The London flight was called again. Clem picked up his bag. Silverman walked to the barrier with him. They embraced. Silverman was crying.

'This is how I am now,' he said. 'All sentiment.'

'There's no shame in it.'

'The boy asked for you last night,' said Silverman, brushing a tear from his cheek. 'He must have a future too, don't you think?'

Clem agreed. A gap opened between them. Silverman reached across it with the envelope. 'Maybe you can do something with this. It's beyond my powers.' Clem took the envelope; Silverman smiled and quickly retreated, waving his newspaper. 'You get my vote, Clem Glass!' he called. 'Better times for us all, eh?'

It was the same crew Clem had flown out with from Heathrow. He recognised the blonde stewardess as she stood by the door greeting and directing. He couldn't tell if she remembered him: though still discernibly new to her work she had learned the indiscriminate smile of a professional, her face lighting up like a torch bulb, one or two seconds, as each passenger shuffled past her.

His seat was at the front of Economy (or what did they call it now? Main Cabin? Family Traveller? World Explorer?), an aisle seat behind the central bulkhead where the film screen was showing reassuring pre-flight images of birds roosting at twilight. Of the other seats in his row only one was occupied, a man who, in short order, had put in the earpieces of his Walkman, put on his complimentary eye mask, and drawn his blanket up to his chin.

They took off, hurtling gently into the lighter sky above the clouds. Announcements were made, a trolley service began. When Clem had a drink he took down his bag from the overhead locker, put it on the empty seat beside him, and unzipped it. Silverman's brown envelope was on top. Clem regarded it for a moment (unwelcome gift!), then reached below for the word-search book whose gloss cover showed a woman holding a pencil to the corner of her mouth in some strange, coquettish mime of rumination. Each puzzle in the book set the same basic problem: how to find a list of words sunk within a block of letters. The words could run in any direction. The trick, it seemed, was to apprehend a word as a pattern, then try to recognise it against a background where it was minimally differentiated. More doggedly, you could take the first three letters of the word and work systematically across the grid, though this approach was made harder by the anticipation of the puzzle-makers who often set letters together as a decoy, thus Clem found the ELE of ELECTRON running down, diagonally and backwards, before uncovering the word itself. There was an extra challenge to the puzzles that employed longer or less familiar words. He completed a puzzle called *Things to Do at Home* – KNITTING, YOGA, BRIDGE – in ten minutes, but made only slow progress with *Varieties of Clematis*. One on this list,

HELSINGBORG, he searched for fruitlessly. The solutions were given in the back pages but he went on, scanning the grid with the nib of his biro until it became, quite suddenly, beyond bearing. He told himself they had certainly left the word out, while at the same time knowing perfectly well they could not have done and that he was simply too blind to see what was there in front of him. The pain above his eye was significantly worse. He pressed around it with the tip of his thumb, a kind of acupressure, until his eye watered and the letters in the grid blurred to the point of being unreadable. He shut the book, brushed it from his lap. He stood up. Both of the toilets at the front of his section were engaged. He went through the curtains into 'Executive' Class. If any-one stopped him he would tell them he was about to vomit, which, from the heat rising into his head, he thought perhaps he was. The only air-crew in his way was the young stewardess, and she was occupied with one of the passengers, leaning in front of him, listening to something she evidently didn't want to listen to, her face attempting an expression of quiet authority. Coming closer, Clem saw that the man talking to her was the one in the white linen jacket he and Silverman had seen in the bar before the flight. On his tray were already four empty mini-bottles, Remy Martins, and from his tone as Clem passed he seemed at the point of deciding whether to go on flirting with the stewardess, or to start becoming very angry with her. ('Oh, rules!' Clem heard him say, as though he were a man for whom rules were both made and broken.)

In the toilet, Clem hung his head over the steel basin. When he realised he wasn't going to throw up he wiped his brow with water and dabbed it dry with a paper serviette. He examined his eye: shut it, opened it, blinked. There was nothing to see. Even the redness he had noticed at the Trillium Inn – or imagined he had noticed – was gone. The face in the mirror, a face for which he now felt only a very minor sense of ownership, regarded him with a curious intensity, a look of excitement he neither understood nor trusted.

He emptied his bladder, washed his hands, and folded open the cubicle door. The stewardess was still leaning beside the man's chair though her posture now was more defensive. He heard her say, 'Sir . . .' two or three times, then saw her hold up her hand, palm out. The man reached up, snatched at her, caught her arm below the shoulder, dragged her down, then thrust her backwards. In her effort to escape him she snagged her feet, one behind the other, lost her balance and fell, heavily, striking her head on the moulding of an unoccupied seat in a way that looked both comical and painful. The man began to stand, already, from his expression, appalled at having done so much so easily. With his eyes fixed on the stewardess he did not notice Clem step forwards. The blow – a noise like the snap of a leather belt – caught him high on the cheek. He grunted, sat back, said, 'Oh!' in a mild voice, and turned up his gaze just as Clem's second punch, a downward slanting right, connected with the wetness at the side of his mouth. By the fourth punch he was bleeding freely, black drops falling on to the lapels of his jacket. He raised his hands, defending himself, or a gesture of surrender perhaps, but Clem, braced by the seat, thrashed at him, flurry-punching until he was seized from the back and dragged clear. Some discreet alarm was sounding. Cabin crew arrived from all parts of the plane. The blonde, helped to her feet, sobbed against a colleague's blouse. Orders were issued, counter-orders. Someone said they should fetch the restraints; someone else said the captain was coming.

Across the aisle, a woman, some ten years older than the stewardess – a tall, shapely woman in an expensively tailored night-blue suit – got out of her seat, inclined her head to Clem in grim salute, and began to clap. A second woman, a few seats further back, stood and joined her, then, more grudgingly, a half-dozen of the men. The steward who had wrapped his arms around Clem's chest loosened his grip. Clem looked down at the beaten man and smiled at him. The man's blue eyes were wild with shame. He tried to speak (*Violar, estoy violada!*), a thread of blood between his yellow teeth. Then he turned in the seat and hid from them.

At Heathrow, the Transport Police were waiting by the gate. They escorted Clem to an interview room, took a statement and held him for four hours. At first they were hostile; then the view developed that he had simply defended a member of the airline staff. As Clem was taken from one room to another he saw in the corridor the woman who had applauded him. The man in the white linen jacket was called Paulus, and in the end, it seemed, nobody cared much about a man like Paulus. By three p.m. Clem was back at his flat. His knuckles were so swollen he could scarcely move his fingers. In the kitchen he used a bag of frozen peas as a cold-pack. When the swelling had reduced he made phone-calls – one to a friend in London, one to Scotland, one (a number he had not called in years) to a house in Somerset. Afterwards, he sat on his front steps. The air was full of the dust of high summer. On the pavement the paint had worn to a faintly orange, faintly purple shadow. He wondered what he should feel about the man he had hit, about Paulus, but when he thought of him, the frightened face turning away, he felt a glee he was too tired to despise in himself. He lit a cigarette, gripping it between ruddy fingers. It was only when he leaned to tap out the butt on the stone between his feet that he realised his headache was entirely gone.

13

He left his bed while the Grove was still lit by its orange lamps. In the kitchen he cleaned out the Bialetti, then filled it with water and fresh coffee. From the kitchen window he could see a scatter of lights in a scatter of buildings. A car passed, then, two or three minutes later, another. The city was at low ebb, as hushed now as it could ever be with so many restless millions packed in for miles in all directions. An hour notorious for ghosts, rummaging foxes, suicides, false clarities. While he waited for the water to boil he calculated the time in Toronto. Eleven, eleven thirty. Silverman would be making his preparations, Defoe or his uncle buttoning his uniform, the Moldovans (if that was what they were) and the Guatemalans keeping their vigil, their practice of an almost infinite patience. And on the island? Was his father asleep, or was he taking his turn in the little chapel, 'the heart of the house'? Old knees, old thighs, old neck bent in prayer. What did he hear above the sea sounds and the settling of his bones? A mail train on the mainland? The dub, dub, dub of a trawler's engine? It was harder to conjure up the night at Ithaca, those concentrations of distress that shaped the darkness there, everyone pressed against his particular confusion, someone whimpering in a dream, the night staff gossiping in the corridors . . .

He poured the coffee into a mug, sugared it, and carried it through to the living room. For a minute he stood there, stalled, irresolute, then crossed to the book-shelf, reached to the top of it, and lifted down a black mock-leather file the size of an attaché case. He took it to his desk and sat in front of it a long time. It was here that he kept the negatives and transparencies from the spring, hundreds of them in acetate pockets, many of them – the negatives – processed in the bathroom at the Bellville Hotel where, stripped to his underwear, he had laboured like an automaton, the films dangling in long bronze curls from a clothes-line above the bath, some curious resource of shock or professionalism allowing him to go on with it.

He had not opened the file since his return – he had not dared – but now he took the light-box from under his desk, plugged it in, shook out frames and strips of film, and scattered them across the lit surface. His Schneider eyeglass was in a velvet pouch in the desk drawer. He polished the lens on the hem of his T-shirt, then ordered the film into rows, leaned, and went from one to the next, from the innocuous to those he could scarcely believe he had had the stomach, the effrontery, to take at all.

What prompted him to look again? Why this morning? Did he fear the wearing thin of his faith in human iniquity? That his disgust was being undermined by petty kindnesses, the rounding-off of memory? Or was it the persistent rankling of Silverman's challenge to him the night they drove to the station – *Do you really know what we saw?* The question then had seemed outrageous, easily answered. He had the evidence in Ektachrome and on rolls of Tri X 400. He could touch it, handle it; he owned it. But knowing what it meant – wasn't that the sense of Silverman's question? Not what it was, but what it *meant*? He roused himself and pressed his eye more keenly to the glass, yet the more he looked the less it seemed the pictures had to tell him, as though, stared at too long, too needily, they shaped themselves into terrible puzzles, the truths they held retracting into tiny points of light, their eloquence suddenly ambiguous, contentious, refutable.

He switched off the light-box, thrust the film anyhow back into the file, zipped the file shut. The day had dawned. Cars passed the house every few seconds; the street-lamps were barely brighter than the air around them. To quieten himself, these waves of agitation, the troubling half-glimpses of the weeks ahead, he pulled one of Clare's books from the shelf (*Delacroix and the Economics of Excitement*), settled into the room's solitary armchair, one leg crooked over the armrest, and read a dozen cool well-written pages from the middle of the book. Delacroix in Paris, Delacroix and Chopin, music and painting, the civilisers. As he read he thought he heard his sister's voice and, growing drowsy, the book slipping from his lap, saw her in the doorway of his box-room bedroom in Bristol telling him it was time to put the light out, time to sleep, that tomorrow was a school day. When she was in the mood she would sometimes come and sit with him for a few minutes, solicitous, serious, a little distracted, as though trying to keep track of all the things she had to do before she went to bed or turned eighteen. Then the light was off, the darkness bloomed, and he was left to swallow his grief until sleep came with dreams that ushered him through empty rooms or left him, house-trapped, listening to a voice from the garden, a calling to be let in that could not be heeded . . .

He was woken by the noise of sirens. A pair of fire engines lumbered past, dementedly. His leg was insensate. He rubbed it hard, wincing as the life flowed back, then hobbled into the kitchen to eat. The fridge contained a carton of UHT milk, the peas he had used to cool his knuckles, a nub of salami hard enough to break his teeth on. He opened a can of tuna and ate the meat from the tin, his chin shiny with oil. When he had finished, he shaved, dressed, and packed a suitcase (this endless packing and unpacking!). It was eight fifty. He had arranged with Toby Rose to pick up the car at ten. He went back to the living room to collect his cigarettes from the desk, but as he reached for them he saw that three leaves of film had, in his haste to hide them all away, floated to the back of the light-box. He hesitated, considered for a moment sweeping them into the bin by his feet, but sharply curious to see which of the images chance had selected (he was drawn increasingly to every manner of portent) he pressed them on to the surface of the box, flicked the switch, and picked up the eyeglass.

The first – vivid enough to make him flinch – was Sylvestre Ruzindana, a shot Clem had taken of a photograph that he and Silverman had found at the Bourgmestre's house when they had driven out there in the hope of confronting him. They had arrived too late: an intense disappointment, though hardly a surprise. The house, a two-storey concrete building on the edge of the commune where most of the murdered once lived, had already been abandoned, broken into, ransacked. The photograph lay under shattered glass on the floor of the office, a portrait, semi-official, of a solidly-built, neatly bearded man in his mid-fifties. A relaxed and confident figure looking at the camera through black-rimmed spectacles, one hand on his hip, the other reaching back to rest on the bright roof of the saloon car behind him. A man on the way up. A man with connections, heft. Someone accustomed to issuing orders and to seeing them swiftly obeyed. Silverman had taken the original print, intending to give it to whomever seemed most serious about hunting the man down.

The next picture showed a classroom in one of the outbuildings beside the church. The legs of upturned desks. A map of the world. The edge of a blackboard with chalk marks from the last lesson. The whitewashed wall at the end of the room was sprayed and thickly smeared with blood. The dead were not in view, though in places their bodies had been stacked three or four deep. He had no recollection of taking the picture, of the moment when he must have looked at the wall and thought, I'll take that.

The third was Odette Semugeshi. She was dressed in a blue cotton pinafore and plastic sandals, and stood at the end of her bed at the Red Cross hospital. Ten years old, bandaged, graceful as a blade of grass. The daughter of murdered parents, the friend of murdered children. She returned the camera's stare with a gaze of the quietest imaginable outrage.

These three images Clem put into his wallet, a compartment with a steel popper, a pouch meant for a bus pass or a library ticket. He would not look at them again – he did not want to weaken them with looking – but he would carry them with him as others carried photographs of a wife, a house, a beloved animal. He would let them tell him who he was (for who *was* he?) and what he believed (for what *did* he believe?). In the end, perhaps, they would excuse him or, if not, they would be the excuse that he offered.

14

It took several minutes of ringing the bell to bring Toby Rose to the window. He dropped the keys down; Clem let himself into the building, went up a flight of bare steps – it was an undistinguished ex-council property two hundred yards from Wandsworth Common – and opened the door to the flat. Rose was in the narrow passageway dressed in a pair of boxer shorts, his large face blurred from heavy sleep. He held up his hands. 'Sorry, mate. Forgot the whole fucking deal.' Clem put his case down and followed him into the living room. The room, in darkness, was pungent with the smell of the previous night's partying. Rose tugged the curtains open. Over the coffee-table, the sofa, the carpet, the mantel-piece, the top of the television, was a litter of glasses and CD covers, newspapers, Rizla papers, contact sheets, ashtrays. On the floor by his feet Clem noticed a heat-discoloured spoon and the length of strapping that Rose used to swell a vein in his arm, a mild heroin habit that did not seem to have affected his work and which, perhaps, made it possible.

'Long time no see,' said Rose.

'No great change here,' said Clem.

Rose collected a pair of empty wine glasses and went to the kitchen to make tea. Clem followed him out, going along the passageway to the toilet at the end. On his way back to the living room he passed the bedroom door. It had been shut before but now was open. There was a girl in the bed, drowsy but awake, naked from the waist up, her hands on the pillow beside her head, the sheets ruffled around her hip-bones like a surf. She smiled unguardedly (a nymph in the sea off Lemnos spied upon by some idiot goatherd on the beach). Clem smiled back and walked on, made dumb for a moment by this intrusion of the lovely, then rueful and half amused that a five-second view of a nude in a sunlit room could make everything, all weighty preoccupation, into so many bubbles of soap. To be alone with a girl like that for an hour! To close the door and run his tongue to the pit of her belly! To breathe her in! He was ready for that, felt, with a little flare of impatience, that he had earned it. Hadn't he?

He stood at the living-room window looking at the scruffy garden, the stray blooms, the unmown grass decorated with lozenges of sunlight. Forgetting what had happened last time, choosing to forget it, he thought of calling Zara again. Would she take a day off work? The spontaneity of it might charm her – a pair of school-kids tiptoeing past the headmaster's study. Buy wine, chocolate, smoked salmon, cigarettes. Flowers! Then back to her flat behind Oxford Street. Lock the doors, pull down the blinds (were there blinds? He couldn't remember). Go at it like dogs. He might even ask Rose to sell him some junk. He had not taken it before – Nora's ghost would be aghast – but now the idea appealed to him powerfully. What was he saving himself for? Wasn't hedonism as good a way as any? He could live in a kind of stumbling dance, show his bare arse to all solemn thinkers, act the fool. He no longer understood why he was going up north. Family obligation? Bad conscience? And what if he didn't go? Who would think about it for more than ten minutes? Surely, like almost everyone else, he suffered from an exaggerated sense of the importance of his own actions. Better to be a clown or a drunk. Better to somehow get past caring and stay there.

Rose returned with a tray, a brass teapot, two little cups. They drank the sugary tea and smoked, meditatively. Rose had been working in the Balkans and was going back at the end of the week. He asked where Clem had been.

'Canada,' said Clem.

'Canada? Shit. What's happening in Canada?'

'Nothing,' said Clem.

'Right,' said Rose.

'The car still works?' asked Clem, quickly. He wanted no descent into the details of his trip.

'The car's all right,' said Rose. They had bought it together from the auction house the other side of Wands-worth Bridge: five hundred pounds each. Out of the country half the year neither had need of a car of his own. Sharing was a sensible plan, though it was Rose who got the greater use of it.

'Going somewhere nice?'

'Dundee.'

'Dundee!' Rose shook his head. 'Another of the world's great trouble-spots. What about the old dark continent? You're not going back?'

'I don't think so.'

'If you're looking for fresh mayhem you can come with me.'

'I'm not.'

'Not?'

'Looking for fresh mayhem.'

'Well, please don't tell me you're going to start doing abstracts like that poor cunt Singer.'

'There are other things.'

'What? Weddings?'

'Other things besides photography.'

'If you're giving up, sell me the Leica.'

'You can't afford it.'

'I could if you gave me a good price.'

Clem nodded. 'I'm going to need the car for a while. I'm not sure how long. A few weeks perhaps. Is that OK?'

'*Wenn du willst*,' said Rose, turning in his chair to watch the girl from the bed entering the room on bare feet. Not a nymph any more, but an ordinary broad-hipped girl in a frayed towelling bathrobe, her hair tangled from the pillow. She looked about fifteen.

'Clem Nina, Nina Clem.'

Clem wished her a good morning.

'Clem's off to Dundee,' said Rose.

'Nice one,' said Nina, without a trace of Rose's irony. 'That's the cake place, right?'

'That's right.'

'Nice one.' She showed off her little pearly teeth in a smile, found her pouch of tobacco under a cushion and started to roll a cigarette.

Clem said it was time he made tracks; Rose went to find the car keys. At the door they slapped hands and wished each other luck. 'And think about the Leica,' called Rose down the stairwell. 'No sense in it gathering dust. I could *do* something with it.'

*   *   *

The car, a white Ford, unwashed in weeks or months, was parked beside the common. There was a penalty notice under one of the windscreen wipers. Clem put his case in the boot, put the notice in the glove compartment (at least two more in there) and wound down the windows to let out some of the cooked, rubbery air. The inside of the car was a scale model of Rose's living room. Clem rooted through the cassettes scattered on the passenger-seat footmat, found one that he knew by the Brazilian singer Caetano Veloso, and put it on. For a minute it was tempting to stay there, secure in the public privacy of the car, listening to the caress of Veloso's voice. He let his eyes shut, then opened them again and rubbed vigorously at his temples. He should be listening to some of Silverman's 'angry boys', not this crooner. He looked again among the cassettes on the mat. No rap there; a good deal of glum British rock; some club stuff that might have been Nina's. He settled for a tape called *Essential Soundtracks 2*, manoeuvring into the noonday traffic to the beat of 'Caught in the Middle with You', glad to be on his way at last, relieved, as though he had survived some subtle trap, the perilous down-suck of hesitation, inaction.

As soon as he had cleared London he filled the tank with petrol, paid with a cheque, then drove hard, a middle-lane driver, pushing the little car to keep up a steady eighty. Near Knaresborough he stopped for coffee. Fifty miles further north the traffic slowed to a crawl, half an hour in first gear until, for no observable reason, no blue lights or fuel spill, they were freed again. He crossed the Tweed at Coldstream – Berwick was only twenty miles down-river. He smiled a greeting to his father, and had a strange brief fantasy of all the old men from the house gathered around an enormous *camera obscura* in which they could see him, the white car, climbing into barren latitudes on a road that ran past dry stone walls and the shadows of hills. At Edinburgh, arriving at that point of the dusk when nothing is clean-edged, he lost his concentration and found himself on the M8 to Glasgow. He changed carriageways at the next junction and drove back, crossing the Forth Bridge in darkness, the lights of the shore-front below him, a sense of flying now, of no longer going north but upwards.

On the far bank, bored by symmetries, he turned off the motorway and took the minor roads, driving through villages and black countryside until a string of bulbs on a roadside inn made him realise how hungry he was. He went in and ate, gratefully, a heaped plate of badly cooked food. Immediately he longed for sleep. He asked behind the bar if they had rooms but there were none. The landlady gave directions to a place that might; Clem nodded but did not listen to her. He bought a bottle of Scotch and went back to the car. The roads were quiet, almost empty. He drove towards the sea (a sign said Tayport), then slowed and turned into a lane, wooded on one side, utterly unlit. Skeins of mist hung over the hedge-tops. His headlights picked out moths and, low beside a barred gate, a flash of yellow eyes. A second turning, narrower, led into the woods. He drove cautiously over trackway, pulled on to a small clearing beneath the trees, turned off the lights and switched off the engine. Quietness, like the hissing in a shell, seeped through the skin of the car. He drummed his fingers on the wheel and peered out at nothing. Did he want to stay here? Or should he press on for Dundee, find a B-and-B there, a cheap hotel? If he had kept the keys to Clare's flat . . . but staying there would have brought the risk of a confrontation with Finola Fiacc. Would she not have tipped off the neighbours, warned them about an errant brother, a troublemaker? God help the pair of them if it came to a showdown in the small hours. What were they not equal to?

He climbed from the car and stretched his back. Above him he could see sprays of tiny stars but their light did not penetrate. The forest floor was black as a cellar, the car itself a bare grey shadow. He fetched the whisky and leaned against the ticking bonnet. Now that he was here he was determined to be at ease, to feel that this space apart from human voice or light was not hostile. Why should it be? If he climbed a tree he would see the glow of some village or other. Did he suppose Ruzindana would suddenly appear, megaphone in hand, as Odette said he had appeared outside the church compound, taunting them, calling them cockroaches, snakes, then urging his men to leave no grave half filled? No. This forest was neutral ground: it did not know him and had not been expecting him. It harboured only itself. If there was fear in this place then he had carried it with him from London.

He broke the seal on the bottle and warmed his mouth. He had the sudden urge to whistle, and he was grinning at himself, the absurdity of it, when he heard a movement, twenty, perhaps thirty yards to his right, a shifting or a falling that startled him so badly he gasped, theatrically, like the heroine in an old film. He crouched by the radiator grille, the bottle in his fist. For a minute he heard nothing; then it came again, a soft crashing ten yards nearer, ceasing as abruptly as it had begun. He bent towards it, listening with his spine, probing the tight, invisible corridors between the trees. The next sequence was longer – four or five seconds, leaf and fern and twig pressed underfoot directly behind the veil of the first trees. Whatever it was, whoever, it had a clear view of him now, his childish hiding by the car. Should he shout a challenge? Throw something? He could run, of course, as he had run away from the Spanish girl, as he had run from Clare too – or thought he had. He pushed himself to his feet and walked to the first trees. Now, if he stretched out his fingers, what would he touch? He went on. After twenty paces he stopped. No hand had clutched at him, no hot breath had blown against his neck. Another ten steps. A clatter of wing beats made him stumble, but he did not fall. Through the boughs he saw a scrap of moon, the moon in its first quarter, the rubbed edge of a coin. He went back to the clearing and smoked, lighting one cigarette from the embers of the last. There was no comfort for him in the knowledge that he had been stalked only by his own mind. He sat inside the car. A sense of aloneness descended, so vast he nearly laughed out loud. The dashboard clock said 10:10. He had been at the clearing for less than forty minutes. He locked the car doors and climbed on to the back seat. He could smell the smoke on his fingers, and something of the woods, clammy and fungal. He thought of Nina; of Toby Rose asking him if he was giving up. When he closed his eyes his head played monotonous views of roads, miles of Tarmac unspooling in real time. He muttered a short prayer, scoffed at himself, and aimed at sleep.

15

He did not know the routine at Ithaca – what time did bi-polars and alcoholics get up in the morning? – nor had he remembered to ask for such information when he had called from London, but he assumed there would be no five a.m. starts. He ate breakfast at a café in Dundee, then idled an hour, leaning on a wall watching gulls patrol the banks of the estuary. At eleven, in light rain, he drove out on the Arbroath road, missed his turning, doubled back, and parked outside the clinic just before midday, relieved to find no green Volkswagen van there. He checked himself in the rear-view mirror. He looked, as he had thought he must look, like a man who had spent the night on the rear seat of his car in the woods (and how benign the woods had been in the morning – birdsong and emerald bracken; a pair of rabbits nibbling at shoots of grass). It was still raining as he crossed the gravel, a persistent summer drizzle, half warm, like being in the basement of a cloud. A small lorry was picking up or delivering laundry, and the clinic's blue door was propped wide open. There was no one in the day-room. Clem knocked on Boswell's door.

'The doctor's away,' said a voice from behind him. He turned: an enormously fat woman with ginger eyebrows was wiping her hands on a piece of damp cloth.

'Away?'

'For the golf at St Andrews. Have you come to see someone? They don't like visitors at lunchtime.'

'Is Pauline here?'

'I'm Sheila, the cook.'

'Clem Glass. My sister's been staying here.'

'That's Clare.'

'Yes.'

'Is she expecting you?'

'I called a couple of days ago. If I could see Pauline.'

'She has a sweet tooth, your sister.'

'Really?'

'Did you not know that?'

'I suppose I'd forgotten.'

The cook made a face as though they had been debating something of substance and she had scored an important point. 'I'll walk you round,' she said. 'I can't let you go on your own. They'd scalp me.'

She led him past some stairs and out through a fire door at the back of the building.

'Hydrotherapy suite,' she said, waving the cloth at a newly built brick block directly ahead of them. 'You can live like a fush in there.'

They veered left and crossed the garden, the cook with the awkward chafing gait of the obese, Clem all gristle and long bones, a stride he could have walked many hours with, untroubled. 'And this wee hoose they call the gazebo,' she said, pronouncing 'gazebo' as though she found the word comically affected. It was a wooden cabin raised off the ground on short stilts, a pair of larches at one end, a veranda at the other. Inside, in soft light, eight or ten residents sat in armchairs or occupied themselves at the table. There was a tape playing, a winding, soporific flow of pan pipes and little bells, a music Clem associated with wholefood stores or the waiting rooms of progressive dentists. He recognised the man he had smoked with on his last visit, though the Paisley gown had been replaced by crumpled cricket whites and a mustard-coloured cravat. He was staring with great avidity at the puzzle on the table in front of him, a big jigsaw of what looked like the mid-Atlantic photographed from the air. He had the edge pieces in place and was moving down from the upper-left quarter, building waves and troughs, searching among the pieces that remained (at least a thousand of them) for a fleck of spume or a particular green wrinkle. To Clem it looked a puzzle to take a month over, though the man had the air of someone determined to finish it in a day, as if, should he succeed – and it would require heroic concentration – somebody would put him into a car and drive him to the nearest distillery.

Pauline came down the room, greeted Clem and smiled her dismissal to the cook. She led Clem on to the veranda. Drops of rain, fine as pins, fell from the edge of the veranda roof and broke on the wooden railing. They sat in a pair of canvas chairs. Clem lit a cigarette. Pauline asked if the weather was better down south. Clem said it was.

'Do you know what Clare's decided?' he asked.

'I think she intends to go with you.'

'She understood, then?'

'Yes. Of course.'

'And she's able to leave?'

'She always was. There's no one here on a section. Certainly not your sister.'

'I mean, you think she's well enough to leave?'

'Yes, I do.'

'Boswell seemed optimistic about her.'

'We're optimistic about everyone at Ithaca. There's no point in being anything else.' She pushed a grey-blonde curl behind her ear, glanced at her watch. 'You're going to be in Somerset?'

'Yes.'

'You'll want to find a good family doctor there. That should be a priority. Ideally someone with some mental-health experience.' She paused. 'Have you ever been a primary carer before?'

Clem shook his head.

'You'll be fine.'

'What about the dark?'

'What about it?'

'Is she still frightened?'

'She likes to keep a light on. More than that she just wants to be reassured.'

'You know what it is she's afraid of?'

'Not specifically.'

'But she feels threatened?'

'Yes.'

'I suppose she'll tell me when she's ready.'

'We recognise a patient's anxieties, Clem, but we're careful not to be drawn into colluding. Clare's fears are largely irrational.'

'Fantasies?'

'Powerful fantasies that are not, by Clare, always experienced as fantasies.'

'Fantasies she believes in.'

'Yes, if you like.'

'So her illness is to believe in things that are not real. Not the case.'

'That's a symptom of the illness. The illness itself, I'm afraid, is very real. The depression is real. The physical effects are real. The suffering is real.'

'I understand.'

'You'll be fine,' she said again.

'We'll manage.'

'What about work?'

'Mine? I'm taking some time off.'

'Clare tells us you're a photojournalist.'

'Yes.'

'She said you were out at – what was the place called?' He reminded her.

'That's stressful work,' she said.

'This too,' said Clem, tilting his thumb towards the door of the cabin.

'I've spoken to Finola,' she said. 'About your coming for Clare.'

'How was she?'

'Not pleased.'

'No.'

'I don't think she'll give up easily.'

'Clare can call her when she's ready. We're not going to be in hiding.'

He put out his cigarette in the sand-tray next to his chair. There were already a dozen butts poking from it, most with the same bright red lipstick print.

'Well,' said Pauline, 'should we go and see her now?'

Their feet leaving silvery tracks in the damp grass, they walked to the main house, went in through french windows to the dining room, then up the stairs to Clare's landing. There was a smell of floral disinfectant, a slightly stronger smell of the meat being roasted for lunch. Clare was sitting on her bed, her hair held back by a band of black or purple velvet. She was wearing dark glasses, the type skiers wore, the shades curling around the sides of her face and hiding her eyes completely. This was new. Pauline said she would wait downstairs in the office.

'Stay if you like,' said Clem. She smiled and shook her head. She would see them both later, she said. She went out; Clem stared at the back of the door and then, with a surge of hopelessness, at the crown of his sister's head. He took the chair from beside the window and sat opposite her, knee to knee.

'How are you?' he asked.

'You've come back?'

'Yes.'

She reached up with her left hand. Her fingertips brushed his lips, his cheek. He shut his eyes and she touched his eyelids. 'I have to know it's you,' she said.

'You can see it's me.'

'And seeing is believing?'

'Who could it be but me?'

'I don't like riddles,' she said.

'Clare. Please listen to me. Do you want to come away? Do you feel strong enough to leave here today? I've spoken to Aunt Laura. You remember the little place she had in the lane? Frankie lived there for a while. Remember? Laura says it's empty and if we want it we can use it for the rest of the summer. It's not in great condition, but there's electricity and water, a little garden. I thought it was a good idea. Better than London. Better than Dundee. I thought we could try it for a while and see how we do.'

'In Colcombe,' she said.

'Yes.'

'I can trust you?'

'Yes.'

'What if it doesn't work?'

'Would you rather stay here?'

'I don't know.'

'It's your choice, Clare.'

'What if I don't get better?'

'You already are. Pauline says so. Boswell says so. I say so.'

'Really? And how would you know? How would *you* know?'

From under the plastic rim of the glasses came tears. Her shoulders shook. He sat next to her on the bed-covers. After a moment he put an arm round her. She tugged a piece of tissue from the sleeve of her dress and blew her nose. 'Can I sleep in the car?' she asked.

'No problem.'

'And I don't have to see Daddy?'

'Not until you want to.'

'I have to be careful.'

'He worries about you.'

'He worries about his immortal soul.'

'About you too.' He looked round the room. 'Have you packed?' There was a suitcase open on the floor behind the bed, though she seemed to have given up the job half-way through. 'Shall I finish it?' he asked.

He checked the wardrobe, found her slippers beneath

the bed, a scarf on a hook by the door. The Géricault picture, *The Raft*, was pinned to a cork board. He unpinned it, rolled it, then packed her washbag, zipped it up, put it into the case and strapped the case shut. He helped her into her coat, a smart fawn raincoat – the same he thought she had worn the night he walked her to her friend's house in Tite Street.

'Did I tell you,' he said, 'that Frankie's getting married? Some character called Ray. I don't think Laura's that impressed with him.'

'Frankie?'

'Yes.'

'Will they have children?'

'I don't know.'

He waited at the open door. She came slowly and took hold of his elbow. He guided her down the stairs to the office. Pauline stood up when she saw them. On the desk was a sealed bag with a pair of grey-blue canisters inside. 'Medication,' she said, handing the bag to Clem. 'Clare knows the drill. As soon as you've registered we'll send the records down. It's very important the dosages are checked regularly. And this is my card. You can call me any time. OK?'

There were some papers to sign: waivers, disclaimers. When it was done they all went out to the front. The laundry lorry had gone; the rain had stopped. A few weak beams of sunlight fell across the dripping trees and the slates of the clinic roof. Pauline hugged Clare and rubbed her back, saying something to her that Clem couldn't hear and didn't try to. He lifted her suitcase into the boot beside his own, then opened the passenger door for her and helped her to buckle her seatbelt. He had cleared away the cassettes and the whisky bottle but the car still had a semi-derelict look to it.

'Good luck,' said Pauline, shaking his hand.

'Has Clare had her eyes examined?' he asked, a quiet voice.

'Clare's eyes are fine.'

'The glasses . . .'

'Her eyes are fine.'

'Our mother . . .'

'I know, I know.'

He got into the car and let the window down. Three of the residents came out to see what was happening, three hunched young women in woollen cardigans who seemed suffused with cold, as though icy springs were bubbling beneath their breasts. As Clem drove past them they lifted their bony arms and waved goodbye. Clare glanced back, then ignored them.

'Who were they?' asked Clem, turning onto the road.

'Clotho, Lachesis, Atropus.' She shrugged into her seat. Clem accelerated up the hill. They did not speak again until they came to the city.

They stopped for an hour at her flat. Clare asked who had taken the tape from the windows and was briefly irritated when he told her. He sat in the kitchen while she collected what she wanted from her bedroom. Again, he was braced for the sudden intrusion of Finola Fiacc, but there was no sign of her, no acid note left on the table. He felt a twinge of guilt. He had been ready to bargain with her, to explain that he was trying, finally, to behave like a brother; that he was repaying old debts of kindness. And he had been ready for her come-backs: the charge that he was using Clare to distract himself from his own difficulties (she would know all about such strategies). That Clare, as usual, was helping *him*, not the other way about. But this non-appearance, a sadly lame quitting of the field, suggested she was more hurt than angry. What if it pushed her to drink again? He did not want that on his conscience as well.

They locked the flat. A neighbour coming up the stairs as they went down greeted them, cautiously. 'It's nice now, isn't it?' responded Clare, as though reciting a line from some phrasebook of normalities.

'Ay,' agreed the neighbour, glancing at Clem. 'Nice enough.'

They lunched in Edinburgh at a place on the edge of the New Town. She ate little. When they returned to the car she wanted to lie on the back seat. She spread her mac over herself as a blanket. Clem put on the Veloso tape. He didn't know if she was sleeping, if she was happy to be out of Ithaca, pleased to be going to Colcombe. On the motorways he several times glimpsed a phantom Volkswagen three or four cars behind them, but once they had passed Gloucester (their grandfather, Nora's father, had been a printer in the city, an alderman too) he felt they were back in their own kingdom, and safe.

The last hour he wound the car through country roads past banks in shadow, fields of blue corn, pubs called the Waggonwheel, the Plough, the Wheatsheaf. Since the petrol stop south of Birmingham Clare had travelled in the passenger seat again. She still wore the glasses. She sipped from a bottle of mineral water, nearly a litre of it since the garage. On the far side of Radstock he pulled over to check the map. The road he remembered was not quite the road in front of him, but coming to the brow of the next hill he saw below them the abbey, its buildings freckled with light. He turned off to the left. Now, half shyly, everything showed itself faithful to memory. The hump-back bridge, the old brick barn, each blind bend where, during the day, you had to sound your horn. Left again by the post office, then the branches of the trees closed over their heads. The cottage they would share was somewhere to the right, set back a little behind scrub. He slowed, peered, thought he saw it, then bumped the car another thousand yards to Aunt Laura's house. The gates were open. His headlights cut through trees, scooped the lawn and, for a moment, held the figure of a child, a concrete boy with an urn on his shoulder, his face to the valley, one stone foot behind the other, spellbound, lost in a dream, waiting, so it seemed, for the sharp clap of hands to send him running home again.

16

Laura explained it to him.

For two years the cottage in the lane had stood empty. Before then she had let it through an agency in Frome, a small but useful income until the agency surveyor wrote to inform her that the house was sinking. He showed her the crack, fine still but unignorable, that ran up the side of the house from ground to guttering. She had not been surprised. There were tunnels in black webs under most of the fields and local villages. Sometimes a garden shed would disappear, sometimes a cow or a parked car. Two hundred years of burrowing, branching off, blocking off old shafts and starting again. Who knew what exactly was down there? Only the later work had been mapped.

No one had suggested repairing the house: cheaper to bulldoze it and build again on firmer ground. The surveyor's opinion was that it would stand another twenty years, perhaps fifty. It was not, however, suitable for renting, so the doors were locked and the house removed from the agency's list of properties.

The last tenants – gone three months by the time of the surveyor's letter – had been a family from Bristol looking for a start somewhere they were not known. A man, a thin older woman, a boy Laura thought was slightly hydrocephalic. The husband – Alan – had had a taste for country ways, striding through the village with a piece of cloth round his neck, a stick in his hand, a little black and white dog running at his heels. Over Laura's gate he told her he had not been happy in Bristol, hinting at a history of family feuds. He found work at one of the local quarries and spent his evenings digging in the garden behind the cottage, sowing vegetables, dahlias, sweet peas. He built a cold frame, a wooden bin for compost, hung new wallpaper in the bedrooms. A model tenant, really.

'And then?'

Then his back was broken in a blast at the quarry. Accidents were not uncommon there. In the post office someone said he had run the wrong way when the klaxon sounded. Laura had helped the wife pack up. Later she learned they had gone back to Bristol, to the wife's mother's place.

'So the man survived?' asked Clem.

'Oh, he *lived*,' said Laura. 'Yes. But not with them any more. It's rather sad, isn't it?'

Clem said that it was.

On the first day, Clem and Kenneth arrived at the cottage with mops and buckets, a bag of detergents, old newspapers for the windows. Other than a patch upstairs outside the bathroom the place was dry, and with all the doors and windows open there was soon a through-breeze scented with grass and a whiff of the honeysuckle that grew round a pole by the back door. Laura had had the electricity reconnected. Clem vacuumed dust and two summers of dead flies from the carpets. He put Kenneth to work in the kitchen, scouring the sink, scouring surfaces. They filled black bags with rubbish, sweated as the sun hit the back of the house. Under the bed-frame in the boy's little room Clem found a toy car, a red Ferrari the length of his finger. He polished it on the leg of his jeans, carried it downstairs and put it on the mantelpiece.

They worked until two o'clock, the hour ringing from the village church, and then, a moment later, from a belfry in the abbey twenty fields to the west. Lunch was wrapped in sheets of greaseproof paper. Ham in slices of white bread, two wedges of cheese, two apples. They had a packet each of salt and vinegar crisps and two small tins of pale ale, Laura having the old-fashioned notion that men working together liked nothing better than beer for their thirst.

They ate outside, brushed the crumbs from their laps, pulled the rings on their beer. Clem tossed his apple core into a patch of wild corn. He saw the cold-frame Laura had mentioned; the glass was broken; a few blackened tomato stalks poked from the waterlogged peat bags. He liked the idea that he would never have to do anything with the garden, that it could go its own way, a haven for hedgehogs, grass snakes, countless thousands of insects. For a few weeks – if all went well – the house would be disturbed once more by the sounds of the living. Then the latch on the front door would click shut for the last time (the last of the last times?) and the rooms would grow quiet again. The house was a coaster, a little tramp ship, sinking so slowly there was no need for anyone to go down with her.

A middle-of-the-day somnolence settled on him. If he had been alone he would have lain in the long grass and slept. He grinned at Kenneth, leaned over and tapped tins with him. His cousin had grown rounder and balder in the years since Clem had last seen him, more stately and deliberate, more silent. Kenneth as a boy – a maker of rudimentary bird tables, a sweeper of leaves, Ron's tame shadow, then Laura's – had struggled to make himself understood in words, his voice a mash of noise in his throat, an effort that must have hurt him and never communicated much beyond his own frustration. Now, in his forties, he had settled on an ABC of gestures – the wave, the nod, the pointed finger. It occurred to Clem he would fit in well at Theophilus House. They should like his silence there, those connoisseurs, and could surely use such a biddable, good-natured charac- ter. He would have to go somewhere when Laura died. Why not there? There he might thrive.

At the sky's zenith a prop plane flew in circuits; in the woods someone started a chainsaw. Clem went back into the house, found the cleaner for the windows, and got to work again, spraying the glass, buffing it with crumpled pages from the *Western Daily Press*. Now and then, growing warm, he paused to read about a Bring and Buy sale, a school production of *My Fair Lady*, a man fined for badger-baiting. He gave Kenneth the job of washing the orange tiles around the fireplace. Later they moved upstairs and set about the bathroom. Clem tried the hot tap over the bath. Yards of old piping juddered, there was a burst of musty air, then the sudden slap of water on the worn enamel. He let it run a few minutes; it began to steam, and when he put his hand under the tap the water almost burned him. The walls were hung with green paper that curled back at the joins. A green light fell from a small square frosted window above the bath. Clem pulled the toilet chain. The flush worked, but the noise of it, the churn of water followed by a final mournful groan from the water tank in the attic, would make it unusable at night. It would wake half the village; it would certainly wake whoever was not in the bathroom. For himself – the primary carer – he would go into the garden and piss on black grass under the stars. Clare could make her own arrangements (somewhere in Aunt Laura's attic there was surely a chamber-pot). They were fastidious people. He did not think they would want to see the unflushed reminder of each other first thing in the morning.

On the landing, two plain doors led into two plain bedrooms. Light came from a window at the top of the stairs, its frame filled with the heads of the trees that arched over the lane. Clem swept a moth's wing from the sill, then leaned there just as Laura and Clare were turning from the lane on to the path that led to the front door. He tapped on the glass but they were not quite close enough to hear him. How awkwardly they came! Laura leaning on her aluminium stick; Clare in her dark glasses (the glasses were starting to exasperate him), gripping the older woman's free hand as though she were being led along the edge of an abyss.

He met them at the open door.

'Would the workers like some tea?' asked Laura. There was a Thermos and some cups in the string bag over her shoulder.

Clem led them through the house. He fetched the chairs from the dining area and arranged them into a half-circle beside the honeysuckle. Laura was sweating from the walk. She fanned herself with her hand and plucked at the yellow cotton of her dress to peel it from her skin. She wore woven leather sandals, the kind boys used to wear in picture books. Her ankles were puffy, dimpled. For an instant, Clem imagined the labouring of her old heart, then took the Thermos from the bag and poured the tea. There were biscuits too, a packet of chocolate bourbons, a packet of Garibaldis. Clare sipped at her tea, holding the cup as though they were huddled on some out-of-season beach in Norfolk. She had washed her hair and it had half dried on the walk down. It needed brushing through; it needed treating with something – a conditioner, a cream, some nourishing oil. Would she go to a salon if he suggested it? How could she be well when every time she looked in a mirror she saw this haggard woman with her bad hair and bad skin? Better to have her hair cropped short than leave it like that. Laura would know somewhere, a local place run by friendly women. They could do her nails too, what was left of them. It worried him that away from Ithaca, away from the institutional backdrop, the company of people equally broken down, she looked more ill rather than less.

'Do you remember,' said Laura, adjusting the hefty strap of a salmon-coloured bra, 'when all of you children camped in the garden? Ron brought you lemon tea and bananas in the morning.'

'We camped?'

'All four of you, on the lawn beside the court. Clare was in charge, of course. None of the rest of you was very sensible. You would have set the tent on fire.'

'I vaguely remember,' said Clem. He tried to picture Uncle Ron crossing the grass with a tray of bananas, a pot of tea – surely he should remember something like that? – but the lawn in his mind was deserted.

'You smoked one of Uncle Ron's cigarettes,' whispered Clare. 'You and Frankie.'

'I didn't know that,' said Laura. 'I hope you put a stop to it, dear.'

'Does Frankie still smoke?' asked Clem.

'You know,' said Laura, 'I think cigarettes are why she gets up in the morning.'

'A grand addiction, then.'

'The one thing she's really stuck at.'

'But now there's Ray.'

'I'm trying to have charitable thoughts about Ray,' said Laura. 'You'll see them both on Sunday.'

'And the wedding?'

'September the twenty-fourth. Though as the invitations still have to be sent out I don't see how it can happen at all. The church will be empty.'

'I'm sure we'll be there,' said Clem, glancing at Clare.

Laura nodded. 'And your father, I hope. Why don't you call him this evening?'

'Yes, I could.'

'I suppose they have telephones there?'

'There's one.'

'Are they allowed a weekend off?'

'I'm not sure.'

'For a wedding.'

'Probably.'

'Well, I would hope so,' said Laura, making a face. 'It's not as if we have them all the time.'

When they had finished their tea they poured the dregs on to the ground. Laura clutched at her stick and rocked herself to her feet. She said she would see Clem and Clare at supper. Seven o'clock? They would have a nice supper, a bottle of wine, a good chat. Kenneth carried the bag with the Thermos and cups. Clem shook his cousin's hand and thanked him for his help. He walked with them to the front door and watched them down the path, then took a deep breath and went back to the garden. 'Like a tour?' he asked. There was a pause, a count of three, then she followed him inside.

'The living room,' he said, seeing suddenly how dispiritingly bare it was. She looked at the carpet, the black mouth of the fire. He showed her the kitchen, a little oblong annexe at the back of the house. 'The hobs work,' he said, 'though I'm not sure I'd want to try the oven.'

Upstairs they went from the small bedroom to the large, then back to the small, where the wallpaper, sunbleached, had a pattern of little biplanes piloted by blond boys through blue clouds. Other than the bed-frame the only furniture was a pine chest of drawers, painted white.

'You prefer this one?' he asked.

Clare went to the wide open window. The view was south across the garden, the fields at the end of the garden, a line of woodland, the Mendip Hills, tawny after so much dry weather.

'There was a woman at Ithaca,' she said. 'Mary Randall.'

Clem waited for the story to go on. When it didn't, he asked if Mary had been a friend of hers.

'She ran away,' said Clare. 'And tried to swim to Denmark.'

'What?'

'I heard the fat cook say it. It was a code they used.'

'For running away?'

'For drowning.'

'Jesus, Clare.'

'If I opened my window on a windy night I could hear the sea.'

'Well, you won't hear it here.'

'The grass is like a sea.'

'But it's not a sea.'

'You don't understand,' she said, turning to him.

'Don't I?'

'I like the sea. So did Mary.'

'Clare?'

'Yes?'

'Are you choosing this room?'

'The light must stay on. And the light on the landing. And in the bathroom.'

'They'll all be on.'

'This is awful,' she said.

'We can give it up,' he said, 'if that's what you want.' She shook her head and turned back to the window. 'What I want,' she said, 'is to believe there's something at the end of this. Something better.'

'You don't believe that yet?'

'How can I?'

'Then I'll believe it for you,' he said. 'Until you're ready.'

At seven, Clem carrying a bunch of yellow roses from the garden, they walked together up the lane. Clare held his arm. He said she would see a lot better if she removed her glasses; she didn't answer him. Above their heads on either side the birds rustled and called from the trees. By seven thirty it would be dark. A month ago it was light until nine.

Laura's dog, a big blunt-headed retriever, was waiting

for them on the drive. It barked once and shambled towards them, whipping its tail. Clem pressed the sleek hair on its skull. The porch lamp was on, and they followed the dog into the house and along a panelled corridor where the wood was almost black with age. The house dated from the 1700s; a home of some sort had stood on the site since the days of the Conqueror.

Laura and Kenneth were in the kitchen.

'Here they are!' cried Laura. 'And what blissful roses! Poor Alan's, I suppose.'

The kitchen smelt of fish pie, the radio was on; the dog circled itself in the corner and lay down on a rug, instantly asleep.

Clem and Clare sat on a bench at the kitchen table. Laura poured white wine for them – a large glass for Clem, a smaller one for Clare. On the wall beside the kitchen door were the lines and dates (he could make out only one: June '65) that Ron had marked with his coloured pens to make a record of the children's heights. All comic gravitas, he had had them stand in turn, backs to the wall, while he levelled a pen along their skulls, drew the line and measured from the floor with one of Laura's dressmaking tapes. Clem tapped Clare's wrist. He pointed to the highest of the lines, marked in red like the flood line on the side of a bridge. 'That's you,' he said. 'The tallest of all.'

Kenneth carried the pie to the table. Clem finished the wine. Laura fetched another bottle from the fridge. The Harwoods had always been generous with their drink. Wine, brandy; in Ron's day a great deal of Bombay gin. It had not been like that in Bristol. There, a little beer at Sunday lunchtime, whisky in single fingers when there was something to celebrate. The Glass family had lived beneath their means somewhere in the middle of the lower middle class, the lower middle being as far down the social maypole as Nora, a lawyer married to an engineer, could possibly impel them. This was politics. The Harwoods, whose season of good money had not, Clem reckoned, lasted more than ten years, probably less, chose differently and lived like minor gentry. In his first year at secondary school, Clem had learned about plebeians and patricians in Ancient Rome. The Harwoods, clearly, were patricians, distinguished not so much by holidays in Corfu or Ron's charcoal Mercedes, as by that freedom in their manner that seemed to come from not really caring about anything, the things other people cared about, that Nora cared about. In Bristol, everything was weighed, everything – homework, bedtimes, pocket money – a matter of principle. Behind life was a web of moral science. A certain seriousness was taken for granted. Blinder each week, Nora lectured them on clarity, the unillusioned eye, the hard edge that thinking needed if thinking was to serve. The Harwoods had garden parties and drove to Cheltenham for the races. Blatant atheists, they went twice a year to the abbey for elaborate rites involving censers and ash. They smoked at the table, went to bed in the middle of the afternoon if it suited them. They were Tories, of course, something Nora must have felt shamed by – her sister in with the landlords, the toffs, the bosses. If one of the dogs farted they roared with laughter.

Odd, though, how two sisters should have gone their separate ways like that, and not only in their politics, their ambitions, their ideas on what constituted the good life, but physically too. As little girls – there was a photograph Clem knew well, the pair of them on a railway platform, 1940-something, pigtails and gas-mask cases – they had been as alike as two drops of water. But Nora in middle age had shrunk into herself as though settling on to the perch of her own bones, a woman stripped for action who, had she lived, would, he thought, have become even leaner, tougher, her atoms packed as tightly as a sharping stone's. Laura, the more luxurious, more sexual character (the stories about boy-friends, May balls, tiptoeing on the stairs at three in the morning, were all hers), had filled out, expanding almost exotically, so that now, to watch her cross a room was like watching one woman drag another with her in her arms. There were half a dozen pill bottles on the shelf above the kitchen sink. Like her house in the lane she was starting to buckle into the ground. Who would come for her in a crisis? Would Kenneth have the sense to sound the alarm? The strength to lift her?

The pie was made with white fish, peas and boiled eggs, a crust of mashed potatoes on top. Laura called it nursery food. They ate; Clare was gently encouraged. Clem could not look at her face. He kept his eyes on his plate, topped up his wine, talked to Laura about the work he and Kenneth had done at the cottage, taking refuge in the homely details of water-heaters, light-fittings, the state of the chimney flue. For pudding there was cold stewed rhubarb. Clare stood up from the table and left the room. Clem counted five minutes on the kitchen clock, then said he would look for her. Laura said that she would go. Clem shook his head. 'I'd better get used to this,' he said.

She was in the drawing room staring at the television, though the set was off. He offered to switch it on for her. 'Forget it,' she said, as though he had broken a promise and would now be made to pay. She went to the sofa and lay with her face to its back. Clem sat in one of the armchairs, a big chair of tobacco-coloured leather that exhaled wearily under his weight. Through the wool of Clare's cardigan he could see her vertebrae, four, five – the knuckles of her spine – and for a moment he had the urge to put his hand between her shoulders and touch her like a faith healer. There was a story he had read at university, a little book, not part of any course he was doing, about a young conquistador wrecked off the South American coast, a man who, losing everything – his country, his comrades, his place in life – discovered in himself, as though remembering what had always been there but had been forgotten, a power to heal. Reading it at nineteen Clem had thought of it as a Christian story: the young Spaniard knelt and prayed before he did his work. Now he thought it was a story about how strong a person could become when enough had been lost. He, Clem Glass, had lost things – illusions, a persisting innocence, much courage – but not enough to be effective. Odette Semugeshi, if she survived her wounds, would be qualified. Hard to think how you could lose more than she had lost (all of childhood hewn out of her head); how you could be stripped barer than she had been. With the wine in his blood it was not such a difficult task to conjure the girl into the room, to tempt her over (she pauses by the door: the modesty of power) and have her push small brown hands against his sister's back until the thing was *shifted*. But this was nonsense.

Clare would not be cured by a touch, whoever's. Time, medication, good luck, those might work. He was becoming as credulous as the old men on the island.

'It's got quite chilly,' said Laura, when she came in. 'Shall we have a fire?'

She lifted away the hinged brass fender. Clem crouched on the hearth-rug, balled sheets of newspaper, made a pyramid of kindling, and snapped a flame from his lighter. When the wood took he laid on one of the previous winter's logs, then went outside to the store and carried back an armful of timber and cobwebs.

'The first since April,' said Laura. 'We'd better have something to celebrate it.' She limped to the drinks tray and poured two brandies from a heavy decanter. 'This should see us out,' she said. The fire popped and snapped, smoked a little, then drew well. Clem yawned, rubbed at his neck, gazed round at walls almost completely unchanged since he had sat in the room as a boy. The last of the last good things were in here: antiques, *objets*, 'art', bought with Ron's money before the money went wherever it went. A walnut escritoire, the black lacquered vases, the Victorian watercolours with their lot numbers still taped to their backs. Would they be sold off? A vase to pay for the wedding reception. *A View of the Hunt on the Marlborough Downs* to cover a private hip replacement. He had realised last night that the drawing room was one of three or four rooms that Laura and Kenneth still used – the drawing room, the kitchen, a couple of rooms upstairs. Lives in slow retreat, each year shutting another door whose handle they would not turn again.

Clare turned over on the sofa. 'Hello, dear,' said

Laura. 'Were you having a lovely snooze?' Clem saw the flames shimmering in his sister's glasses. He drank half his brandy, then walked behind the sofa, making a quick telephoning gesture to Laura as he left the room. There was a phone beside the front door. He had the number for Theophilus House in the breast pocket of his shirt. The ring-tone was the sound of two little silver bells, something quaintly mechanical in a wooden box. Who answered? The guest-master? The voice said how nice it was to hear him again. 'Likewise,' said Clem. The phone was laid on the office desk. Two minutes later, his father came on, slightly winded.

'Dad?'

'Clem?'

'You were in the middle of something?'

'Nothing that can't wait. How are things with you?'

Clem said where he was, that he was there with Clare and that they were going to stay a while in the cottage in the lane.

'Won't you stay in Laura's house? Goodness knows, it's big enough.'

'We're only two minutes away,' said Clem. 'We can be more independent.'

'Laura wouldn't mind what you did.'

'Laura's getting on, Dad.'

'She's a year younger than me.'

'She's not as robust as you.'

'Isn't she? I hadn't thought of that. How is Clare?'

'There's a long way to go still.'

'Should I be down there?'

'Not yet.'

'No. Of course.'

'She's not ready for much. Everything's a strain.'

'You're the man on the ground, Clem. You guide me.'

'In a few weeks, perhaps. Who knows?'

'Then let's hope for that.'

Clem told his father about the wedding.

'Frankie! Now that is a surprise.'

'I think Laura thinks so too.'

'A family wedding. Well, well. A first for your generation.'

'I know.'

'A vote for the future.'

Clem laughed. A second later his father joined him, though perhaps neither could have said what exactly had amused them.

'We'll play it by ear,' said his father.

'Yes,' said Clem. 'I'll call you next week.'

'You'll thank Laura for me, won't you?'

'I will.'

'And give Clare my love. If the right moment presents itself.'

In the drawing room Laura had moved on to the sofa. Clare's head lay pillowed on one of her thighs.

'Asleep,' whispered Laura, smoothing Clare's hair. 'I'll sit up with her for a while.'

'Are you sure?'

'She's exhausted. Absolutely exhausted. I can remember a time a few months after Kenneth was born when I thought if I got any more tired I'd collapse and die. I mean literally. She needs *copious* rest.'

Clem picked up his brandy and went to the fire.

'You should sleep too,' she said. 'Don't think I don't know what's in your head, Clement Glass.'

He grinned at her, and for an instant saw in her face, in her even brown gaze, his mother, sight restored, looking up at him. A look that said, 'Where now, struggler?'

He swallowed the brandy. 'Dad wanted to thank you,' he said.

Laura nodded.

17

He stayed in Frankie's old room, woke early and went down to the kitchen. Kenneth was there, standing at the window. He had misbuttoned his shirt, and his shoelace – why could he not have slip-ons? – hung loose. Clem tied them for him, rebuttoned the shirt, then found them both some breakfast. The dog waited expectantly by the side of the table. Clem shared his toast with it. He asked Kenneth if he had seen Laura or Clare. Kenneth shook his head. They washed their plates and mugs and went upstairs. There were twin beds in the guest room at the lane end of the house (another two guest rooms at the 'court' end). They stripped the beds and carried the mattresses and eiderdowns outside. It had rained in the night and the grass was damp. They lifted the mattresses on to the roof of the car, securing them as best they could with lengths of green gardening twine. From the airing cupboard they brought down sheets and towels. On the back seat of the car Clem put his suitcase and the grey electric fire he had found in an unused dressing room. They drove to the cottage, each of them with an arm out of a window to cling to the mattresses. The dog ran after them and ran around their ankles as they unloaded, barking excitedly as they wrestled the mattresses up the stairs. The bed-frame in the child's room was slightly too narrow, in the other room too broad, but they would serve well enough for the time that they were needed. Clem made the beds. The sheets, shaken out, had a good smell, though it might have been many months since they were laundered and folded and put away. Back at Laura's they began to load up again. She had shown Clem the pans he could take, and in which of the deep cupboards he would find a spare set of crockery (patterns of tangled leaves on the edges of the plates). He was pleased it was just Kenneth with him. They worked without any fuss, already used to each other. If the women were sleeping then let them sleep on; let Clare get her 'copious' rest – Laura too.

The room on the ground floor at the court end was Ron's old study. At first Clem thought the door was locked, but when he pushed harder it gave inwards with the dry snap of an air seal. The curtains were half drawn; on the shelves, the gilded book-spines – collected classics, more furniture than literature – glimmered dully. How strong the dead man's presence was, as though at any moment a newspaper would crackle and a voice politely enquire what it was Clem wanted there. After seven years there seemed to linger still some trace of the cigarettes he had smoked, an aromatic tobacco with the print of an artillery piece on the front, a brand that Clem had never seen on sale anywhere and which he suspected was ordered privately by gentlemen smokers from a shop in Curzon Street. He opened the curtains. Across a flowerbed and a strip of lawn were the remains of the tennis court, its surface broken by powerful weeds that used the side-wiring as a climbing frame.

The main desk was presidential, an utterly solid piece it would have needed four men to move, but by the door there was a smaller one with two hinged leaves and two drawers. Kenneth and the dog were in the corridor, waiting there like a pair of primitives outside a cave where once a local god had lived. Had either been in the study at all since Ron had died? He waved them in; they came reluctantly. 'Take an end of this,' he said to Kenneth. 'We'll give it to Clare. If she has a desk perhaps she'll do some work.'

They laid it in the open boot, draped a blanket over it and used more of the twine to hold it in place. Back in the study Clem rolled the Persian rug and put it over his shoulder. He wondered if he should draw the curtains again and return the room to its mourning. He looked, idly, at the frames on the papered walls. A wedding picture posed in a bower of black and white roses. Kenneth on a beach in shorts holding a bucket. Frankie pretending to be Tinkerbell, Frankie at a gymkhana, Laura and Frankie with one of the dogs. Then three grinning soldiers, Uncle Ron in the middle, a photograph Clem remembered from his earliest visits to the house, though he had not been tall enough then to look at it as he looked at it now, his eyes on a level with the tanned and boyishly handsome Captain Harwood. What was the regiment? Kings Own Rifles? King's African Rifles? They had been in Kenya to put down the Mau-Mau rebellion, that much he knew. These three had posed for the camera at the edge of a village, their faces flushed with heat and the excitement of some recently completed operation. One of them, not Ron, carried a rifle with the bayonet fixed. The photograph had been enlarged without much skill, and the background beyond the shallow depth-of-field was confused, a marbling of light and shadow that made interpretation almost impossible. *Something* was there, however, a blurred shape that was apparently a man, kneeling on the ground, head bowed, his hands behind his back. A man – or nothing but the way the light had fallen that day, forty years ago. There was a magnifying-glass on Ron's desk, a fancy piece with a gold rim and green malachite handle that Ron had used to track share prices in the newspapers. Clem cleaned the lens and held it up to the soldiers' faces, then moved it slowly over the ground behind them.

'Good morning, dear.'

'Laura!'

He had not heard her at all. She was in the doorway of the room, smiling at him, though with something curious and questioning in her expression. She turned slightly to look at the photograph. 'All so terribly long ago,' she said. 'Another world, wasn't it?'

Clem asked if she minded him taking the rug. 'I feel I'm looting the place,' he said.

'Good,' she said. 'It needs a bit of looting. Ronny was terribly fond of you, you know.'

'I was fond of him, Laura.'

'He was always so excited when you were coming down. You and Clare. Thought you were a very promising boy. Very promising.'

Clem put the glass back on the desk, positioning it exactly as he had found it. He felt obscurely ashamed, guilty of some lapse in taste, a clumsy trespass on her feelings. He wanted to say, You must miss him still, but when he looked up towards the door again, she had gone.

*   *   *

At the cottage, they carried the little desk into the living room, setting it between the fireplace and the window. The living room and the dining room were joined by an archway. In each room there was a single window with red and brown curtains. He put the rug in Clare's bedroom, then some flowers – he didn't know what they were called, small purple flowers – in a glass on top of the chest of drawers. In the garden the dog snapped at the bees around the honeysuckle. Clem sat on the back doorstep and wrote out a list of provisions. Behind him, Kenneth waited for fresh orders. Clem tried to dream up a job for him but in the end merely asked him to keep an eye on things. He put the list in his pocket and set out for the village shop.

The road through the old village – Old Colcombe – was steep and narrow and lined with small grey houses. The village hall was there, and on the other side of the road the graveyard and squat tower of the church where Frankie and Ray would marry. Though it was in the old part of the village, this was the 'new' church. The other, Saxon or Norman, had been abandoned with its settlement some time in the fourteen hundreds, an attempt to escape a disease they did not understand and could not fight. How many were there on that journey? Clem knew what a train of refugees looked like – he had photographed such pitiful sights more than once – but found it difficult to envisage English refugees in English lanes, the young on foot, the elderly in carts or on the backs of animals. They had not come far, though to some, unused to straying out of sight of their roofs, the smoke of their own chimneys, it must have seemed an epic distance. Then the raising of a church, the building of houses and barns, the making of new paths while half of them still grieved for those they had left behind in winding-sheets. A huge undertaking! A huge investment in a common future.

Abutting the graveyard – some manner of planning irony – was the recently erected health centre where Clare had her five-thirty appointment with Laura's doctor. The shop was on the junction at the top of the hill. To the right the road ran east towards Frome. To the left was a chip shop, a garage, the British Legion building, the little estates of post-war housing. Clem parked in the forecourt of the British Legion and walked the twenty yards to the store. Nothing much had changed there. The same unlit windows, the milk-crates (metal once, now orange plastic) stacked outside, the door-glass stuck with handwritten notices on squares of card offering rabbits for sale (pets or food?), a second-hand washing-machine, a second-hand coat, barely worn. Other villages, nearby, with their beamed coaching inns and elaborate traffic-calming systems, seemed to have some secret history of affluence and rustic culture that Colcombe was untouched by. There were no quaint traditions here that he knew of, no hunt meetings or mummers' plays, no village green even. A curious lassitude prevailed, as though that five-hundred-year-old escape from pestilence had exhausted all ambition. The village could have been the suburb of some undistinguished county town. Its charms were incidental. There was no interest in the picturesque.

He took out his list and began to fill a basket. A few of the vegetables – mired and unappetising roots – were apparently local, though almost nothing else. The bread was sliced and sealed in plastic bags; the eggs came from Kent. A new freezer cabinet was stocked with brightly coloured boxes of 'Chicago-style' pizza. Clem thought of his local shop in the Grove, the garlic and fresh chillies he could buy there, the sweet potatoes, bell peppers, home-made hummus. You could also make cheap calls – Addis Ababa, Bangalore, Freetown – from one of the makeshift booths at the back of the shop, then get your change from a girl with hennaed hands. Was large-scale immigration the English countryside's best hope? (Who would he have to vote for to get such a measure proposed?) The last new blood in Colcombe – a story Ron had liked to tell – had come with the Italian prisoners-of-war who worked in the fields around the village and left behind them in '45 a clutch of dark-eyed babies, and at the mouth of a track that led nowhere, a pair of white Corinthian pillars that still stood, visible from the road.

Kenneth helped him unpack. Milk, cheese, eggs and yoghurts went into the fridge (a machine that constantly shivered as though with a sense of its own cold). Tins, a box of cereal, a box of rice, the sugar, tea and coffee, they lined up on a shelf. Thinking of the sweet tooth the cook at Ithaca had mentioned, Clem had bought a chocolate cake and two jars of raspberry jam. The bulbs, ten of them, he hid away in a cupboard, then took two out again and put them on the mantelpiece. It was midday. He made a quick tour of the house to see what was still missing. Lamps. A radio. Books? Something for the walls, something decorative, homely. He whistled the dog in from the garden and walked with Kenneth to the pub. There were two in the village; the nearest was the Pump, a place apparently afflicted with the same soft-ening of the foundations that was slowly destroying the cottage. A Union flag hung limply over a car park empty except for a pink caravan propped on bricks. Inside, the pub was dark as a Spanish church. Two men – the only other customers – sat on stools at the bar and now and then grimaced at their reflections in the tinted mirror behind the spirits bottles. Clem asked the landlord if he had something for lunch. The landlord consulted his watch, looked briefly peeved, and called through a hatch. A woman came out followed by a muzzled Alsatian. She told Clem she had some Scotch eggs, otherwise it was just crisps. Clem ordered the eggs and two pints of bitter shandy. He wondered if Kenneth knew how to play bar billiards but when he placed the cue in his hands his cousin gazed at it hopelessly as though it were an old cross-staff he had been asked to go outside with and use to measure the angle of the sun. Clem sank the balls on his own. A bell chimed on the microwave. The woman found a tomato and cut it in half, sharing it between the two plates. Clem ate a mouthful of his egg, then pushed his plate away and smoked. Kenneth finished both their lunches, belched loudly and grinned (a Harwood after all). Clem promised that next time they would go to the chip shop. The dog licked at something under the bench. Clem went to the urinal, a rank shed tacked to the back of the pub. When he collected Kenneth and the dog he did not take the glasses or plates back to the bar. For very little money he would have bounced the landlord's head on the bar and told him to go and buy some Chicago-style pizzas. Two or three times a day he had these fantasies of aggression, minute-long cartoons of havoc that poured the adrenaline into his blood and left him dizzy. Walking in the lane with Kenneth, he thought of the man in the white linen jacket. Where was he now? Was there anything to show still what had happened to him? A little scar, an obstinate bruise? Clem hoped he had drunk it away, the memory of those minutes dissolved by a bottle of Cognac, or changed into a story that, over time, might become almost funny. 'There was this chap on the plane. Never clapped eyes on him before. Completely mad . . .'

They went up to Laura's for a last load. Laura and Clare were in the garden. Clem waved and made a gesture to show he was still working and that he would come back later. He found a lamp with a kitsch turquoise shade for Clare's room, and a pair of Anglepoise lamps for downstairs. On the first-floor landing he stopped in front of an oil painting he liked, a still-life of bread, cherries, an empty glass and a clay pot, all arranged on a white or blue-white tablecloth against a blue background. He lifted it off its hook, mimed hammering to Kenneth – he had already fallen in with Kenneth's style of communicating – and was led to a tool-box in the garage where Laura's dormant Volvo was parked under a faded green tarpaulin. There were tins of paint here too, and brushes stowed neatly in bracket-clips along the wall. They helped themselves, went down to the cottage, and put a layer of white gloss around the frame of the kitchen window, then touched up the woodwork in the bathroom and in Clare's room. In the dining room Clem knocked a pair of nails into the wall and hung up the painting. The quality of the piece was not, he thought, exceptional – the cherries were flat as coins, the table tilted so that nothing could possibly have stayed on it –

but immediately it loaned the room its warmth, the decency of its ambition, an energy Clem ended by describing to himself as 'moral', though, as always, the word confused him. Could a painting be moral? It was an object, a production. Yet in the picture's presence certain wrong acts (who *was* the figure in the background of the photograph? What had those smiling young soldiers done with him?) might be harder to commit. He remembered Boswell speaking airily of 'a power beyond reason'. He was right. Art was nothing if it was not in some way magical. But what did Clare believe? Did she have ideas about art that went beyond the aesthetic, the political, the art-historical? He didn't know.

He washed out the brushes, washed his hands, and drove to Laura's. Laura and Clare had moved their chairs under the boughs of a chestnut tree. There was a folding table there with a jug and some glasses. Clem and Kenneth sat on the grass by the women's feet. Clem told them about the visit to the pub, adding a few touches of his own invention. He had hoped the Pump's absurd failings might make Clare smile, but some anxiety – one of those experienced-as-real fantasies he was supposed not to collude with – was distracting her. Though she tried to follow him she could not prevent herself turning her head every few seconds to the gate, as if, hidden in the deep shade there, something was spying on her, waiting for some lapse in her vigilance.

When the jug was empty Clem went into the house to collect Clare's cases. Tonight they would sleep in the cottage and he would know if this – what was it? an experiment? a salvaging? – was possible or not. On the driveway Laura quietly pressed him to come up for supper but Clem said he had bought things. It was, he said, better this way; she was not to worry about them. She kissed his cheek, kissed Clare's, and waved them off as though they were setting out cross-country and would be gone for months. Five minutes later Clem carried the cases into the bedroom with the Little Prince wallpaper. When he came down Clare was running her fingertips over the polished surface of the desk.

'For you,' he said. 'In case you wanted to do some work.'

'Work?'

'If you fancied it.'

'What would I do?'

'The Géricault?'

She shook her head, mouthed something, and for a moment – several seconds – seemed to forget that he was still in the room with her.

'We should think about going up for that appointment,' he said.

'I can't go,' she said.

'Why not?'

'I can't.'

'It's important.'

'I can't go.'

'Clare?'

She turned the chair by the desk so that it faced away from him. She sat down. He studied the back of her head for a while.

'Then I'll cancel it,' he said, 'if that's what you really want.' He went outside and leaned against the wall of the kitchen where the bricks were warm from the sun. A blackbird made a low pass, right to left, across the width of the garden. It perched on a fence post and began to sing. The sound was delicate as stitching. Clem let his eyes close. He was almost asleep (sleep as enchantment) when Clare came out to tell him she was ready.

At the health centre he gave Clare's name to the receptionist. The woman found the appointment on her computer screen – five thirty with Dr Crawley – pressed a key and sent them through to the waiting room. The room was colour co-ordinated. Blue seats and yellow walls; prints of yellow flowers in blue vases or yellow houses under blue skies. He fetched some magazines and sat with Clare towards the back of the room. The other patients were mostly pensioners or mothers with young children. There was some coughing. A fly buzzed around the leaves of a yucca plant. At intervals a doctor would appear with someone's notes in his hand and call a name. Clare fidgeted with her glasses. Clem read half an article about the daily routine of an actor he had never heard of. He wanted to think of something encouraging to say, then wondered if he had time to go into the car park and smoke. He was about to ask Clare if she minded being alone for a minute when her name was called. A woman in a crumpled linen suit was standing by the passage to the consulting rooms. She called a second time.

'It's OK,' whispered Clem, touching the back of his sister's hand. 'Laura says she's great.'

Clare stood, visibly gathered her courage, and walked to where the doctor was waiting. The doctor looked to see who she had been sitting with, then flashed a smile at Clare and led her away. They were gone for forty minutes. The last mother and child were seen, the last of the pensioners in his summer overcoat. Eventually there was no one but Clem. He ambled round the room, stepped over the ugly toys, read the telephone number for people wanting to quit smoking, then frowned uncomfortably at a poster in which a retired sports personality – someone whose picture Clem had pasted into a teenage scrapbook – exhorted men to talk openly about impotence.

The receptionist came in. She grinned and nodded as though to show Clem that she knew why he was there and respected his involvement in a case of unusual seriousness. She asked if he would go down to the doctor's office. She pointed the way. In the passage there was a soft humming of electrics. Clem stood outside Crawley's door, listening for voices. He knocked; Crawley opened the door. 'Oh,' she said, as if she had already forgotten having sent for him. 'Take a seat.' She pointed to the chair next to Clare's. The black glasses had come off. He could see his sister had been crying but could also see that she liked Crawley and that something useful had happened between them.

'I wanted to say a quick hello,' said Crawley.

'Yes,' said Clem.

'I've arranged with Clare to have a double appointment once a week for as long as you're down here or for as long as we think it's necessary.'

'Thank you.'

'We can review the medication. Monitor her general health. See what extra help may be necessary.'

'Good.'

He thought Crawley looked as if she, too, were in need of copious rest. She had the haven't-slept/just-woken face of a scholar, but she regarded him very steadily. She did not seem afraid of silences between people.

'Clare tells me she's worried about your eyes. Are they troubling you?'

'*My* eyes?' He glanced at Clare. 'No,' he said. He paused. 'Or this one, a little.' He touched his cheek below his right eye.

Crawley picked up a pencil torch from among the clutter on her desk and walked to his chair. She tilted his head back and shone the light in his eye. 'Look up,' she said. 'Right, left . . .' His eye began to water. She turned off the torch and sat down.

'I'll write a prescription for eye-drops. Something to take any irritation away. I'm afraid you'll have to go to Radstock for it. There's no chemist in the village.'

'Is there a problem?' asked Clem.

'I doubt it,' she said, 'but with your family history you should have a proper examination.'

'What about Clare's eyes?'

'There's nothing wrong with Clare's eyes.' She scribbled on a pad. 'I can arrange an appointment for you at the eye hospital in Bristol. It may take a while to come through.'

He thanked her for this and tried to guess what it was that made her someone to whom he immediately wanted to tell everything. There was no obvious effort on her part to appear noticeably zealous in her work, more compassionate than other doctors, more competent. Her style was somewhat dry, shy even, as though she might have been more in her element in the pure sciences. What was it, then? What was this atmosphere radiating through her skin, the creased linen of her suit? It was a case, he decided, of 'principled bones' – one of Nora's expressions. A person with principled bones, which meant, he thought, the ability, innate or learned, to take another person's difficulties as seriously as your own. It was exceptional. If she asked him what he had seen on the hill with Silverman he would tell her. He would take the pictures from his wallet and line them up on her desk.

She tore the prescription from the pad and handed it to him.

'I'm a photographer,' he said, surprising himself and wondering if it could be true any more.

'I know,' she said. She smiled at him, gravely, as if she knew far more than that. 'And tell your aunt it's time she came in again.' The smile lightened. 'We're missing her.'

Outside the health centre Clare put on her glasses again. Clem said nothing; nothing even when she reached for his elbow and let him lead her as though she could see barely a yard in front of her. He had no doubt that her interview with Crawley had had a good effect, that they had found, as Pauline Diamond said they must, the right person to oversee her care, but this thing, a malignancy that ran as deep as thought, was intractable, and perhaps permanently so. Fiacc had not wanted to tell him why the windows at the flat in Dundee were taped, but now he believed he understood. All of it was about trying to stay alive. A tremendous undertow was drawing Clare out, like Mary Randall, into a cold sea. Amazing, then, that in the midst of such a struggle she should concern herself with his sight! She must have caught him rubbing at his eye, something he might have been doing far more often than he was fully conscious of. And if there really was a problem? The idea unnerved him, though he seemed to have been thinking about it for a long time, as long, in fact, as he could remember. Long before Africa, before the night at N—. Do the children of blind parents spend a lifetime preparing for a blindness of their own? Do they store the world away for a time when they will have to navigate by touch and memory? As they drew level with the village hall (a poster in the window announcing the harvest disco in September), the road curving gently downwards towards the Pump and the lane, he slowed his pace and closed his eyes. Now, he thought, let's see who guides whom.

At eight o'clock, the lights on, the lamps on, the curtains drawn, Clem set the table for supper. In the kitchen he opened a tin of baked beans, a tin of sweetcorn, a tin of mackerel fillets. He broke the leaves from a lettuce and sprinkled them with oil and salt (a benediction). He buttered the bread and cut the slices into halves, shredded the white bulbs of two spring onions. He uncorked a bottle of white wine, poured unequal measures into two glasses, and carried the smaller through to Clare. A mouthful of wine would, he believed, do her more good than harm, and to drink wine together would be a little marker of a normal life, something to set against the sheer strangeness of their situation. For the first night or two they would need to defend themselves against any stark accounting of the facts. Whatever was ordinary – and the ordinary could always be found because it was rooted in the routines and appetites of the body – they needed to make use of it.

She was sitting next to the electric heater on the other

side of the archway. While there was still daylight she had gone to her bedroom and brought things down: a few books, an academic journal, the Géricault print, some pens and paper. He had hoped she might do something with them – read a line, write a line, a single line – but having tidied them on to the desk she had apparently lost all interest.

He held out the wine to her. When she didn't take it from him he put the glass on the mantelpiece between the light bulbs and the toy Ferrari. 'Supper when you're ready,' he said.

He served up in the kitchen. A spoonful of beans, a spoonful of corn, two fillets of mackerel each. He carried the plates through, brought in the bread and the lettuce, the wine bottle. Clare sat at her place as though she hadn't the strength to pick up her fork.

'Try something,' he said. 'If you won't eat, what's the point?'

She ate some of her beans and afterwards the cherry yoghurt he gave her. He asked if she approved of the painting he had put up. He said how much he had liked Crawley. 'Have you ever been to Toronto?' he asked. She didn't say a word. He decided he would take her back to Ithaca the next day. How ugly she had become! Skin the colour of uncooked potato. Her hair, her ridiculous glasses. What was he making such an effort for? If Fiacc wanted her, let Fiacc have her.

He gathered the plates and hurried through to the kitchen to keep himself from shouting at her. By doing everything at the speed Kenneth might have done it, he made the clearing up last for a full hour. When he went through the archway again, Clare was sitting at the desk with a book in her hand. He slipped on to the chair by the heater. Some of the newspapers he had brought down for the window-cleaning, all local papers, were still in the room. He reached for them; they were months old. One had a front-page photograph of cars abandoned in the snow. More weather pictures appeared on pages two and three – children tobogganing, a snowman with a carrot nose, a cheery postman trudging up a snowy front path.

Over the top of the paper he watched Clare 'reading'. She held the book as though, should she relax her grip, it would fly violently into her face. The veins stood proud on the backs of her hands. She moaned. The skin twitched at the corners of her mouth. Clem waited. When he gauged that she could no longer bear it, that something was about to break out, to shatter the evening, he said, 'Postmaster Christopher Dee has made a personal pledge to readers of the *Somerset Standard*.'

She looked at him.

'Collections and deliveries will go on as normal, though he asks people to be patient.'

'What?'

He read it again.

'It doesn't make any sense,' she said. She put down the book. Clem saw that it was one of her own, *The Death of Polite Nature: Poussin to the Fauves*. 'If deliveries go on as normal why do people need to be patient?'

'There may be more snow.'

'Then he should say that. He should say what he means.'

'Are you feeling tired yet?'

She nodded.

'You want to go up?'

She shrugged.

Clem folded the paper. 'I'll come with you,' he said. 'Check that everything's working.'

They climbed the stairs in single file, Clem first, Clare just behind him. Clem thought of the children pursued by the evil preacher in the Laughton film, *The Night of the Hunter*. He remembered a scene of them sleeping in the hayloft of a barn, the boy waking at first light to see on a theatrical horizon the silhouette of the preacher on horseback, a man who apparently needed no sleep, who was relentless. Clem had liked that boy, the slight stiffness of his character, the way he stood up to the adult world. He had a less clear memory of how things had ended. The children overcame, of course. Weren't they taken in somewhere? Some stern old lady with a heart of gold who taught them to be children again?

While Clare was in the bathroom he waited on the landing inspecting the red-brown moth-wing stain in the corner where the damp had come through. In the bathroom the pipes banged; the flush released its weight of frantic water. When Clare came out she had the red robe on and paused at the bathroom door as if for effect, though with the glasses she looked what she was: a woman in trouble made freakish by things that had recently made her attractive.

'You go first,' she said.

He went into her bedroom. The overhead light and the bedside lamp were already on (what kind of electricity bill would they have?). Clare took off the robe. She had on a white knee-length nightdress. There was nowhere to hang the robe. Clem took it from her and draped it over the end of the bed. She got into the bed and pulled up the sheets. 'What are you going to do?' she asked.

'Do? I don't know. Is there something you want me to fetch you?'

'You could read to me,' she said.

There were no books in the room. He asked if she wanted one of the books from her desk. She shook her head, rolling it on the pillow, forty-five reduced to ten. He went to the other bedroom, the one the quarryman and his thin wife must have slept in. From his case he took the book he had borrowed from Frankie's room, a guide to Italy that he imagined she had bought or been given to prepare for one of those Harwood holidays in the south (certain pages had the corners turned down; on others there were tanning-oil fingerprints in the margins). He did not know Italy. He had been at Rome airport a few times, napping on a bench in the transit lounge. He knew Pakistan better, Brazil, Northern Ireland. He had taken the book because flicking through it had proved an effective way to edge himself towards sleep, a sort of harmless romance, the traveller as unnamed hero, his place set at a recommended table, his room aired, a famous view of the lake and the mountains awaiting his gaze.

He carried it through. There was no chair. He folded the robe and sat on the end of the bed. He showed her the cover of the book; then, as he had done the previous night, he opened it at random and started to read. 'Montalcino, with its full circuit of walls and fairy-tale castle, has long been a place of pilgrimage for lovers of Tuscan Hill towns . . .' The Hotel dei Capitani was apparently the place to stay. In August there was a festival with dressing-up and archery competitions. He listed the restaurants, the Madonnas on view at the

Museo Civico, described the neighbouring vineyards, the bus schedule from Sienna. Was she sleeping? He thought she had soporifics among her medicines, temazepam or some such. He moved on to the sulphur cures at Bagnio Vignoni, the Renaissance façade of the cathedral at Pienza with its three-tiered veneer of Istrian marble. He whispered her name, whispered it again. When she didn't answer he eased himself from the mattress, tiptoed to the door and switched off the overhead light. The bulb in the turquoise shade flickered, then burned steadily.

In the kitchen he drank the last of the white wine, then went upstairs and tugged from the front pocket of his suitcase the brown envelope Frank Silverman had passed to him with such sleight-of-hand at the airport in Toronto. He opened it at the dining-table. There were sixteen sheets of paper inside. He fanned them out over the table-top. 'Maybe *you* can do something with it,' Silverman had said. But do what? Finish it? Find the conclusion he had been unable, or unwilling, to find? He started to sort through. None of the pages was numbered; all of them were heavily corrected; corrections to corrections in some places, each modification a degree more impenetrable than the last. He looked for a way in and found a page, two pages, that dealt in précis with the colonial backdrop, the divisions of power, the parties, the factions, the secret committees, the growth of extremism.

Even the president's wife was talking about it: the need to hunt down the enemies within and show no mercy. Weapons were collected. Bands of men were trained, quite openly, to go to war against their neighbors . . .

A third page gave glimpses of the physical country. The tightly terraced hills, the jagged shoulders of old volcanoes, the abandoned plantations, the starburst green of banana trees, the marshes, the rusted iron roofs of the houses, the churned red earth of the roads, the fast rivers brown with upland silt. There was a description of the Bellville Hotel,

abandoned by its foreign masters, left to its fate. Penile, though several stories less tumescent than Mobuto's Intercontinental. The hotel bar was called the Shangri-La and boasted a pianola that every night some over-refreshed member of the press corp would pretend to play . . . In some of the rooms on the top floor, wanted men and women, people with their names on death-lists drawn up months earlier, hid out with their families . . .

Then the beginning of a narrative:

For the westerner, a citizen of the so-called developed world, used to taking his night walks under a flow of silver and orange neon, an unlit city has a special menace. The road behind the hotel where we waited for Major Nemo and our escort had not a single source of light, the whole quarter sunk into almost palpable darkness, a shuttered maze where the sense of someone being very close to you but unseen and unseeable becomes, in short time, a source of real and escalating disquiet.

The next six lines were inked out. The last paragraph began with a sketch of Major Nemo.

I do not know if Nemo liked being a soldier. To me he lacked that appearance of animated iron most of his caste aspires to. But he was a man whom you sensed would keep his authority however a situation turned out. On several occasions in the Shangri-La he had shared information with us and given advice. We had come to think of him as a friend . . .

Another line erased, then:

. . . the first roadblock was a barrier rigged from a sapling balanced across a pair of oil drums. Nemo lowered his window and spoke in French, his tone so pitched as to suggest the respect between fellow professionals, though the men at the roadblock were militia, and no more or less than an armed gang, the local sansculottes, full of banana beer and ready for any criminal enterprise, though not, that night, quite drunk or brave enough to take on a body of disciplined soldiers. They spat into the dust at their feet, drew back the pole, and let us pass . . .

It took Clem a minute of shuffling and scanning to find the page that followed this. Here, too, much had been defaced, only becoming readable again a third of the way down the page, and half-way through a sentence:

. . . of shacks and lean-tos and at last into the country. For ten miles or so we traveled on tar roads and made good progress but the road gave way to track and we had to cling to what we could while the driver wrestled the steering-wheel to keep us from tipping into a ditch. I was thrown repeatedly against the thigh and shoulder of the soldier beside me. Each time we hit a larger stone or deeper rut we grunted like boxers. The track narrowed. Elephant grass scratched at the windows. Nemo picked out our route on a square of crumpled map, though it was hard to have much confidence in those lines, or to believe they bore any close relation to the forested vastness we drove through. I tried to read my watch but could not hold my arm steadily enough. After forty minutes of this, longer perhaps, Nemo spoke to the driver and we braked hard. I was afraid he had seen something – shadows flitting over the track ahead of us – but he was looking for the turning that would take us up to the church at N—. We went on more slowly, stopped, went on again, then found on our right a sanded incline like an old riverbed, ascending steeply. We drove now at walking pace, the headlights swinging over the forest walls. The sensation was of having entered a long tunnel into the side of the hill. The soldiers gripped their weapons more tightly; we all peered forward, straining our sight. Then the trees were gone and we were on the crown of a hill, a spacious grassy clearing beneath an expanse of stars. Ahead of us I could make out a cluster of low buildings gathered under the bulking shadow of a much larger one. As we came closer I saw that the larger building was the church, and that above its main door was a statue of Jesus Christ, ghostly white, his arms thrown back in the universal gesture of welcome . . .

The cars deployed in a line. Little clouds of golden insects danced in our lights. We sat a while in stillness. Through the vehicle's air vents there came the smell I had become almost accustomed to during the worst days in the Lebanon and El Salvador, though, of course, no one can become entirely used to the smell of death. Something deep in us rebels, quails, aches to flee from it, but once you have it in your mouth and nose it clings to the soft lining, the little hairs, lingering there for days or weeks. It becomes part of the taste of the food you eat, part of the odor of your own living body. More troublingly, it penetrates the imagination, and there it stays much longer.

Nemo's soldiers were skittish. He issued commands in a low voice, positioning two of his men by the rear of one of the Land Rovers, their weapons trained on the tree-line behind us. The photographer and I tied cloths around our faces. Someone threw up, unrestrainedly. Nemo, pistol in one hand, flashlight in the other, led us along a gravelled path until we reached the first of the corpses, a boy of seven or eight years of age, lying on his back in khaki shorts and what had once been a white T-shirt. There was a deep wound to the side of his head, and half of his left arm was missing, severed just below the elbow. His right eye was destroyed, but the other was open in a fixed and unmeetable gaze that traveled over our heads to some infinite mid-point of the sky. We paused, then passed by without a word, following the beam of Nemo's flashlight. Two more corpses lay across the path, then five together like a family group, then suddenly hundreds of them in crazy ranks, face up, face down, twisted and swollen, their limbs tangled like wire. Many had been decapitated, apparently with machete blows or axe blows, or the sawing of a knife. One child I saw – there were very many children at N— – had been sliced almost in two, skull to hip, by the force of a blade.

The buildings around the church – most of them constructed with brick and stone, for religion here, as in most places, has a certain call on people's money – had served a variety of purposes. Offices, meeting rooms, a small clinic. Some had been used as classrooms, and in one of these, among the kicked-over desks, we found fifteen teenagers, their hands bound behind them, puncture wounds to the backs of their legs where the tendons had been cut to keep them from running while their killers rested.

More lines erased. Then:

Rats squeezing between the bodies. They go for the viscera first, burrow into the abdomens . . . Maggots move under the skin making it ripple. A soldier fired a round at a dog that ran from us carrying something in its jaws . . .

A line missing.

So much blood! Did the killers leave their bloody footprints behind? Could they be trailed?

Another line missing.

Beside me the shup! shup! of the photographer's flashgun. When I turned to look, I saw him crouched over what was left of a woman, a matronly figure, the type a well-bred Frenchman might describe as 'une femme d'un certain âge'. Her dress had been hauled above her hips, and something – a stick or truncheon – thrust into her vagina . . .

And so it went on – a little more, a little further: horror as a list – but Clem had had his fill. He turned over the page. On the back of it were a half-dozen lines in hurried pencil strokes:

> And there is another thing he has in mind
> Like a grave Sienese face a thousand years
> Would fail to blur the still profiled reproach of. Ghastly,
> With open eyes, he attends, blind.
> All the bells say: too late.

From the Berryman poems? One of the Dream Songs? He did not recognise it. He gathered the pages together, tapped their edges on the table-top and returned them to the envelope. From Clare's desk he fetched a marker-pen, a red-ink fibre-tip, and wrote on the front of the envelope FRANK SILVERMAN'S WORK. Then he licked the unused strip of adhesive on the flap of the envelope and sealed it, pressing down hard with the side of his fist.

Outside, the garden air was cool and slightly sweet. He lit a cigarette, found the Plough, the Pole Star, the square of Pegasus over the Mendip Hills. Then he saw the firefly light of an airliner moving east to west, Heathrow to the States perhaps, or Amsterdam to Rio, Paris to Toronto. There would not be much for them to look down upon –

a little patch of darkness between the orange glittering of the cities – but Clem gazed up at them with interest and, snared by some perversity of hope, some blind fellow-feeling that disregarded every high black thought that Silverman's unfinishable article had reawoken in him, he raised an arm and waved, as his father, under the old lighthouse on the island, waved to ships too far out at sea to see him.

18

'What are you doing?' she called.

Clem looked up to the window. 'Don't lean out too far,' he said.

'Are you gardening?'

He held up the sickle. 'Thought I'd try to clear some ground.'

'Why?'

'Why not?'

'It's going to rain,' she said.

'I know.'

'We have to go to Laura's.'

'Not for another couple of hours.'

She drew her head inside. He wondered if she was anxious about seeing Frankie. He imagined she must be: all such meetings had to be a hardship for her. But he was pleased with what amounted to a conversation between them, a simple to-and-fro of question and answer. Each occasion when she took her gaze from her troubles and glanced into the world again he counted as a small victory. There had not been many during the last four days.

The sickle was from Laura's garage – Ron's garage. Several times he had come close to gashing his leg with it. The required posture, a lopsided stooping, made his back throb, but he went on with it, swinging, chopping, adjusting the angle of the blade, looking for a rhythm. It was work he had not intended to do at all – what could be more dreamily senseless than tending the garden of a collapsing house? – but sleeping in the quarryman's room, looking at the same ceiling cracks he must have looked at, it had been impossible not to enter the man's head a little, and feel some admiration, envy even, for the determined and practical way he had set about changing his life. He had come to the village with a project in mind, a new idea of himself that was surely something more than just running away from whatever dogged him in the city, those feuds he had mentioned to Laura. Under the briars, the bowed grass, the waist-high nettles, the print of his labour was visible everywhere. In the flowerbeds there were pegs hand-labelled with the names of the plants, and at the bottom of the garden, laid out beside the wall that divided the garden from the field where sheep grazed under the watchful green eyes of a billy-goat, there were the remains of fruit and vegetable plots – strawberry leaves under torn netting, a half-devoured marrow, a pile of grey potatoes like slingshot. There was even a vine, its tendrils wrapped round a collapsed wooden frame, the grapes themselves hanging in shrivelled green strings. An arbour? The quarryman had aimed to sit there with his wife perhaps, a shade and silence tantamount to love, while the sun went down and sixty square miles of Somerset were folded into night.

At noon, Clem went inside, sucking at a blister on his thumb. Always, on entering the cottage, he listened for Clare, locating her, monitoring her. It wasn't difficult: the walls were thin and every board complained the moment it was pressed upon. As he filled the wash-basin in the bathroom he heard her leave her bedroom and cross the landing, then a soft diminuendo of creaks as she went down the stairs. In a moment he would hear the door into the living room, then perhaps the faint click of the back door if she wanted to smell the rain that had begun its pattering on the tiles over his head.

He shaved, washed beneath his arms, changed his shirt. In the living room they stood in silence by the window waiting for the rain to stop. She wore no makeup. Her hair (the night before last he had found a sticky whorl of it in the plug-hole of the bath) was fixed with an elastic band. No earrings, no rings or bracelets or brooch. The only colour, other than the patch of eczema or psoriasis below her ear, and the fawn of her raincoat, was a sea-green shawl she must have packed in Dundee.

The rain lengthened, grew briefly fierce, then eased to drizzle. With her hand on his arm they set off under the dripping trees, picking their way round shallow puddles where the water was already draining into the earth. In a field hidden from them by the bank and the trees, they could hear the tractor of a Sabbath-breaking farmer. The harvest was coming in; not a village enterprise any more but the private industry of a few dozen professionals. Going into Radstock to collect his eye-drops and buy a radio, Clem had seen the combines in the larger open fields moving like dredgers on a brass sea. They worked after nightfall too, their arc lights criss-crossing the darkness, then sweeping like the beams of a lighthouse as the machine turned at the end of the field. No reason to regret any of it, but neither did you need to be an anthropologist or village archivist to know that something had gone out of the life of the country for good, and that a Saturday night disco was not the old 'Harvest Home' Laura and Nora, as little girls, must have heard hallooed in the lanes around Gloucester.

Frankie's Alfa Romeo Spider – Clem was astonished she still had it – was parked in Laura's drive under the dining-room windows, a classic sports car reduced to something chaotic by London street-life and years of botched parking. A Harwood car, and left in typical Harwood manner, the driver's door, despite the rain, wide open, as though shutting it were something too tedious to bother with, something for others to do.

In the kitchen Laura was crouched like a sumo in front of the Aga, pushing a tray of roast potatoes into the oven.

'They're in the drawing room,' she said, her head in a scarf of steam. Clem said they'd go through but Clare immediately sat at the kitchen table and started to pick at her nails.

'Clare can help me in here if she wants,' said Laura. 'I've no idea where Kenneth's gone. I'm afraid he's been caught in the rain.'

'He'll be under a tree somewhere,' said Clem.

'Colds always settle on his chest,' she said, gripping the steel rail on the front of the Aga and using it to heave herself upright. 'But I can't make him wear vests in the summer, can I?'

Clem poured her a glass of Soave from the open bottle in the fridge, then went along the passage to find Frankie. He had not seen her since Ron's funeral, when he had arrived at the crematorium in a taxi two hours off a flight from Colombo, coming into the back of the chapel with his suitcase and camera bag just as the coffin was beginning its descent to the furnace. In those days Frankie was still calling herself an actress, though she had not worked for many months and had never worked much. A play called *Header Garbled* at the Edinburgh Fringe, a stint as the weather-girl on the HTV lunchtime news, a season or two of pantomime. At various times – her life to him, as his to her, no doubt, was a spilt file: no clear order to anything – there were periods of English teaching, modelling, Buddhism, the dole. The men he had heard about were mostly older and mostly married. At Ron's wake she had mentioned a recent abortion and somehow given the impression it was one of a series. Her newest venture – explained to Clem by Laura in that half-anxious, half-amused tone that coloured most of her comments about her daughter – was an interior-design consultancy operated out of a friend's basement in Finsbury Park, though it was hard to know what exactly could have qualified her for such work.

She was standing by the drinks tray in the drawing room slopping gin into a pair of tumblers. She had her coat on still, a shiny mock-snakeskin mac that fell to shiny black boots. Her auburn hair was piled under a large tortoiseshell grip decorated with an orchid of red and white silk. Clem kissed her cheek.

'I wish these clouds would fuck off,' she said.

'We need the rain,' said Clem, grinning.

'Balls!' She smiled at him over the rim of her glass. 'How very peculiar that you're living at the cottage.'

'Just for a while.'

'Oh God, yes.'

'It's nice to see you again, Frankie.'

'It's nice to see you too. Isn't Clare with you?'

'She's with Laura in the kitchen.'

'How is she?'

He made a see-saw movement with his hand.

'I remember the first time,' said Frankie, lowering her voice. 'Some heartbreaker in Paris, wasn't it?'

'That was part of it, I think.'

'*Poverina.*' She swilled the ice around the sides of her tumbler and looked for a moment vexed by memories of her own heartbreakers. Then she smiled and pointed to the sofa. 'Meet Ray,' she said. Clem looked over the back of the sofa and found a small man with a brown moustache lying there. He was not asleep. His clear blue eyes were wide open. He reached up a hand and Clem shook it.

'Gemini?' asked Ray.

'Capricorn,' said Clem.

For a while Ray seemed to ponder this, then, with a little moan, he swung his feet off the sofa. Frankie patted his hair into place and gave him his gin. Clem poured one for himself.

'You're coming to the do?' asked Frankie.

'Of course. And Dad will come down.'

'It's going to be a terrible bore,' she said, a light of excitement dancing in her eyes. She started to tell him about the preparations, the woman from her boarding-school days who was doing the catering, the flowers they would have, the dresses she had tried.

'You have to help Ray choose a new suit,' she said.

'OK.'

'Have a boys' day out or something. You could bond.'

'Sure.'

'Do you have a girlfriend?' She leaned towards him as though she would sniff his breath.

'Not at the moment.'

'That's why you look a bit musty,' she said.

'Well, you look good.'

'She looks great,' said Ray to the fireplace.

'A triumph of cream over experience,' said Frankie, touching her very white face with pleasure.

'I like experienced women,' said Ray, chuckling to himself. His neck and spine seemed fused in a way that made it hard for him to turn round. Frankie leaned and kissed his temple. In the doorway, Kenneth, his grey hair bright with rain, waved a tea-towel at them.

'An attempt at lunch,' drawled Frankie, draining her glass. 'Tell her we're coming, Kenny.' She put a hand on Clem's arm. 'And don't worry about Clare,' she said. 'We know tons of people like her. These days it's practically an epidemic.'

Lunch was ribs of beef. Clem was given the carving knife and Ron's old steel to sharpen it on. The heavy cutlery from the dining room had been brought out, and the tall glasses. Bottles of wine stood along the table, and in a vase at its centre, the yellow roses Clem had brought dropped their petals as the meal wore on. Clare was next to Ray. Clem, at the other end of the table, heard snatches of what Ray said to her, something about little frogs that lived under the sand in the deserts of California, waiting for rain. He talked to Clare as if there was nothing wrong with her at all and Clem was grateful to him, though could not yet tell if it was good style or plain ignorance. He asked Frankie what Ray did for a living. 'Oh, everything!' she said immediately, tapping ash on to the side of her plate as though ash were a condiment. On

Clem's right Laura huffed through her nose, and he remembered the answer she had given him to the same question, her equally emphatic 'Nothing! He does nothing whatsoever.'

By the time they had finished eating and the dishes were piled in the sink, it was late afternoon. They went back to the drawing room. The television was switched on. Laura sat on the sofa, her arm round Clare's shoulders. Ray fell asleep in the armchair. Kenneth went walking again, though this time was made to wear his father's Barbour. Frankie and Clem sat on the window-seat at the back of the room. Frankie tipped her head to her lap to show off a tattoo on the nape of her neck, a blue heart the size of a baby's fingernail. She hinted at other designs, more intimately sited, that Ray had asked her to have done. She seemed keen for Clem to under-stand that, despite some appearances to the contrary, the relationship was not just healthy but athletic. On the television a horse race entered its excitable last furlong. Clem asked Frankie if she knew a good local hairdresser. He nodded towards the sofa.

'There's Donatello's in Frome,' said Frankie. 'Mum-my's been going there for about a thousand years.'

'Can we get an appointment?'

'It's Frome. Of course we can get an appointment. If it can wait a couple of weeks I'll take her myself.'

'You're coming down again?'

'Blah blah with the vicar,' she said. 'What does *he* want to know?'

'I could take Ray into Bath and look for that suit.'

'Something nice,' she said. 'But not too expensive.' She peeled the Cellophane off a fresh packet of cigarettes. 'I don't suppose you want to do the pictures of the wedding, do you?'

'Not really,' said Clem.

'No,' she said. 'I didn't think so. It wouldn't be the same with no one shooting at you.'

'I'd be afraid of screwing up,' he said.

'Liar,' she said. 'Bare-faced liar.' She offered him a cigarette.

When Ray woke up they had tea. Once tea was out of the way Frankie poured the early-evening drinks. They watched, without the slightest interest, a programme of hymn singing, then the start of a soap opera about chirrupy and resourceful people whose lives were issue-based and comically disastrous. Through the drawing-room windows the light suddenly flooded as the sun rolled below the level of the clouds.

'We have to go,' said Clare, standing up.

'Do you?' asked Laura, looking at Clem.

'Yes,' said Clem, 'we probably do.' He fetched his jacket from the back of a chair in the kitchen. The others came out to the hall to say their goodbyes.

Laura gave Clem a carrier-bag with the remains of the beef in it. 'It makes the best sandwiches,' she said.

Clem squeezed her hand. 'Remember that appointment with Crawley,' he said.

She promised him she would.

At the cottage that night, Clem, searching for his lighter in the side-pockets of his jacket, found a white postcard written over with the type of gold ink people used for writing names on birthday presents. He read the card, then took it through to where Clare was drinking a mug of sweetened milk by the heater. He read it again, out loud: 'Near Picota southern Portugal 6-year-old Luna Vargas missing from home for 9 days has been found alive at the bottom of a dry well 12km from her village. Dr Pires 43 who treated Luna for cuts and bruises described her survival as "a miracle"!'

'I know,' said Clare. 'I've got one too.' She went to her raincoat, pulled out another of the cards, and passed it to Clem.

A 16-hour operation in Osaka Japan to sew a woman's arm back on after it was severed in a freak bicycling accident has been declared 'entirely successful'! 20-year-old literature student Izumi Kuzuu hopes to be in the saddle again before her 21st birthday!

'Where do they come from?' asked Clem, turning the cards over to see if there was some clue.

'It's Ray,' said Clare. 'I saw him put yours in your jacket when you went to the loo.'

'Ray?'

'Frankie's marrying Don Quixote,' she said.

19

On Monday morning, so early it was barely light, the chimney sweeps arrived: an aged man with his chest full of coal-dust, followed by a bland, incurious boy who carried the equipment, an outsize vacuum cleaner like a Max Ernst elephant. Though the nights were mostly mild and would be perhaps for weeks to come, Clare wore her jumpers and cardigans in the evening and was not much helped by the threads of warm air from the electric heater. Another source of heat and light would be welcome (and had fires not kept off the human fear of darkness for two hundred thousand years?). The old man called Clare 'Mrs Glass'. Clem made him a cup of tea that he drank scalding hot, sucking the liquid noisily through pursed lips, then coughing and spitting into a handkerchief. He had never, he said, in response to an unasked, an unimagined question, found any riches in a chimney. 'Just soot and dead birds. The rest is all mad talk.'

There was a coal merchant's in the lane, a place that had continued from the days when there were working mines around the village. Later in the morning Clem bought a twenty-kilo sack, carrying it back in his arms like a sleeping child. At twilight, his first attempts to set a fire choked the room with wraiths of kerosene-scented smoke, but after fifty minutes of blowing and fanning, the use of many more matches and several chunks of firelighter, the little flames finally adhered and the coals began to give up their heat. Clare drew her chair close and held out her palms. 'Thank you,' she said, and stayed up late watching the coals burn down to a bowl of bright embers, sometimes naming the colours she saw there. Copper, violet, viridian. Deep red, chrome yellow. Magenta.

At her bedtimes they went on with the guide. Tuesday they toured Sorrento. Wednesday it was Calabria. By Thursday they had reached the northern coast of Sicily. She slept for ten hours a night, sometimes twelve, then another two hours in the afternoons. It was hard to believe that anyone could need so much sleep but apparently she did. This, surely, was the 'copious rest' Laura had spoken of, the calm in which confusion's material base, its root in chemistry, was altered for the better.

At the health centre on Friday Clem was not invited into Crawley's consulting room, though he had hoped he would be. He was left among the local unwell, leafing through creased magazines and noting how almost none of the patients who emerged from the passage after seeing their doctor met the eyes of those still waiting, as though they chose to forget as soon as possible the enforced neighbourliness of such places, the queasy knowledge that the body as it failed would be increasingly spectated.

He was at the back of the room rereading the health-advice posters when she came out. 'How was it?' he asked.

'Hard,' she said, biting down on the word, but when, on the walk home, she offered to help with the supper

(Crawley's suggestion?) he realised that 'hard' meant something more useful than simply difficult and tiring. He told her he'd found a little sage bush in the garden. They could have pasta with butter and pepper and sage leaves. Would she like that? She said she would. She was hungry, she said.

At the cottage she rested in her room, then came downstairs and made herself busy in the kitchen.

'Jane was pleased with me,' she said, crushing a garlic clove with the heel of a knife.

'Jane?'

'That's her name. Jane Crawley.'

'She's right to be pleased.'

'Is she?'

'Of course.'

'You think I've come a long way but you didn't see me at the beginning. How I was then.'

'No.'

'Only Finola saw me. You don't like her but she helped me when no one else did.'

'I like her for that,' said Clem.

'You had your work to do.'

'Yes. My work.'

'I told Jane you bought the eye-drops.'

'Did she say anything?'

'What would she say?'

He shrugged. 'She might have been pleased with me too.'

At supper he introduced the subject of Frankie and Ray. 'They'll be down again next Friday,' he said.

'I know.'

'I said I'd go into Bath with Ray on Saturday after

they'd seen the vicar. Help him choose a new suit for the wedding. Why don't you spend some of the day with Frankie?'

'Is that what you've arranged?' she asked.

'You could have a girls' day out,' he said.

'In Bath?'

'Or Frome. Frankie wondered if you'd like to get your hair done. There's a place Laura goes to. Donatello's.'

'This was Frankie's idea?'

'Wouldn't you like to get your hair done?'

'If you think I need it.'

'It's not that,' he said. 'It's not that at all.'

He was worried that he had spoiled the evening's delicate mood, but after supper they sat by the fire together listening to the radio: a programme of film reviews, a preview of the weekend sport, then a comedy quiz that made her laugh, a sound that startled them both. On that night, as on all the others, he kept her away from the news – the hard news and that dark halo of analysis and opinion that surrounds it; kept himself away too, imagining well enough the material it carried, the echo and dull report of that mayhem Toby Rose had invited him to share.

Saturday afternoon, Clem called the island from the phone-box by the post office. His father was in Berwick. Clem left a message for him (he assumed whoever he was speaking to knew enough of the family story to make sense of what he said), a cautious update that hinted at progress, but gave no grounds for complacency.

The following morning, Kenneth appeared. He helped Clem to build a bonfire at the bottom of the garden: lopped boughs, pieces of the cold-frame, a dozen wooden pallets somebody had dumped, an old and rotten door, coils of bindweed. In the early evening Laura joined them and they cooked potatoes in the hot ashes, drank wine and talked about the past as though it were an entirely untroubled place.

'Her skin is very much improved,' said Laura, as Clem drove her and Kenneth back to the house at the end of the evening. 'Don't you think? You both look a great deal healthier than when you arrived. I can't tell you how worried I was about you then.'

It was true. The dry, angry-looking marks on Clare's skin had almost gone, and some of the telltale pallor from her cheeks. His own face had darkened from working in the sun. He felt fit; he liked it, and began to have thoughts about the future, ideas that came, it seemed, from quite a different mind to the one he had grown used to since coming back from Africa. Was he learning to forget? Was that *possible*? He felt as though, here at the cottage with Clare, with Laura, with Kenneth, with the appealing tedium of days spent doing simple chores, he was being borne away, slowly, on slow currents, from the stench of blood, the dead boy's stare, those conclusions that Silverman had so determinedly shied from. Was he forgetting, then? It struck him (he was carrying breeze-blocks from a sledgehammered outhouse down to a far corner of the garden where they could be hidden) that forgetting might, in some way, in accordance with some law of paradox, be memory's truest function, a means of great necessity and ingenuity for the slow erasure of experience and knowledge. He wondered – a pang – if he should tear open the brown envelope or look at the pictures in his wallet again, but he put the moment off, repeatedly.

*   *   *

The next week began with a curious dense mist, chill to the skin, damp, smelling of estuaries and the high Atlantic. The bells of the abbey and the village church sounded the hours with the flat clanging of warning buoys. Clare stayed in bed. Downstairs, Clem drank mugs of coffee and smoked. Even the radio reception was affected. It crackled, grew faint, then suddenly too loud. He swept out the grate. The ashes were exactly the colour of the mist.

By noon it had gone. The afternoon appeared, delicately blue, thin, cool, good to breathe. Clare came down in her coat and sat on a cushion outside the back door while Clem finished shifting the last of the breeze-blocks. (The hollow where he was hiding them, he realised now, was subsidence. He did not mention this.) A few bees still visited the honeysuckle. There were brown-green apples on the tree whose boughs reached over the fence from the neighbouring land. Clem picked Clare a sprig of rosemary. She pinched it between bitten-down nails and held it to her nose. He tested her on the names of the plants, though he knew them himself only because he had read the quarryman's pegs. Most of them she named correctly. Then they recalled to each other, a conversation like some leisurely game of tennis, the garden at Bristol, a thirty-yard spit of meticulously tended land that had sloped from the back of the house towards the road, the park, the red-brick railway bridge. The lawn had been steep enough to roll down, and as you rolled you crushed the grass and earned the marvellous green smell of it. Their father had been – still was, no doubt – a useful gardener, but the garden was always Nora's. Even when her sight had failed completely she would kneel on a hassock of yellow foam at the edge of a flowerbed, bare fingers winding between the stems and leaves, telling weeds by the feel of them, hoicking them out, her head turned to the side and slightly upwards, an expression of finely tuned abstraction on her face as though attending to that secret music only the blind are privy to.

'You're like her,' said Clare, when Clem stopped for a smoke. 'More so than me.'

'Really?'

'Single-minded.'

'Stubborn, you mean.'

'High-minded.'

'Stubborn!'

'Yes, stubborn.' She smiled. 'Horribly stubborn.'

'I wonder what she would say if she saw us now.'

'It would sadden her.'

'I think you're wrong.'

'She'd chase us out with a broom.'

'A broom?' He laughed. 'You're wrong. Or we remember her differently.'

The morning after this, a Tuesday, he suggested a picnic. Clare said she wasn't in the mood. He repeated the offer on Wednesday and this time she agreed. They made sandwiches from whatever was left in the fridge – a scooped half-moon of Edam cheese, some onion chutney, lettuce leaves, ham paste from a little jar, half a beetroot, some coleslaw. They drove south, looped up the side of the Mendips, became increasingly lost at each unmarked crossroads, then parked on the verge by a wooden gate, climbed the gate, and walked along an overgrown footpath to the stump of a huge felled tree by the side of a pond. They spread a rug and sat down to eat. When

Clare had finished a sandwich and drunk some mouth-fuls of iced tea from the flask, she curled on the rug to sleep. Briefly, she cried in her sleep. Clem wondered if he should rouse her or if, in some way, the crying was necessary: grief, fear – whatever it was – expelled through the eyes like a toxin. He let her be; the crying subsided. For several minutes he watched a pair of dragonflies hunting over their reflections in the pond water, then grew drowsy himself and, with a pleasant sense of letting go, he slept with his back against the tree stump, his head filled with the monotonous cooing of wood pigeons.

When he opened his eyes, the light had deepened and the field was wound in shadows. Clare was crouching at the grassy lip of the pond, staring down at what, pre-sumably, was her own face. Then she raked her fingers over the surface of the water and stood up, abruptly.

'All right?' he asked.

She said she was fine. They packed up the remains of the picnic and walked back to the car, not quite at ease with each other.

In the blue and yellow waiting room that week (the whole week orbited these sessions) Clem was nodded to by other Friday regulars. A young mother, a game old fellow with a heavily bandaged hand, a teenage asth-matic, a red-faced man of about Clem's own age who looked like an actor with a drink problem. Greetings so restrained, so brief and embarrassed, they verged upon the subliminal. Again, he had hoped to be summoned into Crawley's consulting room but after only twenty minutes Clare was out, and they were walking home in slants of evening sunlight, stopping now and then to pick blackberries out of the hedgerow.

That night, having been sold quite enough Italian towns and beaches, they started a new book, *Cider with Rosie*, a fifth-year set book of Frankie's that Clem had taken from the shelf in her room when he returned the guide. There were no oily fingerprints on this one. The marginalia amounted to a few pencilled question marks, someone's phone number, the word 'bucolic' misspelt at the top of page two. He read for half an hour (*I was set down from the carrier's cart at the age of three; and there with a sense of bewilderment and terror my life in the village began . . .*), then put off the overhead light, went down to the living room and washed the supper dishes.

At a quarter to one he put on the radio and listened to the shipping forecast, following the announcer's voice, the vocal tread, clockwise around the coast, listening in particular for that reach of water – Cromarty, Tyne, Dogger – where his father was.

In the bathroom he cleaned his teeth and put in his eye-drops. The windows of his bedroom were open. He lounged beside them, hearing from somewhere the sound of flowing water, some small murmurous stream he hadn't heard before, or hadn't attended to. He smoked a last cigarette, scraped it out carefully on the stone below his windowsill and left the butt on top of the cigarette packet. A fox barked. He closed the windows, stripped off, and climbed into bed, pondering how he would survive a day with Ray, then finding himself in an idle half-dream about Frankie, how it would be to fuck her, this mature woman of forty-whatever he had fumbled with in the attic as a boy. Were her thighs as white as her face? What tricks had she learned with her older men? She had, it seemed, found happiness now, and like all happy people she made it look easy, a simple adjustment, like leaving the house through a different door or changing the parting in her hair. Had she *earned* it? Was she getting what she deserved? He hoped so, if only because it was nice for a minute, very nice and very soothing, to believe that such economies of cause and effect, of deserving and receiving, existed; that goodness, even quite a small and secret goodness, might be handsomely rewarded. He rolled on to his side and sighed contentedly. From far off he heard the anxious barking of the fox again, then saw, rising in swoops from the purple of his almost sleeping brain, the butterfly he had startled into flight that morning as he worked in the garden. And there before him, his long toes barely grazing the grass-tips, his great wings folded at his back, was Frank Silverman, a bottle of Four Roses in one hand, the other hand pointing like Plato's to the sky where the lone butterfly had become many, tens of them, scores, brilliantly coloured and bobbing in the air like an infant's mobile.

'Didn't I tell you, Clem?' sang the older man, exultantly. 'Didn't I tell you how it is? Well, didn't I?'

For several moments after he woke Clem was unsure which way he was lying, then realised he was turned towards the door and that the line of light at its bottom was not there any more. He kicked back the sheets and tried the switch above his bed. Nothing. He went on to the landing. There was no sound from Clare's room. The entire house was sunk into a breathless hush, a silence that seemed to lean over him, self-suppressed, alert to him, listening to his listening. He went back to his room. By the milk-light of the stars he retrieved his lighter from the window-sill and followed its flame down the stairs to the hall. The fuse box and circuit breaker were in a cupboard under the stairs. He found the finger hole, opened the cupboard, and ducked his head inside. His thumb began to burn with the heat of the flame. He looked along a double row of black switches, saw one that was out of sequence and flicked it up; saw another, flicked it. Light fell on to his shoulders. He dropped the lighter, stuck his thumb into his mouth and ran up the stairs. He pressed his ear to Clare's door, then opened it wide enough to see that the lamp was on but the bed was empty. He went in. Clare was squatting in the furthest corner of the room wrapped in her own arms, her stare fixed on a zone of air directly over her bed. He turned on the overhead light then knelt at her side. He didn't touch her at first. In a steady voice he explained what had happened. He told her he was going to help her stand and walk to the bed, that they would do it together, that it was only a few steps. She had had a scare, he said, a bad one, but it was over now. 'Look,' he said, 'there's light everywhere.'

From being rigid she became suddenly limp; he had to tighten his grip on her to stop her falling. He nursed her to the edge of the bed. She lay down. He pulled the covers up. She closed her eyes, then opened them again and stared at him.

'How are you?' he asked (the question he tried to keep himself from putting to her twenty times a day). 'Would you like some water?'

She nodded. The glass by the bed was knocked over. He took it to the bathroom and filled it. When he saw himself in the mirror he realised he was naked. He went to his room and pulled on some jeans. She was weeping when he went through, but as soon as she saw him she wiped the tears away with the blades of her thumbs. She took the glass from him and drank the water in gulps.

'More?'

She shook her head.

'I'll sit up with you,' he said. 'Do you want me to sit up with you?'

She shook her head again.

'It'll be morning before long,' he said. 'A few hours at most.'

'Go to bed,' she whispered.

'Will you be able to sleep?'

'I've no idea. But if I can't be on my own – if I can't even . . .' Her breath caught on a sob. There was a box of tissues on the chest of drawers. He tugged out a handful and gave them to her. She blew her nose and pushed the tissues under her pillow. 'Please,' she said. 'Go to bed now.'

'You're sure?'

'Go to bed, Clem.'

He walked to the door. When he looked back she had turned on to her side, away from him. 'I can put Frankie off tomorrow,' he said. 'Tell her you're too tired or something.'

She didn't answer. He went on to the landing, stood there a minute, then went down again to the hall. What had she seen above her bed that frightened her so? A ghoul? A thing with horns and a flickering tongue? Or just the blackness itself, black as the hollow seams that fanned under the walls of the cottage? He sat on the carpet, his knees drawn up, the lighter in his fist, and pictured the sunrise as though – crude magic! – picturing it might bring it on the sooner. Then he remembered the sunrise he had watched from the fifteenth floor of the Bellville Hotel the morning after they had driven back from N—, how it had rooted him in front of the windows, and not just the routine magnificence of it, the way the sun ignited the edges of every leaf and building, the way the hills, instant by instant, reinvented themselves with such perfection, but that it could happen at all, that such a darkness, such a night, such a concentration of darkness, could be swept away like any other.

At ten the next morning he tapped at her door but got no reply. An hour later he went back with a cup of tea. She was lying in bed with her eyes open. She took the tea from him, muttered her thanks. They were due at Laura's at midday. At a quarter past she came downstairs. She was wearing the glasses again but would probably have been wearing them anyway. She stood in the kitchen and swallowed her medicines.

'I'll get someone to have a look at the wiring,' said Clem. 'There must be somebody in the village.' Privately he considered that if they could not depend on the lights then they could not stay. How was either one of them to have any peace with the nightly prospect of a melting wire – a wire thin as a hair – plunging them into darkness?

Frankie and Ray were sitting on Laura's lawn, holding hands and smoking. Ray had on a white shirt buttoned to the neck. Frankie wore a lemon trouser suit with peppermint-coloured beads and peppermint shoes with cork soles. They had had their talk with the vicar, who had called it a getting-to-know-you session and explained some of the ground rules to them. No confetti and no rice, please. Confetti got among the gravestones, which apparently upset people; rice attracted vermin. 'We're going to ignore him, of course,' said Frankie. 'You can throw whatever you like. Grape seeds, peacock feathers. You could throw money if you wanted to, in envelopes.'

As they moved to the cars Clem caught her elbow and held her back. He told her that Clare had had a bad night.

'We're only going to the hairdresser's,' said Frankie. 'She doesn't need to sparkle.'

'She's in your hands,' he said sternly.

'Well, Ray's in yours.'

He intended to say, Ray's not sick, Frankie, but then wondered if in fact he was. Was Ray sick? Something was wrong. 'You needn't worry about him,' he said, more gently.

At the end of the drive the Spider turned left towards New Colcombe. Clem turned right, passed the cottage, the post office, then twisted through a mile of high-hedged lanes to the main road, the old Roman road. Ray found one of Nina's clubland cassettes in the glove compartment. He put it on and turned up the volume, his little body jerking to the beat as they drove into Radstock, then up the hill towards Peasedown. Watching Ray from the corner of his eye, Clem pictured him as a boy in a tightly buttoned duffel coat being led up the steps of various Victorian hospitals by a harassed woman. Polio? Something hormonal perhaps, something that had stopped his body growing as it should have. His head was out of scale with the rest of him, and there was a flush of colour in his cheeks as though he suffered from some chronic low-grade fever, but his eyes were bright, and his brown hair and ragged brown moustache grew vigorously. He talked about Frankie; Clem hardly recognised her. His cousin had profound thoughts, acute insights into other lives. Had Clem seen her with animals? Babies?

'What about this interior-design thing?' asked Clem. 'Are you going to be part of that?'

Ray shrugged. 'I'll probably just envisage things,' he said. 'Back-room stuff.'

'I wish you luck,' said Clem.

'Your sister,' said Ray. 'Wow!'

'Wow?'

'Those books.'

'You've read them?'

'Haven't you?'

'Not all of them.'

'She's this close,' said Ray, holding his thumb and first finger an inch apart, 'to greatness. And she's still young.'

'Tell her that. About being young too.'

'You think I'm full of shit?'

'No, I don't.'

'Your photographs are some of the best I've ever seen.'

'You're full of shit,' said Clem, laughing.

They came down the Wellsway into Bath. The city below them – a place Nora had never quite liked or approved of, a Tory stronghold she called it, a den of blue-rinse admirals and trinket-sellers – held the after-noon sun in thousands of tall windows and on the windscreens of thousands of parked cars. Clem left the

Ford in a multi-storey by the river. When they got out of the car Ray took a small pile of postcards from his shoulder-bag, divided them like a playing pack, and gave half to Clem. Clem looked at the gold writing on the top card: the story of Russian sweethearts reunited after fifty years of searching for each other.

'Just leave them where people can come across them,' said Ray. 'There's a knack to it but you'll soon get the idea.'

They had bacon sandwiches in a café by the railway station, then walked to the good shops on New Bond Street and Milsom Street. 'No dark colours,' said Ray, fingering the suits on their rails. 'No black or navy.' He tried on green suits, sky blue, silver. While Ray was changing, Clem left cards in the pockets of unsold jackets or slipped them between the Cellophane of new shirts. One, good news about increasing life expectancy in Mexico, he slid like a press card into the hatband of an expensive snap-brim trilby. In the fourth shop they found a white cotton three-piece with a lining of poppy-red silk. Ray thought John Lennon had married Yoko Ono in something very similar. When he tried it on and stood in front of the mirror (the salesman behind him pinching the slack cloth) he wanted it. Clem told him that it cost almost four hundred pounds. 'Do you have four hundred pounds?' he asked. Ray didn't think he did.

'What do you have?'

'I can stretch to sixty,' said Ray. 'Sixty-five.'

He changed out of the suit and they went to the Marie Curie shop, then tried Oxfam and the British Heart Foundation. In the covered market by the Assembly

Rooms there was a stall called 'Dudes and Debs'. They had a second-hand plum-coloured suit with big lapels that cost seventeen pounds. The trousers were long but the jacket fitted well. Ray bought it, then bought a lilac shirt and a plain green tie with some of the money he had left. They went to a pub to celebrate. Clem got rid of his last card in the pub toilets, propping it on top of the urinal where the successful reintroduction of sea eagles into the Hebrides could be read about without the use of hands.

It was half past five before they got back to the car. They put more music on and wound the windows down. Ray talked about the life he hoped for after the wedding, of the flat he and Frankie were trying to buy in Poplar. Clem, he hoped, would often stay with them; Clare too, of course.

'Were you happy as a child?' asked Clem, who had again seen the little boy, this time with his face pressed to the window, watching other children at play in the street.

'I was loved by inarticulate people,' said Ray. 'You?'

'Mine were articulate all right. Just busy.'

'People do what they can,' said Ray. 'I find it helps to think of them as slightly better than they are.'

'You do it well,' said Clem.

'You've no idea the practice I've had,' said Ray, baring his teeth in a grin.

At Laura's, the Alfa was in the drive again. Clem helped Ray with the bags. Frankie was in the drawing room, mixing something in a tall glass filled with ice. Over her shoulder she told Clem that Clare had gone back to the cottage and that he would like very much what the woman at Donatello's had done with her.

'To the cottage?'

'Yes.'

'Right.'

He went to the car, waved to Kenneth, who was mowing the grass around the feet of the concrete boy, then reversed into the lane. Though he was nettled by the slackness of Frankie's manner, by how coolly Frankie-centred she was, he remained in an excellent mood after his day out with Ray. The dark thoughts occasioned by the previous night's broken sleep had left him entirely. And if Clare's day had gone well? Perhaps then there would be no setback, no lost ground for them to make up.

He called her name as he came through the front door, leaned into the living room, then went up the stairs. The door to her bedroom was wide open. The bed had been stripped, the blankets folded neatly on the mattress. On the chest of drawers, next to the tissues and the half-drunk mug of tea he had brought her that morning, were her dark glasses. He tugged a hair from one of the plastic hinges then went to the window. In the garden the evening shadows were stretched over the grass. A fine evening, warm still, though he saw how the trees in the fields – quite suddenly it seemed – had all begun to turn, to have among their green some flare of red or brown. He went back to the chest of drawers and picked up the glasses again. A coldness he could not check spread along his spine to the tight skin at the back of his skull. He went from room to room looking for some sign, something to tell where she might have gone, something to return the moment to its innocence, but there was nothing. He got into the car. As he started the engine the dashboard clock said ten to seven.

In the drawing room, Ray was wearing the new suit. Frankie was on her knees in front of him pinning the hems of his trousers.

'He looks like a god,' she said to Clem, taking a pin from her mouth. 'You've both been unbelievably clever.'

'When did Clare go to the cottage?' asked Clem.

'When we got back,' said Frankie, her voice shifting pitch as she took in Clem's expression.

'When?'

'I don't know. An hour and a half ago. Two hours.'

'Did something happen?'

'What do you mean?'

'Between you?'

'What are you talking about?'

'She was in your fucking hands,' he said.

'I could hardly tie her to a chair. Clem? Clem!'

When he reached the driveway he stopped and looked around the lawns as if he might spot Clare, entirely at ease, reading under a tree. Frankie touched his arm and he flinched. 'Clem?' she said. He saw that he had frightened her. He was glad. He wanted her to be frightened. Then Ray came out in his plum-coloured suit, and behind him Laura in a dress of billowing white cotton as though the wedding were already under way.

'What's happened?' asked Laura.

'Clem's angry with me,' said Frankie.

'Clare?' asked Laura.

'She's not here,' said Clem. 'She's not at the cottage.'

'Why couldn't she just be having a *walk*?' asked Frankie.

Laura shook her head. 'If Clem's worried then we must assume there's a problem.'

'Search parties?' said Ray.

'We've got two cars,' said Laura. 'I wonder if the old Volvo would start?'

'I could tinker with it,' said Ray.

'Don't be silly, dear,' said Laura.

'Leave him alone!' cried Frankie, furiously.

The lawnmower revved, sputtered, and fell silent. Kenneth bent to unhook the full bin of grass at the front of it. Laura, stick in hand, swung over to him. The others followed. Kenneth put the bin down and straightened up.

'Clare,' said Laura. 'Have you seen Clare?'

He nodded.

'Did she tell you where she was going? Kenneth? Did she say anything to you?'

He paused for several seconds as though in his head film of the recent past were screening frame by frame. Then, with slow hands, he began to draw small circles in the air in front of his belly.

'I don't understand,' said Clem.

'It means swimming,' said Laura.

'Swimming?'

'The quarry,' said Frankie. 'Where else could she swim?'

'Then we must drive there,' said Laura, becoming shrill. 'We must drive there right away.'

To Clem, Frankie said, 'You remember the way across the fields? You can be there quicker than a car.'

He was running. Laura called something but already his head had filled with the noise of his own blood. He found the stile into the fields and ran down to the farm in the crease of the valley where a dog in the yard barked madly at him from the end of its chain. Then the way climbed, more and more steeply. His pace slowed. Had Clare come this way? He was sure she had: it was the way they had always come as children; she would remember as clearly as he did. He stopped, his hands on his knees, mouth open, hauling in the air, then he clambered over a metal gate and on across the next field, struck now with the loathsome fantasy that a woman was running just ahead of him and that the woman was Mary Randall. The quarry was beyond the woods at the top of the hill. He stopped again and spat between his feet, wiping a thread of drool from his chin with the back of his hand. The woods were only a few hundred yards away. He pushed on with gritted teeth, sprinting the last stretch and staggering into the sudden coolness beneath the trees.

From here the path was roots and stones and beaten earth winding upwards under crossed branches. He strode, then jogged, brushing the evening insects from his eyes. The track broadened: he saw the old engine, a piece of quarry hardware left behind when the works were abandoned, massy, bright with rust, like some lame plated creature that had crawled into the bracken to die. The trees drew back. There was the sour smell of wild garlic, the furtive damp-ashes smell of teenage campfires. He waded through spikes of willowherb to the edge of the quarry. He had forgotten how big it was: the roads for miles about had been built with its rubble. On the western side the water was black; on the other, blue and rose from the sunset. He cupped his hands and called her name, then started down the rock steps to the side where the water was still touched by the sun. By the bottom step, on the ledge that circled the inner wall, he saw a plastic bag with a bundle of clothes inside. In the water nearby, a man's head floated on the blue surface, watching him.

'Have you seen a woman here?' asked Clem, panting. 'Tall, forties . . .' He was going to describe her hair but realised he didn't know what it looked like now.

'The one you were calling for?'

'Yes.'

'There was a young crowd up on the car park,' he said, 'but they've gone.'

Clem could not see how the man was staying afloat. He did not appear to be treading water, and the water below him was at least sixty feet deep.

'She would have been on her own,' said Clem.

'I don't pay much mind to comings and goings,' said the man. His head slowly turned until he faced out across the water. 'There was some girl bathing nuddy in the shadows over there.'

'Long ago?'

'Not long.'

'An hour?'

'I'm not a timepiece, friend.' His limbs stirred. He began to drift further off.

Clem ran to the line of shadow, a violet penumbra, shifting by the minute, where the light was eclipsed by the height of the quarry walls. From here he had to go more cautiously. He called again and cocked his head. Twenty paces ahead of him he saw the corroded metal uprights of an old ladder. He heard the water pooling there, then a white hand reached out and gripped the ladder's topmost rung. She pushed the water from her eyes and looked up at him. Her hair had been cut to the curves of her shoulders. She was smiling.

'There's a man over there,' said Clem, 'who knows you're skinny-dipping.'

'Have I set off the alarms?' she asked.

'Some.'

'I'm sorry.'

'I was calling you.'

'I'm sorry.'

'It doesn't matter.'

'You should come in,' she said. 'There's no reason for us to be shy any more, is there?'

'No,' he said. 'There's no reason.'

He left his clothes beside hers, curled his toes over the rock and dived, gasping with shock and pleasure as he parted the water. He swam a half-dozen strokes under the surface. When he came up, the sky above the walls seemed immensely distant. He found it very strange that ten minutes earlier he had been running through the woods thinking his sister had drowned herself.

'I've got lots to tell you,' he called.

'Good,' she called back.

'Aren't you cold?'

'Not yet. Are you?'

'Not at all.'

He looked across to the lit side to see if the man was still swimming there, but the light, packed into a narrower crescent, had grown more brilliant, as though the water were sown with thousands of small golden flowers. It dazzled him and he looked away. From the car park he heard the slamming of doors. A moment later three shapes of colour appeared and three small faces peered down from the quarry ramparts. 'Coo-eeee!' cried Laura. Clem, laughing, waved to her, then filled his lungs with air and floated on to his back, his limbs in a star, the water slowly turning him.

20

She climbed from the quarry's water as though from one of those healing pools or rivers in the myths. Lethe? Acheron? Stepped on to the rock ledge with long white dripping legs and dried herself, unselfconsciously. Back at the cottage she slept for eleven hours, then came down in the morning and cooked scrambled eggs, eating them out of the pan with a wooden spoon, wiping her lips with her fingers, and laughing at Clem's expression as he watched her through the kitchen window.

Later she went for a walk. She did not say where she was going and did not ask him to join her. He considered following her, but how did you follow someone through empty lanes? It was ridiculous.

When she came back she ran a bath. Clem, standing half-way up the stairs, heard her singing. 'Clare?'

'What?'

'All right in there?'

'Of course!'

After three days of this he called Ithaca, dialling the number on Pauline Diamond's card but somehow getting routed through to Boswell. The doctor was delighted to hear from him. There was no reason, he said, for Clem not to believe the evidence of his eyes. An improvement was what he had expected. Had he not said he was optimistic?

'She seems a little manic,' said Clem.

'Only, I would suggest, by comparison,' said Boswell. Clem must encourage her to keep up her medication. When patients started to feel better they sometimes thought they could manage without it. That would be a mistake. 'A pill a day keeps the doctor away.' He chuckled. 'And tell me, how is the male half of the Glass team progressing?'

'My father?'

'Or yourself, indeed?'

'Nothing clinical,' said Clem.

Boswell laughed again, more loudly. 'Heaven forfend! But next time business brings you this way, why not stop by for a chat?'

The morning that followed this conversation, Clem, having failed in his attempt to discover a village electrician, went shopping at the ironmonger's in Radstock (by far the most interesting shop in the town) and bought a pair of battery-powered lamps called Easy Lites. If the fuses failed again, the Easy Lites would stave off darkness for a guaranteed four hours. He was pleased with them. He put one beside Clare's bed and another on the landing by the top of the stairs, then showed her how to turn them off and on, aware that she was regarding him with an expression of exaggerated patience, regarding him, he thought, as though he might be losing his mind.

It went on. Friday, while she was up at the health centre, he found an envelope on the dining-table addressed to the Principal of Dundee University. He held it to the window, squinted, but could make out nothing of its contents. Just an update perhaps, a progress report. He hoped she had not said something foolish about going back in October, or if she had, he hoped they would have the sense to stall her. 'Slow down,' he said to her that night, as she collected the dishes after supper. 'Don't overdo things.' Politely, she asked him not to fuss. He said he wasn't fussing; she said he was. 'Let me breathe,' she said. But was this the request of a competent person? What if he dropped his guard and found her in the garden one night tearing out her hair, howling at the moon? *He* was the primary carer, not Boswell or Fiacc, or Laura even. He would be the one who picked up the pieces.

On Sunday, as though to confirm the working of a spell, she insisted they went back to the quarry together. This time they wore costumes – Clare in a tiger-striped one-piece of Frankie's, Clem in a pair of Ron's old trunks that sagged at the crotch. The day was cool and the quarry was quiet. A pair of skinny boys dived from a rock; a tattooed girl in a bikini necked with her boyfriend. Clem and Clare swam slow curves in contrary directions. As they passed each other for the second time, Clare said she had a plan.

Clem turned and trod the water a yard in front of her.

'Ray,' she said, 'his mother, Frankie. They're all coming on Friday.'

'Yes.'

'I'm going to cook.'

'Cook?'

'Lunch. Saturday. We can eat outside.'

'At the cottage?'

'Going to cook a salmon,' she said. 'Keep dreaming of them.'

'Won't Laura have organised something?'

'Laura's done enough.'

'Sounds like a lot of work,' he said.

'You won't be doing it. So it doesn't matter, does it?'

'Let's talk about it at home.'

'No need,' she said, leaning back from him and starting to swim again. 'Already decided.'

But the new week brought rain. The cottage's broken guttering spilled water down the walls; the patch outside the bathroom darkened and spread. On Tuesday, Clare stayed all day in her bedroom, coming down in the evening, sullen, distracted, something of the old fear in her eyes. Clem braced himself (was it not all as he had predicted?), but on Wednesday her mood brightened, and on Thursday morning she appeared at the kitchen door in her coat while Clem was brewing coffee. She told him that she needed to go into Bath. Bath was where she would buy the salmon. They would need other things too, of course. Some good wine for a start. Sancerre, some white Bordeaux. Clem pointed to the rain on the window.

'It's you or the bus,' she said.

'The bus will take two hours. Probably three.'

She shrugged.

'Do I have time for my coffee?' he asked.

This was unmysteriously the Clare he had grown up with. The more he attempted to balk her the more determined she would become. And why balk her at all? He drank his coffee while she watched him, then went upstairs to collect the car keys and his jacket.

In Bath they bought an umbrella and then a fish, a whole salmon, farmed but organic, that they found curled on the chipped ice of the fish counter at the supermarket. It was expensive. Clem offered the last of his Scottish twenties from the cashpoint in Dundee, but Clare paid with a card, for the wine too and the ice-cream and half a dozen boxes and bottles of toiletries. In Waterstone's on Milsom Street, a light of physical appetite in her eyes, she bought books – nineteenth-century French history, a George Sand novel, a new edition of Coleridge's *Table Talk*, as expensive and heavy as the salmon.

The car was in the car park under the supermarket. They were almost back there – Clare holding the umbrella, Clem carrying the bags – when she stopped him outside a barber's on the high street.

He, too, she said, needed some attention. He was getting ragged, wild-looking. Didn't he know? He thought she was teasing him but she bustled him inside. The barbers in their blue aprons were sitting on the adjustable chairs, reading newspapers. There was no business on a wet mid-week afternoon; they did Clem straight away.

'Day off?' asked the barber.

'That's right,' said Clem. He waited to be asked what he was taking a day off from but the question didn't come. He shut his eyes and let the barber tilt his head with fingers smelling of nicotine and the various oils and balms of his trade. When it was done, Clem looked like all the others there – in a blue apron he would have been indistinguishable – but the event amused him, and as they went out into the rain with their bags and new hair he decided that Boswell had been right. Why not accept the evidence of his eyes? Let what seemed to be be in fact. Where did it get him to assume the worst, to wait on disasters? He saw them together reflected in a store window, two ghostly shoppers, tall, half elegant in the splashed street.

'What about calling Dad tonight?' he asked.

She shook her head. 'I wouldn't know what to say to him.'

'I don't think that matters.'

'Of course it matters.'

'I don't think so.'

'I hate the thought of his being kind to me. Forgiving me.'

'He has nothing to forgive you for.'

'He'll find something.'

'He's not angry with you.'

'Are you?'

'Angry?'

'Having to be your big sister's keeper.'

'No one's angry with you, Clare.'

'It might be easier,' she said, as they took the concrete steps down to the car park. 'People's goodness rather terrifies me.'

At seven they went up to eat with Laura and Kenneth. Clem's hair was admired; Clare's admired again. Tidying peas on to his fork, Clem said that Clare had a plan for Saturday. Laura looked at Clare. Clare faltered a moment.

'Lunch,' prompted Clem.

'Yes,' said Clare. 'I'm going to cook lunch. For every-one.'

'Lunch, dear?'

'At the cottage on Saturday.'

'Are you sure?'

'Outside.'

'Outside?'

'I need a fish-kettle.'

'Goodness,' said Laura. 'I've had a fish kettle for forty years or more but I don't think I've ever cooked anything in it. It might even have been a wedding present. People give you so many silly things.'

After supper they found the kettle's lid at the back of the cupboard beside the Aga. The copper base was on the kitchen window sill filled with earth and planted with hyacinth bulbs. They repotted the bulbs in an ice bucket. The kettle was scrubbed and put into a bag. It was nine thirty. Clem went along the passage to ring the island.

'I think she might want to talk to you tonight,' he said, when his father had been fetched to the phone.

'Oh, Clem! That's *marvellous* news. Marvellous!'

'It would be good to keep things fairly light.'

'Yes. Very. Don't worry on that score. What do you suggest?'

'If you have any recipes for salmon you could pass them on. She's cooking on Saturday.'

'Cooking! Gracious. Is she there now?'

'She's with Laura. Give me a moment.'

In the kitchen Clare had put on her coat. She was smoking one of Clem's cigarettes. He took the cigarette from her. She hesitated, then went out to the passage. Clem waited with Laura and Kenneth. They could hear Clare's voice but not what she said. She was gone for two or three minutes. When she came back she nodded to him, then pressed her face against Laura's bosom and cried noisily. The dog woke from its slumbers and growled. Kenneth shifted awkwardly from foot to foot. Laura stroked her niece's hair. 'There,' she said. 'There now. That's another fence jumped.'

The fish was cooked on Friday afternoon, poached in a *court-bouillon* of white wine and onion, bay leaves and fennel, the kettle slanted across two of the electric coils. At four o'clock Clare left for her appointment with Crawley. She didn't suggest that Clem accompany her (she hadn't suggested it last time). When she returned, ninety minutes later, her pockets were filled with Sicilian lemons from the village shop.

'A good session?' he asked.

'Yes, thanks.'

'Great.' He was not even sure she had gone.

Towards sunset he walked down the garden to the vine arbour. The weather was on the move, the clouds breaking up in the west. Streams of light, as in a child's drawing, picked out certain favoured fields. 'Could go either way,' he said, scraping his shoes on the door-step.

'Oh, Mr Gloom,' called Clare from the kitchen. 'Mr Caution.' The fish was cool now. She said she was going to peel off its skin. Clem sat down at the desk. The books, pens and pencils had all been tidied together. Next to them was her print of the Géricault painting, *The Raft of the Medusa*, which she had never, for whatever reason, bothered to put up. He switched on the lamp. He could remember some of what he had read in her essay in Dundee – the body parts in the studio, the scandal when the painting was exhibited (one of the critics running home to write it up as a painting for vultures, the delight of vultures). He adjusted the articulated stem of the lamp to bring its light closer. The storm that had wrecked the *Medusa* was over, though the sea was still rough and the raft was wallowing in a deep swell. They had a mast of sorts, an improvised affair with rope stays and a sail, blood-brown, bellied out by the wind. In the foreground, a man with grey curls and the beard of a philosopher, his head protected from the sun by a cloth, was sitting with the naked corpse of a youth across his lap, the dead boy's feet trailing in the foam behind the raft. More corpses, face up or face down, lay over the timbers like fallen statuary. Among the survivors only the older man was turned towards the audience (those ladies and gentlemen of the salon). The others – Clem counted twelve of them – were meshed into a frantic pyramid at the right-hand side of the painting, backs and arms and necks straining upwards to where a muscular black sailor, stripped to the waist and held high on his comrade's shoulders, signalled with his shirt to a vessel they had spied on the remote horizon.

How thoroughly the moment's terrible urgency had been caught, though on Clare's print – a colour photo-copy, very imperfect – the other ship, if it was there at all, was nothing but a scratch of black paint above the wave tips. Were they keeping good watch out there? Only the sharpest eyes could hope to see something as small as the raft at such a distance. Certainly no voice would carry. And if someone *had* seen, through a telescope perhaps, the pyramid of men balanced like a circus act, would the captain change course for a raft full of strangers, people who would need attending to, who might bring disease with them? Distress at such a range would look almost ridiculous; it could arouse as much contempt as pity. How difficult then, separated by those leagues of heaving sea, to snap shut the telescope, thank God it wasn't them, and sail by?

'Clare,' said Clem, going to the arch and looking through to where she worked in the kitchen, 'were the people on the raft picked up in the end?'

She lifted a length of silk-thin skin from the salmon's side, then turned to him with the knife in her hand. 'The original,' she said, 'is huge. Almost five metres high. When I was staying in Paris I used to see it at the Louvre two or three times a week. If you look at it long enough the sea begins to move. It's a masterpiece.'

'The dead don't look quite dead enough,' he said.

'Oh, it's not one of your photographs,' she answered. 'In Géricault's day the dead were still sacred.' She smiled and turned back to her work (the fish shone now, moist and coral). 'Someone saw them,' she said, speaking over her shoulder. 'Two of them wrote a book about it. *Naufrage de la Frégate la Méduse*'.

Early on Saturday morning she came into his room. She shook his feet to wake him and told him to look out of the window. A few white clouds, but the southern sky was mostly blue. On the wall of his bedroom was a block of early orange sunlight.

'In all the rushing today,' he said, passing a hand over his face, 'make sure you take your stuff.'

'You can watch if you like,' she said, a giddy voice, flirtatious.

Downstairs she handed him an envelope (it was addressed to 'The Occupiers', unopened). The list on the back was headed 'Things We Need'. He drank a mug of tea and drove to Laura's. The front door was locked; he had to tap on the kitchen window. Kenneth let him in, then helped him carry stuff to the car. He was choosing cloths from the drawer under the kitchen table when Laura came down in her dressing-gown, her hair held in a net of the type he had had no idea people wore any more. 'Still looting, I'm afraid,' he said.

'I wish you'd take it all,' she said. 'I wish you were going to stay.'

'We are,' he said. 'For a while.'

'How is she today?'

'A little high.'

'And how are you?'

'Nervous.' He asked her how she was getting on with Ray's mother.

'It's like a house on fire,' she said, taking a crumpet from the bread bin and dropping it into the toaster.

Clem took Kenneth with him to the cottage. On a fifth attempt they manoeuvred the dining-table through the back door and into the garden. The ground was rain-softened but there was a good warmth in the sunlight and it would be firm enough by the time the guests arrived. He set the table, then picked a dozen vine leaves and scattered them on to the cloth as decoration. In the kitchen the salads and the dressings were ready, the lemons quartered, the salmon snug beneath its sheet of foil in the fridge.

'They won't be here for another hour at least,' said Clem, catching Clare again at the front door looking down the path to the lane. 'There's plenty of time to relax.'

'Mmm,' she said. She walked away to the bottom of the stairs, paused. 'Clem . . .'

'It'll go beautifully,' he said. 'You'll see.'

He took a bottle of white wine from the fridge door, pulled its cork, poured himself a large glass, and went outside for a last inspection of the table and the garden. There was something finely unEnglish about the heavily laid table on the grass – or not unEnglish at all, just unGlass-like. Would the quarryman have approved? The work Clem had done in the garden did not now, as he looked at it, amount to much, less even than he had thought. Some ground cleared, some of the beds dug over. The place was irreclaimable perhaps, or needed skills beyond any he would have time to learn there. He would not give up on it just yet, but this lunch in the open air should, he decided, be the 'project's' official end (its true end, he knew well enough, was in the tunnels underground). 'To Alan,' he said, and raised his wine, seeing, as he did so, Clare at the window of her room looking down at him. They smiled at each other, but did not wave.

Ray's mother was called Jean. Her small round face was like the button of an inconspicuous flower. She shied from things as though quite ordinary objects, her cutlery, Clem's lighter, a slice of salmon on a plate, might strike at her without any warning. To cover her discomfort she began to drink. By the time the first course was cleared she had become hopelessly free, describing herself to Clem as 'a decayed housekeeper'. Ray seemed hardly to notice her. On arriving at the cottage from Laura's he had hugged Clem, a bony clinging that lasted many seconds. Frankie had been cooler with him, remembering his anger. She was dressed in a polka-dot frock of the sort worn by flamenco dancers in tourist nightclubs. Jean regarded her with undisguised awe. Clem kept Jean's glass topped up. She told him he looked like a man she had once known called Alfie. Later, she started calling him Alfie. Clare talked to Frankie. Ray talked to Laura. Kenneth attended solemnly to his food. Toasts were drunk: to the cook, to Jean, to absent friends, to family. A van passed in the lane. The ice cream was a Viennetta, described on the box as *extra-dolce*. Clem cut it into seven portions, then brought more wine from the kitchen. He told Jean about Silverman's work in Toronto. There were people, he said, hiding out in little rooms in the railway station. Jean said she hoped he wouldn't be offended but it was her opinion that a lot of down-and-outs needed a swift kick up the backside. Clare went into the house. Laura and Clem swapped places. The sun was sliding towards the abbey. The table's complicated shadow grew over the grass. Clem smoked with Frankie. He reminded her of their moment in the attic. She blew smoke between her teeth, laughing. 'Be honest,' she said, holding open the little sateen jacket she had put on. 'Do I still have great tits?' Clem assured her she did. He noticed that Clare had shut the back door. He thought she'd been away perhaps ten minutes. He lit another cigarette, rubbed his eyes. Ray dragged his chair over. Clem asked him if Jean knew about the good-news cards and what she thought of them. Ray said the cards frightened her, he didn't know why. Clem threw his cigarette away, excused himself, and walked to the cottage.

In the living room Clare was standing beside the empty fireplace. Next to her, her hand on Clare's shoulder, was Finola Fiacc. She looked much as she had the last time Clem had seen her – the plimsolls, the scarlet lipstick, the vulcanised coat – though instead of the tracksuit she wore a black woollen dress that hung to the middle of her long bright shins.

'Well, well,' said Clem. He glanced at Clare. 'A surprise?'

'I wanted to tell you,' said Clare. 'I tried to.'

He shrugged. 'The more the merrier.' He asked Fiacc if she had eaten. She said she wasn't hungry.

'I've brought you something,' she said.

'Really?'

'I tried to tell you,' said Clare.

'Tell me what?'

'Your sister called me,' said Fiacc. 'Or did you think we never spoke to each other? I told her I had seen something and asked her if she thought you had seen it too. I was concerned that in your hideaway the great world was passing you by.'

'I've no idea what you're talking about,' said Clem.

'I was going to tell you,' said Clare, softly. 'I wanted to . . .'

'I thought,' said Fiacc, 'it would be more the thing if I told you myself. Showed you.'

She dug in one of the pockets of her mac and took out a small square of folded newspaper. She held it between two fingers and straightened her arm towards Clem. He took it from her. It was a foreign-news round-up piece, an unadorned paragraph explaining that a man wanted in connection with the atrocity at N— had been detained in Brussels. He had been living in the Matongé district of the city. Apparently he had family there. The man's name was given and Clem read it several times. There was no doubt about who it was.

'I dare say,' said Fiacc, 'they'd let you get a sight of him. Your monster. That's what you wanted, wasn't it?'

Clem folded the paper again, carefully. He studied the carpet, then looked up at Fiacc. He had not seen her so happy before. 'The date?'

'Wednesday's *Scotsman*,' she said.

'Wednesday's?'

'Wednesday's.'

He thanked her. She told him he was welcome.

Part Three

That same night Theseus did as he was told; but whether he killed the Minotaur with a sword given him by Ariadne, or with his bare hands, or with his celebrated club, is much disputed. A sculptured frieze at Amyclae shows the Minotaur bound and led in triumph by Theseus to Athens; but this is not the generally accepted story.

Robert Graves, *The Greek Myths*

21

Six hours after Fiacc had handed him the piece of newspaper, Clem parked the white Ford on Faraday Road and
walked to his flat. On his desk he had a book, old, the
binding held together with silver gaffer's tape. Anyone
who had been useful to him – night editors, hotel door-
men, managers of car-hire companies, staff at an embassy,
at an airport – anyone who might be useful again, was
noted down in the dog-eared pages of the book. By the
light of the desk lamp he found Kirsty Schneider's name.
Four or five years ago, their lives overlapping between
jobs, they had spent a dozen evenings flirting in various
West London pubs, a non-affair that had ended with an
embrace on a street corner and the exchange of unfulfilled
promises to stay in touch. She was an economist writing
freelance for the broadsheets. She had moved to Brussels
to specialise in Community finances and Community
fraud, he knew that much, and had seen her pieces, part
technical, part satirical, lodged between Obituaries and
Sport. In the book there were two numbers for her. The
first was defunct; the other, a mobile number, she answered after four rings. She was on holiday, she said,
having told him how nice it was to hear from him again, a
village near Arles with her husband Hein and her little girl
Beatrice.

'I hadn't even realised you were married,' said Clem.

'A wife and mother,' she said. 'I adore it.'

He congratulated her.

'Is this business or pleasure?' she asked.

'Business,' he said. 'Business mostly.' He asked what she had heard about Ruzindana.

'The crimes against humanity thing?'

'Yes.'

'Only that they arrested him, then had to let him go again.'

'Let him *go*?'

'Something technical with the warrant. Perhaps they misspelled his name. Isn't this a story you did with Frank Silverman?'

'I want to find this man,' said Clem. 'Can you help me?'

'I'm supposed to be on holiday,' she said.

He said he was sorry.

'There are a couple of people I can try tomorrow,' she said. 'Els Claus at De Morgan might have something.'

'Anything you can get.'

'I'll do what I can, but no promises.'

He apologised again. She told him to forget it. 'A story's a story,' she said. 'We're all addicted.'

They wished each other a good night. Clem took out his wallet and found the scrap of paper with Silverman's cellphone number on it. He copied it into the book below the New York number, then rang the cellphone. A voice – a voice he had grown half used to in Toronto – informed him that the handset he was trying to connect to was switched off. He took a shower, tried again an hour later but got the same message. He went to bed.

* * *

In the morning he bought milk and bread, margarine, three tins of tuna fish, four newspapers. He sat on the floor of the living room drinking tea and eating tuna sandwiches. He spread the papers over the carpet and read carefully through the foreign news but there was nothing to help him. From the bookshelf he took down his copy of *501 French Verbs*. He started to test himself – *blesser, blesser à mort, demolir, se demolir, mordre, moudre* – then started translating in his head paragraphs picked randomly from the papers on the floor. Clare, who had carried on with the language at university as part of her art-history degree, who had lived in the country for over a year, was proficient in a way he was not and would never be, but he had, he believed, all that he would need.

Kirsty Schneider called at one fifteen. She had spoken to her contact at De Morgan. 'Els thinks they'll pick him up again soon,' she said.

'How soon?'

'A couple of weeks. Probably less.'

'Did she have an address for him?'

'Afraid not. But she gave me the number of someone who might. Have you got a pen? A woman called Laurencie Karamera. She's a relative of Ruzindana's. A cousin, a niece, I'm not sure. Works at one of the lobbyist associations, a place called the FIA. They have an office on the rue du Sceptre, just outside the EU quarter.'

She read out a number. Clem wrote it down in large numerals on the paper in front of him.

'Do you know a place called Matongé?' he asked.

'It's an African section,' she said, 'near the avenue Louise. They took the name from one of the suburbs of Kinshasa. Pretty lively. Some good bars.'

He thanked her.

'Hope it works,' she said. 'Whatever it is.'

When she rang off he stared a while at the piece of paper on the desk. In the past there had always been someone else to make these contacts – Facey, Gentellini, Keane, Silverman, someone; it had not really occurred to him before that there might be some specific skill in what they did.

He picked up the receiver, added the code for Belgium, and dialled. The woman who answered told him that Laurencie Karamera was not back from her lunch. Clem left his name and telephone number, then went to his bank in Notting Hill and wrote a cheque at the counter for four hundred pounds. He didn't know what he had in his account, he thought perhaps he had nothing at all, but the bank was busy and the teller knew his face. She counted out the money in twenties, flicking the notes with the stained rubber thimble on her index finger. At a second counter he changed a hundred pounds into Belgian francs, then went to one of the cut-price travel shops on Queensway and bought a return flight, Heathrow–Brussels, leaving at ten a.m. the following morning.

It was four o'clock when he got back to the flat. No one had called. He drank a glass of tap water and pressed the redial button on his phone. A woman again, but a different woman.

'My name is Glass,' he said. 'I called earlier. I would like to speak to Laurencie Karamera.'

'What is it,' asked the woman, 'that you wish to speak about?'

'Are you Laurencie Karamera?'

She paused; he felt her search for some way of probing

him without declaring herself, but finding nothing, as unpractised it seemed as he was himself to the feints and ruses of the game, she finally confessed her identity and repeated her question.

'I'm looking for Sylvestre Ruzindana,' said Clem.

'I have never heard of this man,' she said.

'The former Bourgmestre of R—, wanted by the International Tribunal on a charge of complicity in genocide. I understand he is a relation of yours.'

'Understand? From whom?' A voice outraged.

'I want to see him,' said Clem. 'I want to meet him.'

'Who are you?'

'I have given you my name.'

'You are a journalist?'

'I'm somebody interested in the truth.'

'You have made a mistake,' she said. 'I have nothing to say to you. Do you understand? Nothing to say to you.'

She broke the connection.

In the bathroom Clem put red Cellophane over the shaving light, set up his chemical trays, plugged in the enlarger, and made a set of prints from the negatives he kept in the black folder on the bookshelf. He washed the prints and clipped them up to dry, then went to his bedroom, unpacked the case from Colcombe, threw the dirty clothes into a corner of the room, and packed the bag he had taken with him to Canada. He put the bag, his passport and the plane tickets by the front door of the flat. He tried Silverman again but the handset was still off (lost? stolen?). For a moment he was tempted to call Laura and had typed in half the area code before he changed his mind. He had no right to task her with some manner of snooping mission. Clare would be as safe with Fiacc as she had ever been with him – Fiacc who had been there at the beginning, who had helped at the beginning. He pictured the two of them snug beside the cottage fire. Pictured Fiacc cooking in the little kitchen where Ray's good-news cards were propped on the shelf. Then Fiacc in his bed, or in Clare's perhaps (would they fit?), a pair of middle-aged women soothing each other in a child's bedroom.

He checked the prints and took off the last of the moisture with a hairdryer. He looked at them in the only way he was able to: a disengaged and tensionless focus that kept the images on the surface of his eyes, no deeper. He found a plastic folder for them, then slid the folder into one of the side pockets of his bag. There was still time to change all this. Time to unpack, to put things away, to take some quite different path. He was not fated to any of this; nor was he being goaded on by ghosts, that company he had imagined following him as the plane made its descent to Toronto. Whatever he was doing now he was choosing it. The consequences, the responsibility, were purely his own. He lit a cigarette, rolled the smoke over his tongue. It was the last few minutes of the dusk. On the other side of the Grove, thin lines of light showed between the drawn curtains.

22

He had picked the hotel from a sheet supplied by the tourist desk at the airport, selecting it because it was close to Matongé and because its rates were reasonable. The sheet described it as 'clean and modern' and this was exact. The corridors were pale grey, his room also, a Magritte print (bowler hats, rain) on the wall over the bed. The view – he was on the fourth floor at the back of the building – was of tall windows opening on to balconies, a narrow, quiet street below. He lay down and shut his eyes, then roused himself, sat on the edge of the bed and picked up the phone.

'I'm in Brussels,' he said.

She said she didn't care where he was. She threatened to call the police.

'How did the police behave with your uncle?' he asked.

'He is not my uncle!'

'This man you have never heard of?'

She rang off. Clem unfolded a map of the city (his gift from the tourism office), smoothing it out over the counterpane. He found the rue du Sceptre, found his own street, Matongé, the EU quarter. Around each of these he drew a careful circle, then called Laurencie Karamera again.

'Don't put the phone down,' he said. 'All I want you to do is help me to meet Sylvestre Ruzindana.'

'And why should I do this? Why should I help you?'

'You know what he is accused of. You know how serious it is. That must mean something to you.'

She paused. 'But it is not my business,' she said. 'You understand? I know nothing about this. Why are you trying to make this my business?'

He sat a moment with the phone in his hand, then slowly put it down. He looked again at the map and went out. At the end of his street he turned left and walked until he came to the Porte de Namur Métro at the edge of the Boulevard de Waterloo. He picked out a black face, a man he thought was about Ruzindana's age, and followed him. He knew very well the man was not Ruzindana but hoped there might be a café or social club where men of that age went to gossip and play cards. They headed away from the boulevard and had walked for less than ten minutes before they crossed into Matongé. Suddenly, Clem was among scenes, scents, accents he had left behind in May, though then it had been the ruin of such scenes, with empty stores and silent markets, and underfoot a litter of broken glass and cartridge cases. Here in Matongé the shops had sacks full of sweet potatoes for sale, maize, red chillis, stalks of sugar-cane, dried locusts, palm leaves, dried fish like the soles of old sandals. There were bolts of vividly dyed cloth on display, tresses of false hair, a heavy jewellery of gold or mock-gold. Along the pavements, men in slacks and safari shirts, a few with dreadlocks, a few in ankle-length robes of light cotton, were gathered in animated conversations, shaking hands, holding hands, laughing open-mouthed at each other's stories. Clem, distracted, lost sight of the man he had been following, his target.

For an hour he explored the place, entering the tatty arcades, losing and finding his bearings at street-corners, then stepping into a bar and ordering a bottle of beer that came with the print of an elephant on the label. He flicked through an African newspaper (*Le Phare*), listened to the twang of Soukous and Juju on the radio. The whole quarter had something lush and improbable about it, like those tough, brilliant flowers that cling to the soot-blackened walls of old railway cuttings. A community – more recent, he thought, more improvised than its equivalents in London – arriving piecemeal on cheap flights from the south and threading itself on to strings of nineteenth-century Bruxellois real estate. He ordered a second beer. The waitress who served him was a waddling, laughing, yellow-toothed woman with a purple and gold turban on her head. She winked at him. He wondered what would happen if he mentioned the Bourgmestre to her. Did she know him? Did everyone know him? Did she see him walk by her windows in the morning, an unlucky figure she glanced away from?

He went back to the hotel. It was mid-afternoon. For a third time he dialled the number of the FIA. A man answered: a young man's voice, suspicious, ready for a fight. Clem asked for Laurencie Karamera.

'She cannot speak on the phone now,' said the voice, decisively.

'She's occupied?'

'What is it you want to talk to her about?'

'Not knowing who you are, that is not something I can discuss.'

'You're the journalist, yes?'

'Is she still at the office?'

'Shall I tell you what I think of journalists? Of people like you?'

'Why don't you give me your name?' asked Clem. 'You have mine.'

'Worse than dogs.'

'Are you a colleague? A friend of hers?'

'You can kill a street dog with an axe. Nobody cares.'

'Is that what you would do?'

'Nobody cares what happens to them.'

Clem took a bath, then performed some vaguely remembered yoga exercises in the space between the foot of the bed and the cupboard where the television was stored. At half past five he rang again. The phone was not answered and no answering-machine clicked on. He turned on the television and channel-surfed, looking for news. He heard the news in French, in American, in Flemish. He turned off the television, dressed, and went out. It surprised him how chill it was; he only had his denim jacket for warmth. He walked quickly, then stopped at a bar to drink a brandy. The man beside him had pale eyes in a long, bearded face, a northern face, like some stern northern smallholder or predestination elder of the Kirk. In French, Clem asked for directions to the city centre. The man answered him in English, sketching the route in the air with the stem of his pipe. 'Twenty minutes,' he said, but Clem, stopping at two more bars on the way, took an hour to reach Grande Place. There, he toured the square with several hundred others from the despised and leaderless army of tourists, trudging under the spotlit guild-houses, peering up at their blank windows, their stone insignia, and remembering the gross geometries of Toronto's financial district; remembering too, with something like a flash of panic, that he had still not spoken to Silverman, had not been advised or warned off, was navigating alone.

Behind the square he found a restaurant and sat at his table writing notes on whatever clear paper he found in his pockets. The restaurant – small, underlit – had a ripe and oily perfume of fried onions, fried fish, garlic, tobacco smoke. He wrote: *Is Europe finished? A well-run corpse, maggoty.* He ordered six oysters, steak *frites*, a bottle of house red. *Who is the man who threatened me today? His connection to LK? What am I doing here? This is not journalism! I know less all the time.*

The oysters were over-chilled, his steak bloody and hard-sinewed. He chewed on it and drank his wine, then ordered coffee and brandy. On the card wallet of his airline ticket he wrote, 'I am lonely', then very carefully scrubbed the words out. He settled his bill and went on to the street. The city was busier, noisier. A gang of Scotsmen in their kilts roared and staggered, though without much menace. Clem moved away in what he hoped was the right direction for his hotel. He tried to wave down a taxi but it sped past. On the side of a bus-stop he found a street plan and studied it profitlessly for many minutes before travelling on, trusting to instinct and drunk's luck. The streets he turned into now were quieter. He recognised a cobbled square, a statue, a bar he thought he had been into earlier. He went in (it was not the same place at all), found a stool and studied the names of the beers. Kwak, Brigand, Judas, Faro, Bonne Espérance. Was there a meaning to any of this? A young pianist played tangos on an old piano; a pregnant waitress gathered glasses.

Clem talked expansively to a girl who was waiting at the bar, then caught sight of his face in the mirror, jabbering, feverish. He slid from the stool and made a clumsy exit, unsure whether or not he had paid for his drink, not caring much. It was beginning to rain. He turned up his collar. Tall windows, iron balustrades, here and there a gleam of light but mostly darkness. The rain grew heavier. Water pooled in the gutters of his ears. He sheltered for twenty minutes in a doorway, then realised that the building on the other side of the street with the half-familiar glass frontage was his hotel. The doors were locked. He couldn't find a bell. He tapped on the glass until the night porter came, a man of middle years, a boatless Charon, who let Clem pass without a word.

Upstairs he towelled his head dry, climbed from his damp clothes and left them on the bathroom floor. His gaffer-taped contact book was on the bedside table. He found 'Silverman' and rang the number.

'Hello?' said a woman's voice.

'Hello,' said Clem, letting his head loll on to the pillows.

'Hello? Who is that?' she asked.

'Shelley-Anne?' He had rung the New York number.

'Well, that's me,' she said. 'Who you?'

'Clem Glass. A friend of . . .'

'Oh, yeah. OK. How are you doing, Clem?'

'I'm in Belgium,' he said.

'Wow. It must be pretty late there.'

He agreed it was, though in fact he had no idea of the time.

'Clem,' she said, 'I've got some friends here for dinner. Maybe we could talk tomorrow?'

'I liked your book,' he said.

'You did? Which one?'

'*The Stitches of Time.*'

'That one I just called *A Stitch in Time*. You know, like the proverb?'

'I like it anyway.'

'That's sweet of you. Thank you.'

'Silverman says he can get a picture of you in any good bookshop.'

She laughed. 'Maybe that's why he doesn't feel the need to come home too often.'

'I wanted to speak to him.'

'I guess we'd all like to speak to him.'

'I'm sorry.'

'There's nothing to be sorry about. He's working something out up there. Maybe when he's ready . . .'

'You know,' said Clem, 'he thinks that people are basically good but he only thinks it to keep himself sober. Really he believes what I believe.'

'Well, I think that people are basically good too. I mean, don't we have to believe something like that if we're not to go completely crazy? There are *some*, of course—'

'The first,' said Clem, cutting across her, 'the first we saw was a child, a young boy lying on the path with his—'

'No,' she said.

'No?'

'I don't want to hear it.'

'No,' said Clem. 'Why would you?' The heat of the room was unpicking him. Inside his skull a voice nagged, telling him to end the call.

'Have you seen someone?' she asked. 'Someone you could talk this through with?'

'A doctor?'

'It doesn't have to be a doctor.'

'A priest?'

'A priest if you're a believer,' she said. 'Which I'm guessing you're not.'

'I had a drink tonight,' he said.

'You guys got too close,' she said. 'Way too close.'

'We thought we were involuble.'

'In what?'

'Inviolable.'

'Invincible?'

'What are you cooking?' he asked.

'Cannelloni with pork and dried apricot and chestnuts.'

'It sounds wonderful. You sound wonderful.'

'You should get some sleep now, Clem.'

'I hope he comes back,' he said. 'I hope he finds his way.'

'Oh, he'll be back,' she said. He heard her smile. 'I always insist on a happy ending. You should too.'

In the morning he caught the last five minutes of the breakfast buffet. He drank lukewarm coffee, filled his pockets with fruit. In his room he took a painkiller and spent twenty minutes under the shower, trying to remember what he had said to Shelley-Anne. He searched in his jacket pocket for his cigarettes but found only a handful of francs, a receipt from the restaurant, his air ticket in its written-over folder. He watched the news updates on CNN and the BBC. Naked on the side of the bed he called Laurencie Karamera.

'Do I have to come to the office?' he said. 'How much do they know there?'

'I cannot help you,' she said. 'Please. Please go away.'

'You're on the rue du Sceptre, yes? That shouldn't take me long.' He waited, giving her some time to picture it, the unknown man shouldering his way into the office talking of bloodbaths, fugitives.

'Give me your number,' she said. 'I will call you later.'

'When?'

'Today.'

'Call me in one hour,' he said. 'One hour from now. If I don't hear from you, then you can expect to see me at the office.'

He ate the fruit he had put into his pockets, watched some of the local daytime TV, then dressed and stood at the window. He opened it. The wet weather had blown through: the day was mild, clear, the street below washed clean by the rain. The houses opposite were no more than thirty feet away. Through the line of windows he could spy on the lives being lived in the various rooms of the apartment facing him. He saw a young woman sitting behind a music stand bowing a cello, or something smaller than a cello – a *viola da gamba*? – sounding her chords tentatively, though, as far as Clem could make out from across the street, without error. He did not recognise the piece, guessed it was something slow by J. S. Bach. She was so close he could have called across to ask her. Would she answer? What a nice, neighbourly exchange that would be! The next window showed a family room – rugs and paintings, chairs that didn't match each other, a vase of white flowers. The end window belonged to an office or study. At the table, a man with a garland of grey hair sat writing, his arm crook'd, his back stooped, absorbed in his labours. A letter? A story? Or a memoir perhaps (yes, let it be a memoir), the History of My Life written for the girl whose music seeped under his study door. Lines to help her make sense of the mystery, to tie life down on its back and show her its belly.

The telephone rang. He clambered over the bed to pick it up.

'There is a café,' she said, 'by the church of St Boniface.' She gave him the name. He scribbled it down on the notepad beside the phone. 'Come at five thirty,' she said. 'At five thirty exactly.'

'Ruzindana will be there?'

'You must come on your own. No camera and no tape-recorder.'

'He'll be there?'

'I have legal training,' she said.

'We all have legal training,' said Clem.

He took his map and left the hotel. He bought cigarettes at the local *tabac*. Half an hour later he found the church (blackened façade, turreted roof), standing, warder-like, at one side of a small semi-circular *place* on the edge of Matongé. A scattering of cafés and restaurants gave to the area a character of well-heeled bohemianism. The café Laurencie Karamera had mentioned – Une Vue de Mars – was not what he had anticipated. The walls were hung with pop art; the music was American swing from the fifties; the clientele – students, young professionals, liberal arts types – almost exclusively white. Had she chosen it for its size? Full, it would hold two hundred customers, probably more. Or was it that in Matongé proper there were too many people who might be capable of piecing together snatches of the conversation – people for whom the events of April were more than a foreign news item buried now beneath a weight of other wars and new atrocities? He had assumed Matongé to be a refuge for Ruzindana, but had assumed it for no better reason than that most of its inhabitants shared the Bourgmestre's skin colour. This made him what? A fool? A racist? What other unexamined assumptions was he carrying? Matongé might not at all be the sanctuary he had supposed.

At the hotel he slept until he woke himself with the noise of his own snoring. There were still two hours to fill. In the house across the street the chair by the music stand was empty and the man had left off his writing (it had been a tax-return perhaps, a shopping list). In the bathroom he shaved, then tilted back his head for the eye-drops. At four fifteen, tired of pacing, unable to stay in the room, he put on his jacket, put the plastic folder under his arm, and rode the small mirrored lift to the ground floor. He made himself walk slowly, stroll like some *flâneur* with nothing more to worry him than where he would take his first aperitif of the evening. It was ten to five when he reached the rue St Boniface. He sat in a café diagonally opposite the open corner-door of Une Vue de Mars. He had no idea, of course, what Laurencie Karamera looked like but thought it would not be difficult to pick her out, a woman in the frame of mind she was surely in. And wouldn't Ruzindana be with her? There had been no explicit promise of it, and yet why else would they be doing this? It occurred to him that in dealing with Laurencie Karamera he might, in fact, have been dealing with Ruzindana all along. Would he surface now? Break cover? Or was this to be the first of a series of unfulfilled meetings in which she brought not the Bourg-mestre of R— but a tangle of stories, lies, excuses, stalling him until he lost the will to go on with it? It would not be such a bad strategy.

At five thirty-five, a taxi – a white Mercedes – coming from the direction of avenue Louise, turned into the *place*. It drove through, but returned a few minutes later and pulled up outside Une Vue de Mars. A woman and two men climbed from the rear of the car and went inside. The car moved off. Clem waited another half-minute, then scattered change beside his coffee cup and crossed the street. Through the windows he saw them at a table by the back wall, underneath a poster, several feet square, of the Martian desert. They were sitting like a committee, all three of them along the same side of the table, facing outwards. The woman was on the left. Beside her was a muscular young man in a tight-fitting short-sleeved shirt, and next to him, a much older man, gaunt and grizzle-bearded, who sat with his head bowed, gazing at the table-top through black-framed spectacles.

'You have five minutes,' said the young man, who, through narrowed and unblinking eyes, had watched Clem's progress across the café. 'Five minutes to say what you want. Then you go away. You don't come back.'

Clem sat on the chair opposite him, catching, as he settled, the whiff of an aftershave or hair tonic, some-thing with sweet rum and spices, though which of the two men was wearing it he couldn't yet tell. He turned to the older man. 'Sylvestre Ruzindana?'

Slowly, as if the movement pained him, the older man raised his head.

'I've been wanting to meet you for a long time,' said Clem, reciting words he had rehearsed a dozen times in the quiet of his hotel room. 'I have even been to your home. Though others had been there first.'

There was no response. No look of alarm or defiance or shame. 'Your home is in ruins,' said Clem. 'Destroyed.'

Still there was nothing. Clem unclipped the folder and took out the prints he had made in London. His heart had beaten wildly as he walked over to the table but now he felt calm, and something more than calm, as though the note of outrage in his voice were not quite authentic.

'I took these in April,' he said, 'at the church in N—. I don't think you need me to explain them to you.'

He slid the prints across the table. Ruzindana picked them up. He began to go through them, carefully, without haste. At one he paused as though to make some comment, but he shuffled it to the back of the pile and studied the next. The waitress came for Clem's order. 'Nothing,' he said. 'Nothing, thank you.'

'What type of human being,' hissed the young man when the waitress was out of earshot, 'can take photographs like these?'

'I don't know,' said Clem. He saw that Laurencie Karamera had turned in her seat towards the far corner of the café. 'Would you like to see them too?' he asked. She ignored him. He looked back at Ruzindana.

'There are witnesses,' he said, 'who identify you as the man who led the killers. The one who encouraged them when they were tired, who ordered them to leave no grave half filled. There are people who say they saw you handing out weapons and that you were smiling.'

By the side of the Bourgmestre's chair was a string bag filled with shopping. Clem could see oranges, a bar of chocolate; something – meat or fish – wrapped in white greaseproof paper.

'Listen,' said the young man, heavily, as though it had fallen to him to explain the glaringly obvious, 'we are educated people. We are successful people. We own land. We have a business. We are not living in mud huts, OK? Because of this we have enemies. They lie because they are envious of us. They want to drag us down. To destroy us.'

'One of the witnesses,' said Clem, 'is a ten-year-old girl.'

'A girl?' He laughed. 'A little girl? She will tell what she is told to tell.'

'Then let me hear it from him,' said Clem. 'Let me hear him say that it's all lies.'

Ruzindana shook his head. He looked as though what he had been listening to was a story he knew, but only vaguely, a parable of human folly, something to sigh over. Through the not-quite-clean lenses of his glasses his eyes focused on Clem. He smiled. A broad, sad smile. 'Tell me,' he said, softly, 'have you been blessed with children?'

'I'm glad you mention them,' said Clem. 'I wanted your opinion on whether killing children is more unpleasant than killing adults, or if, once the killing starts, it really makes no difference at all.'

The young man leaned across the table. He jerked a finger two inches from the end of Clem's nose. 'You think we will let you insult us? Are you shameless? Are you a fool?' He stood, pinching the older man's sleeve so that he was forced to stand up alongside him. The woman stayed where she was, ignoring them still. Clem gathered the prints and returned them to the file. He snapped the file shut. To the young man he said, 'I haven't come here to insult you. I don't even know you.'

He left the café and walked down to the church steps, picked out a piece of shadow there, lit a cigarette, and waited. Was that *it*? Was it over now? Where had his anger been? His righteousness? That rage he had squandered on poor Paulus? The whole interview – this long-imagined confrontation – had played out as a failure of a kind he had not prepared himself for. Why had he not climbed on to his chair and announced to the whole café that there, sitting among them, among the Warhols and the Lichtenstein prints, was one of the *genocidaires*? Yet it had been hard to believe that the man across the table was the same whose image he carried in his wallet. No suavely turned-out politician on the make any more; more the demeanour of some retired academic, some dreamy former expert on quasars or Babylonian dynasties, the type who regularly leaves the house without his keys. Depravity should not appear in the guise of someone's elderly relative who has spent the afternoon food shopping. It was as though the man he wanted to grapple with no longer even existed. As if time had smuggled him to safety while he, Clem, avenging angel, swordless and wingless, had dug in a little garden and grown oblivious.

After a quarter of an hour they came out. Whatever it

was they had needed to say to each other after he left them they had obviously already said it. The two men immediately moved off together, leaving Laurencie Karamera alone on the pavement outside the café doors. Her presence there – intentionally or otherwise – effectively ended any thoughts Clem had had of following Ruzindana: he could not have pursued the men without first walking in front of her. He watched her smooth her brow, brush something from the sleeve of her charcoal-grey jacket, then look up and down the road. Once the men were out of sight he approached her, speaking her name while still some distance from her, hoping not to startle her, but startling her anyway. Whoever she was waiting for it had not been him.

'I wanted to thank you,' he said.

'Thank me?'

'For arranging the meeting.'

'What choice did I have?'

'They were angry with you?'

'What do you want?'

'Who was the young man?'

'Go away,' she said.

'Is he Ruzindana's son?'

She shook her head.

'Does he have sons?'

'His sons are dead.'

'How?'

'I don't know.'

'No?'

'In the camps.'

'The refugee camps?'

She nodded.

'What happened to them?'

'Maybe they were sick. Maybe someone killed them. You're the journalist. You find out.'

'Did you know them?'

'This is not my business,' she said. 'Why are you trying to make it my business?'

'He's accused of a terrible crime,' said Clem.

'Accused by you.'

'Accused by the International Tribunal.'

'It was war.'

'War? It was murder!'

He saw the word's blunt force – *assassinat!* – go through her. She stiffened, then fumbled inside her bag for her cigarettes. When she had one between her lips Clem lit it for her.

'You believe that he's innocent?' he asked.

'He's old,' she said. 'You saw him. Old and sick.'

'He'll stand trial,' said Clem.

'Perhaps.'

'He'll be convicted.'

'He has friends there still. Powerful people.'

'It will make no difference.'

'None of it,' she said, 'will make a difference.'

On the kerb opposite, a young boy in shorts and a crisply ironed shirt was watching them. Laurencie gestured to him to stay where he was.

'He's yours?' asked Clem.

She said he was.

'He's grown up here?'

'Yes.'

'I'd like to talk to you,' said Clem.

'You have already talked to me.'

'To talk to you again.'

'Why?'

'Because you're the only one I trust.'

'I should be grateful for that?'

'Can we meet tomorrow?'

'I have to work.'

'After work.'

'I am taking him swimming.'

'The boy?'

'Yes.'

'What's his name?'

'Emile.'

'I'll meet you at the pool.'

'That's impossible.'

'It's not impossible. It's very simple.'

'If I am seen with you . . .'

'Do they control you? Does Ruzindana control you?'

'I have done what you asked,' she said.

'You're afraid of him.'

'I'm afraid of no one.'

'Then talk to me again. Let me meet you. Even for half an hour.'

'And then?'

'Then I'll leave you in peace.'

'Why should I believe you?'

'Laurencie, please. Where is the pool?'

For the first time in their conversation she turned to look directly at him, weighing him, this wilful foreigner. He saw that her eyes, though brown, had hints of green in them, like the green of glass under river water.

'Twenty minutes,' he said. 'That's all I'm asking for. Fifteen minutes.'

'Fifteen?'

'Ten minutes.'

'And I won't have to see you again?'

'Not if you choose not to.'

She shrugged, as though in fact the whole affair was a matter of the greatest indifference to her. 'The rue de la Perche,' she said, tossing her half-smoked cigarette into the gutter. He thanked her. She crossed the road and took her son's hand, leading him away towards Matongé. The boy looked back at Clem over his shoulder. Clem raised a hand and smiled.

That night, Clem dreamed he was having sex in the garden at Colcombe with one of the young mothers he used to see at the health centre, and that from the tunnel below them there came a muted crying for help that they, in their thrashings, ignored; a piteous chorus, among which Clem thought he detected certain familiar voices, and certain others that he had only imagined, like that of the quarryman, who – so the young mother explained in gasps into his ear – had been condemned to wander through the underworld of the mines for ever, sentenced to it by his own folly in running firewards when the klaxon sounded. 'Can't his wife save him, then?' Clem had asked (some muddled idea in his head of Orpheus and Eurydice, Silverman and Shelley-Anne), but to this large question he received no answer, or none he remembered on waking.

He breakfasted in the basement dining room – more grey paint, more Magrittes – then asked the woman at Reception where he could have some prints made. She gave him the name of a street in the Lower Town and marked it for him on his map. He found the street by ten o'clock. There were at least four places there equipped to give him what he wanted, but one, its window shelves lined with old Leicas, Leitz lenses, Hasselblads, each with its neatly inked price-tag, had a character of seriousness and old-world professionalism that drew him inside. From his wallet he took the transparency of the class-room wall at N— and passed it to the man at the counter. 'How soon can you make fifty postcard-sized prints of this?'

The man held up the picture and frowned. 'Matt or gloss?'

'Matt.'

'Tomorrow morning?'

'I need them today.'

'Wait here.' The man went to the rear of the shop and spoke to someone Clem couldn't see. When he came back he nodded. 'OK. He'll do them for you now. Give him a couple of hours.'

Clem filled the time by walking to the canal, the Porte de Flandre, then circling slowly back. At the shop the prints were waiting for him in a white envelope.

'It's quite a picture,' said the man. 'Nice contrasts.'

Clem checked the prints, paid, and carried the envelope to the nearest café. He ordered an espresso, took out his pen and began to write on the back of the prints. On each, in English and French, he wrote the same question.

WHERE IS THE MAN RESPONSIBLE FOR THE MASSACRE AT N—?

He would have preferred a hundred, or two hundred, but fifty would be a start. He left the first of them in the café, tucked inside the menu. The next ten he left in shops and bars across the city centre. One he slipped between the pages of a fashion magazine, another among the brochures at the American Express office. He went into the Métro and found his way to the EU district. Here he targeted the sandwich bars and spaghetti houses where the *fonctionnaires* were having their lunch. From every street-corner he saw the brightly painted heads of cranes rearing up, a city-within-a-city on the brick dust and bulldozed squares of the old quarter. He left cards behind the windscreen wipers of luxury cars, was shooed away by someone's chauffeur. The last of the cards he took back to Matongé, hid half along the rue de Longue Vie, the rest in shops on the chaussée d'Ixelles.

At the hotel he sat on the bed watching satellite TV. At five o'clock he showered, changed his shirt and checked the map. He reached the pool on the rue de la Perche at twenty to six. There was no sign of Laurencie Karamera. He went up to the viewing area, a balcony with rows of tiered seating above the pool's deep-end. A dozen others were there, parents presumably, keeping watch over their charges. After ten minutes he saw Emile climbing confidently down into the lime-green water. A minute later, the boy's mother came through the door at the back of the area. Clem gestured to her. She looked quickly at the scattered others, noted faces, then came and sat beside him.

'He's already a good swimmer,' said Clem.

'We come every week,' she said.

'Sometimes his father comes?'

'He would have to come a long way.'

'You're not together?'

'You ask too many questions.'

'You don't ask any.'

'Are you married?'

'No.'

'I didn't think so.'

'It shows?'

'Of course.'

'How?'

He waited, genuinely curious to hear her answer, but none came. 'I didn't come here to make things difficult for you,' he said.

'But you have done it anyway.'

'How close are you to Ruzindana?'

'I hardly know him.'

'You're not a relative?'

'I said I hardly know him.'

'How long have you lived here?'

'Fifteen years.'

'You like it?'

'Yes.'

'Why wouldn't you look at the pictures yesterday?'

'I don't need to look at them.'

'Perhaps you do.'

'Because you took them? Because you want me to feel the same as you?' She shook her head. 'I know people like you,' she said. 'I've seen people like you before.'

'Really?'

'You go to Africa. You see something, something bad. Then you believe what was in your heart all the time. These blacks are savages. You go there ignorant. You come back ignorant.'

'This is not a racial matter,' said Clem. 'It's not about black and white.'

She smiled sourly.

'It's not a racial matter,' he repeated, though even to his own ears his voice seemed marked by some uncertainty.

They watched the boy swimming. The noise of the swimmers, most of them children, echoed under the roof, a sound not entirely human, more like a colony of sea birds.

'He goes to a good school,' she said, after some minutes of silence between them. 'He is never in trouble. His heroes are football players and cyclists. His favourite food is pizza. His best friend is a little boy with a Turkish father and a Polish mother. At school the children raise money to provide clean drinking water for villages in India. Do you understand?'

'He's in a new world.'

'He has never been taught to hate, or to look down on people.'

'People need to be taught to hate?'

'Of course.'

'And what does he want to be in this new world?'

She shrugged. 'A lawyer. A lawyer or perhaps a professional cyclist.'

Clem nodded. 'Can we smoke up here?'

'No.'

'If it was Ruzindana,' he said, 'if Ruzindana is responsible . . .'

She sighed. 'If it was him, he must go back.'

'And stand trial?'

'Yes.'

'And if they find him guilty?'

'They can send for you to hang him.'

'Or send for you?'

'Why me?'

'Wouldn't you want to hang a man who had slaughtered three thousand people? Who had murdered hundreds of children? Schoolchildren like Emile?'

'He is always kind to Emile. He buys him presents.'

'Hitler was fond of children. He used to have parties for them at his house in Berchtesgaden.'

'Hitler? What are you talking about Hitler for?'

'Where is Ruzindana staying?' asked Clem. 'Who has he been living with here?'

'Enough of this!'

He should, he knew, leave her be. It was strange to him that he didn't, for clearly she had not the slightest connection with the events at the church of N—, and her relationship with Ruzindana, whatever its exact nature, was, he decided, an irrelevance, some accident of blood or marriage, a source of temporary grave embarrassment that his prying made much worse for her. What question could she answer, what answers could she possibly give that would satisfy him? Had she heard Ruzindana confess? Did she have stories of his sadism? Did she know of some plan to get him to safety? No. She was what she seemed to be: a single mother, hard-working, determined to make her life her own and not be sucked down by the undertow of this miserable affair.

'I was thinking,' he said, 'that when Emile finishes his swim I could take you both for something to eat.'

'As payment?'

'No.'

'Then why?'

'Why not?'

'You want us to be friends?'

'We don't have to be enemies.'

'Perhaps we do.'

'I hope not.'

'You like me?' she asked.

'Yes.'

She laughed. 'You think I like you?'

They stared at each other – a second full of fierce enquiry – then turned their faces back to the pool. Emile, clinging at the shallow end, waved up at his mother. She lifted her arm and tapped her watch.

'I don't want to eat with you,' she said, 'but I will do one thing for you. A last thing. I will show you something.'

'Show me?'

'Do you know where Tervuren is?'

'I think I've seen it on the map.'

'You take a tram. A number forty-four tram from Montgomery station. Tervuren is the last stop. Meet me outside the station there at two o'clock tomorrow afternoon.'

'You're not going to the office?'

'Not until Monday.'

'And what's at Tervuren?'

'Something for your arrogance,' she said. 'Something to make you silent.'

'You want to open my eyes,' he said.

'Yes.' She stood up and straightened her jacket. 'I'm going to open your eyes.'

23

The 44 tram began its journey like a yellow grub in the twilight of Montgomery station, but soon it swung into the light, accelerating through the suburban lunch-hour along an avenue of young chestnut trees until the city abruptly ended and they were hastening under the boughs of true, broadleaf woodland. Autumn here was further on than it had been at home, though the latitude could not have been very different from Colcombe's or London's. Many trees were already bare, the ground below them vivid with the reds and various golds of their leaf-fall.

He knew now – his informant at the hotel reception again – that the African museum, the Musée Royal de l'Afrique Central, was in Tervuren, and this, he assumed, was where Laurencie Karamera would take him. He arrived early and sat on the grass behind the terminus shelter. When she came, he stood up. He had only seen her in her work clothes before, her office uniform. Now she was wearing a cream-coloured, loose-fitting dress, sleeveless, and on her arms, bangles of silver and old ivory. He held out his hand to her. Briefly, she took it.

'No Emile this afternoon?' he asked.

'Emile has his piano lesson.'

'And me? What sort of lesson do I have?' He felt suddenly in high spirits out here in the semi-countryside with this interesting woman, but she, remembering their parts more accurately perhaps, neither smiled nor replied.

They crossed the road and passed between tall gates into the grounds of the museum, a spread of formal gardens with box hedges, gravelled walks, a large pond where exotic-looking ducks paddled across cloudscapes. The museum, a neo-classical juggernaut, was ranged at the top of a flight of broad, shallow steps. Clem purchased tickets from a woman in the marble foyer, then followed Laurencie, the heels of her sandals slapping on the wooden floors, through camphor-scented halls of headdresses, mealie pots, tree-trunk canoes, spirit masks. There were exhibits of natural rubber, timber from the equatorial forests, a termite's nest, cross-sectioned. In a glass case a pair of dowdy zebras, like articles left behind in some repository of belle-époque furniture, grazed on painted grass before a painted sky, while in the neighbouring box a varnished crocodile strained its jaws in an endless yawn. There were not many visitors that afternoon. An elderly gent, dark suit and walking cane, stood before a show of illustrative skulls; a boy listened to his father gloss on a display of hunting spears; three nuns rested on a bench. The place was august, crammed, sepia-tinted; a museum that was itself its own principal exhibit, but which looked now as though it were learning to be ashamed and might prefer to drag its great stone hide into the woods and be seen no more.

Laurencie, standing at the side of a cabinet that ran at waist height along the wall of one of the smaller halls, beckoned to Clem. He went, and leaning beside her saw at first only the image of their faces in the glass, then saw below, pinned to the papered wooden base of the cabinet as though it were the remaining wing of some giant African moth, a photograph of two uniformed white men presiding over the public whipping of a black man. Next to the photograph, curled and dirty grey, was an example of the whip itself, an item known as a *chicotte*, and made, so the caption explained, from a strip of hippopotamus hide dried in the sun.

Clem looked from the whip to the photograph, back to the whip, and again to the photograph. The uniformed men, members of the colonial service or representatives of some industrial concern, did not appear to be taking any sinister pleasure from the sight of a man being whipped, but neither were they shirking what they must have called to each other their 'duty'. They stood ten feet or so from where their prisoner was stretched on the ground, their poses characterised by a kind of double awkwardness – white men among natives; also, the subjects of a photograph they might not have much wanted taken. The younger man, clean-shaven, expressionless, was standing with feet apart and arms akimbo, while his older colleague (moustache) jotted something in a notebook – how the Negro bears up to a thorough flogging, or something for the company records, even, conceivably, something (a sketch or data of a loosely scientific type) for the celebrated collection at Tervuren.

'Here,' said Laurencie, 'is an exact record of our history.'

'Our history?'

'The history of your people and mine.'

'In one photograph?'

'Why not? You believe in photographs, don't you?'

She tapped the glass with a fingernail. 'This picture is not as old as you think. These men may still be alive, enjoying their retirements, playing with their great-grandchildren. Who will look for them now? Will you? And what about those who gave them their orders? The businesses that grew fat on blood and theft? Half of Brussels is built on what they stole from us. You want to find savages? Then here they are. They have Belgian names and white faces. English names too, and French names and German names and Portuguese. You tell me Ruzindana killed three thousand. I tell you these pigs killed millions!'

The elderly gentleman Clem had seen earlier studying the skulls, the Descent of Man, paused at the entrance to the hall, observed them both – this excitable couple – and turned back.

'What was done then,' said Clem, searching his stock of borrowed language for words of an adequate weight, 'is beyond any defending.'

'You admit that much.'

'Of course! But none of this can excuse Ruzindana.'

'You would like to use the *chicotte* on him,' she said. 'You would like to have him tied to a post.'

'The people who died at N— were not colonial officials, Laurencie. Not the police or someone's army. They were farmers and teachers and shopkeepers and school-children. Are you saying the massacre was caused by a colonialism that ended a generation ago? The whip is in a museum now. It's not in anybody's hand or on anyone's back.'

'So we should forget about it?'

'I'm not saying that—'

'That's exactly what you're saying! The humiliation and murder of millions of Africans belongs in the past. We should forgive and forget. We should move on.'

'These are two separate issues. Two separate disasters. We can't—'

'You just don't get it at all,' she said, sighing and turning again to the photograph as though she might still find some detail there to make him see the utter rightness of what she said.

'Perhaps I don't get it,' said Clem. 'Maybe I *can't*. But I won't accept one crime being used to justify another.'

She rolled her eyes. 'Oh, Monsieur Won't-accept!'

'Why are you being like this?' he asked. 'Because I didn't say when we first met that I despise what these men were part of? Should I have said that? Is it still necessary for anyone to say such a thing? Or are you angry because I have disturbed the comfortable life you have made for yourself here? I think,' he went on, taking a kind of pleasure in the injustice of the comment, 'that you would prefer to see Ruzindana free than make even the smallest change to your routine.'

'That is not true,' she said. 'And you have no right to say it.'

'No?'

'You really believe I have nothing better to do with my time? Nothing more pleasant? The question,' she said, regarding him very steadily, 'is what you are doing here. I mean, what you are really doing.'

'You know the answer to that,' he said.

She shook her head. 'I thought I did. Now, truly, I am not sure.'

*   *   *

268

The museum had a café. Smokers were required to sit outside in a grassed courtyard. Clem brought out two coffees. They sat, not quite face to face but at a slight angle, so that sipping coffee and smoking they gazed past each other's shoulders to the windows and pillars of the courtyard walls. It was mid-afternoon; they were the only people there. The other tables and chairs already had an out-of-season look to them, ready to be stacked and carried in, stored somewhere until the spring.

For several minutes they made small-talk. Clem asked her what she did when she went out in the evenings. She said she didn't go out much; when she did she liked to see films. He said he liked films too. He saw a lot of films in London. She nodded. The spark seemed to have gone out of them, as if each was secretly disappointed with the force of his or her argument. Nothing much had been settled at the Musée Royal, though neither of them seemed to know quite what had been missed.

'Now,' she said, lighting her second cigarette, 'now that I have made you look at a photograph, you will expect me to look at the ones you showed to the old man. You will call me a hypocrite.'

'Those are at the hotel,' said Clem. 'I don't carry them around with me.'

'I'm glad.'

'But if you want a picture for a picture . . .' He pulled his wallet from his trouser pocket, flipped it open, undid the popper, selected one of the transparencies, and passed it to her. 'Hold it up to the light,' he said.

She held it up.

'Can you see her? Her name is Odette. She's ten years old . . .' He told her what he knew about the girl. How she had suffered her wound at N— when the killers hacked through the leg of the woman she was hiding beneath. How she lay in the dark for many hours believing herself to be dead, until she heard another child crying and went with her to find water, not knowing, of course, if the men with the machetes were still waiting. He described the Red Cross hospital, the rows of narrow beds, the unreal calm with which she had answered Silverman's questions, then gone out to sit in the shade of a tree.

'So she is alone?'

'Except for the others like her.'

'No mother and father?'

'Among the victims. Her brothers too.'

Laurencie gave the film back to him. As he returned it to his wallet she stood and walked, hurriedly, towards the café. Through the window Clem saw her pushing open the swing door to the toilets. He wondered if he had upset her; he assumed that he had, and that it had been an easy and shameless trick, a point-scoring trick that proved nothing other than her ownership of a heart more feeling than his own.

He carried the coffee cups inside and waited for her by the toilet door. When she came out they returned together through the marble foyer and into the gardens again. The grounds, merely impressive when they first arrived, had taken on a brief late-afternoon splendour. The fountains played, the birds sang from the trained branches of the trees, and the whole softening world seemed to tremble at the point of melting into a pool of liquid bronze. They walked slowly, pensively, the width of a hand between them, though on the raked gravel of the path their shadows overlapped. Clem said he would be flying home the next day. Laurencie nodded. 'You've finished with us?' she asked.

'I don't know what else I can do here.'

'When the time comes,' she said, 'the police will know where to look for him.'

'For Ruzindana?'

'Of course.'

'No one will hide him?'

'No.'

'The young man?'

'Jean?' She shook her head. 'What will you do in England?' she asked.

'There's lots to do,' he said.

'You'll write about this?'

'I'm not really a writer.'

'You're a photographer with no camera,' she said.

'That's one way of putting it.'

She smiled. 'Is there another way?'

They drove back to the city in her car, an old Peugeot she drove well. Emile was waiting outside his piano teacher's house. He had a brightly coloured music satchel over his shoulder. When the car pulled up he clambered on to the back seat. Clem reached around and shook the boy's hand.

'Good morning,' said the boy, in English.

'Good afternoon,' said Clem.

'He learns at school,' said Laurencie. 'He always wants to practise.'

'Then let's speak English,' said Clem. 'I'm sure you speak some.'

'I could not do my job unless.' Her voice in English

seemed entirely different. Emile clapped his hands in pleasure at hearing her.

'We are shops!' he cried.

'Shopping,' said Laurencie. 'Yes. I have to buy food. I will leave you in a street near the hotel.'

'I don't mind shopping,' said Clem.

'Mind?'

'I like it,' he said. 'I like shopping.'

She laughed. 'A man who likes shopping!'

'Is it OK?'

'As it pleases you,' she said, pulling out into the road.

They went to a local supermarket. A man inside a smoked-glass booth read out the special offers of the day. Emile pushed the trolley. Clem tested him on the names of the groceries Laurencie picked from the shelves. 'And this?' he asked.

'It is the chicken.'

'And this?'

'It is the egg!'

Clem carried the bags to the car. They drove to Laurencie's apartment block, a grey substantial building in a grey stone street. 'It looks nice,' said Clem. They were speaking French again.

'Not so great inside,' she said.

'Am I far from the hotel here?'

She shook her head. 'Go down on to the avenue. Turn right, then right again on to Toison d'Or. After ten minutes you will see your street.'

'Can you manage the bags?' he asked.

'There is an elevator.'

'Good.'

'Yes.'

'If you want to eat with us,' said Emile, 'we have a lot of food.'

Clem thanked him. 'I have some things to do,' he said. 'Another time?'

The boy shrugged. They shook hands again. Clem turned to Laurencie. 'Right on the avenue?'

'Yes.'

'Then I'll say goodbye.' He thanked her for her help and started walking. When he had crossed the street he looked round in time to see them go through the door into the building. He waited, thinking she might step outside again for some reason, but the door swung slowly shut and they were gone.

On the avenue Louise the shopping day was coming to a close. Heavy traffic edged past the plate-glass windows of fashion emporia where girls in heels, Italian dresses, drew down security grilles and cashed up. Clem stopped at a bar near the place Louise. He ordered a bottle of Leffe and took it to an empty table. The clientele was a dozen middle-aged men in a purple twilight, most, like Clem, at tables on their own. He lit a cigarette. The music was a low-level whining about heartbreak, impossible to listen to but impossible to ignore. He considered getting drunk again but the prospect immediately disgusted him. He left his half-full bottle on the tabletop, left the bar, and crossed the road on to Toison d'Or. Tonight was his last night: surely there was something useful for him to do? Try Silverman again, call Laura. His father too? Then he could sit down with some paper – there were a dozen sheets of writing-paper in a drawer in his room – and fire down some bullet points. One to ten, one to five. He was rolling to a standstill! Rolling like the year itself towards a mid-winter stasis. Vital now that he stay occupied, interested in things. He lengthened his stride, moving in conscious mimicry of the home-bound business types on either side of him, but by the time he turned into the narrow dog-leg of rue Capitaine Crespel he felt as much a ghost as those others for whom, in the end, he had done nothing but distribute a few macabre postcards.

At the hotel they were having a party. Balloons dangled in clusters from arches and door-frames; from the underground breakfast room there came a noise of uninhibited singing. Clem went upstairs and curled on the bed. He tried to sleep but his eyes kept opening to the light. After several minutes he realised the singing was coming closer – men and women's voices echoing from the grey walls as they advanced up the stairs. It was a song they obviously all knew well. Now and then some responsible person tried to hush them, and one of the verses would be whispered, but at the chorus, unable to contain themselves, they burst out again, more vigorously than ever. Clem stood by his door. There was no peephole, no way, short of opening the door, that he could see them. They passed by, inches from him, then sang their way to the next floor and on to the next. The game, perhaps, was to go to the very top and sing from the roof, to serenade the chimney-pots and aerials, the first stars. It was just after six thirty. He went to the bathroom, washed his hair in the sink, cleaned his teeth. He picked up the brown glass vial of his eye medicine and put three drops in either eye. Some of the liquid leaked down his cheeks. He wiped it away with a corner of the towel, then held the vial by the side of his face, raising it a little, lowering it, moving it slowly forwards and slowly back. Healthy eyes have a greater than two-hundred-degree arc of vision: objects slightly to the rear of a line drawn across the front of the eyes should still be apparent. But were they? He could not, with any certainty, say so.

At a store on the chaussée d'Ixelles he bought a bottle of French red, a bottle of white from the cold cabinet. Back on Toison d'Or, then on the avenue, he fixed his attention on the physical. How many cars, what kind of cars. He counted the steps between one street-lamp and the next, counted trees, litter-bins. His plan was to arrive without a plan, to arrive like someone who falls in through a door in the midst of a rainstorm at the start of a story in which almost nothing about the past will be explained.

When he reached her building he found '*KARAMERA*' on the bell panel and rang, leaning his ear by the speaker. He rang again. He thought perhaps he had completely forgotten how to behave with people. He was, he was sure, about to make himself ridiculous.

'Yes?'

'It's me,' he said. 'Clem Glass.'

Silence.

'May I come in?'

He heard her sigh, though it might have been the static in the speaker. 'Laurencie?'

'Fourth floor,' she said.

He rode the lift. The fourth floor was unlit, though a feeble shaft of twilight descended by the wooden stairwell. There were smells of cooking, and the sound of water stuttering through old plumbing. The door opposite Clem swung open. He saw that she had changed out of her dress and put on jeans and a red shirt. 'I brought some wine,' he said.

She glanced at the bag. 'Are you going to ask more questions? If you are going to ask more . . .'

'I came to apologise,' he said. 'To tell you that I know you have nothing to do with this business. That Ruzindana is not your problem.'

'Nor yours,' she said.

'I came to ask you to excuse me,' he said.

'To pardon you?'

'Yes. To pardon me.'

He watched her think it through (think something through); then she turned and walked into the apartment. 'We have a visitor,' she called. Clem followed her into the kitchen. There was a table in the middle of the room with a light over it. Emile was sitting on a chair, reading a comic and swinging his feet. He was pleased to see Clem. He took him to his room to show off the bicycle he had been given for his last birthday, a cherry-red racer propped against the wall underneath a poster of all-time champion Eddie Merckx. Clem, though he knew little about such things and had not ridden a bike in years, could see it was an expensive piece, particularly for a small boy who might have outgrown it by his next birthday. He listened as Emile explained the gearing, the fancy alloys. It was, said Clem, one of the best bikes he had ever seen. He did not ask whose present it had been. He preferred to think it had come from Laurencie, from whatever it was they paid her at the FIA.

In the kitchen she was jointing the chicken they had bought at the supermarket. She used a long knife and a cleaver. She rolled the joints in flour and herbs. There was a smell of hot oil, the papery smell of steaming rice. Clem opened the white wine. He put her glass beside the chopping-board. 'Thank you,' she said.

'Aren't you afraid for your fingers?' he asked.

She shook her head. She had a streak of flour dust on her cheek. Clem sat at the table with Emile. Behind the boy at the back of the kitchen was a doorway covered by a red or red-brown curtain. He talked to Emile about music, bikes, and *bandes dessinées*. Laurencie fried the chicken pieces. The oil spat and bubbled. At a quarter to eight they sat down to eat. Clem poured out more of the wine. The food was good and he said so, three or four times. She asked if he cooked for himself in London. He said that he often wasn't there and when he was he was often too lazy to make anything. Some nights he ate out of tins.

'Like a bear,' she said.

'A bear?'

'We watched a film about bears going through people's rubbish,' she said. 'When they find something in a tin they push their long tongues inside, very carefully.'

Emile giggled.

'That's exactly how it is,' said Clem.

When the meal was over they left the dishes and went through to the living room. There was an upright piano against the wall opposite the window. Emile played a tune on it; Clem applauded; then the three of them sat on the sofa watching television until it was time for Emile to get ready for bed. He came back to the living room in blue and black soccer-strip pyjamas. He said goodnight to Clem in French and in English. Laurencie took the boy to his room to settle him. Clem went to the kitchen. He started the washing-up. Plates, pans, the knife and cleaver.

'That isn't necessary,' she said, finding him at the sink still when she had finished with Emile.

'It's nearly done,' he said. He wiped his hands and turned round. She was standing in the frame of the kitchen door, and he saw again, clearly, what he had first seen as he walked towards her on the pavement outside Une Vue de Mars: her aloneness, and the pride with which she tried to hide it.

'There's some wine left,' he said. 'Enough for a glass each.'

'You should go soon,' she said.

'I know.' He poured the wine into the glasses and they went back to the living room. They sat on the sofa; she left the television on. 'The noise of it helps him to sleep,' she said.

'Does he miss his father much?'

She shrugged. 'He doesn't mention him often. He thinks it will make me sad.'

'Would it?'

'I don't live in the past,' she said.

'And the future?'

'I'm not afraid of it.'

'You were very young when you came here.'

'I was seventeen.'

'That's young.'

'Yes.'

'It must have been difficult.'

'You think you can imagine it?'

'Some, I think.'

'No,' she said. 'You cannot.'

He disagreed, though feared she was right. What could he know about such a thing? Yet it seemed to him that the effort of trying was important, and he told her so.

She asked him about his work. In his answer he concentrated on the early stuff, the comical perils of his apprenticeship; then the good luck of finding himself in a hotel in Lubbock, Texas, at four in the morning sitting across the room from an election-weary Ronald Reagan. After that he had begun to travel, six, seven months of the year.

'To wars?'

He went, he said, where his employers wanted him to go. He had photographed many different things. The horse fair in the Camargue. Riots in Karachi. The Rio Carnival. The blind writer, J. L. Borges. He had photographed a fifteen-year-old Tamil suicide bomber whose explosive belt had failed to detonate. That picture, the girl held up between two soldiers not much older than her, had made the cover of *Time*.

'Her disaster,' said Laurencie, 'was your good fortune.' There was no venom in the remark. He agreed with it.

'You think about the people afterwards?' she asked.

'Sometimes.'

He said nothing about April, stayed years away from it. On the television a sports programme came on. They watched the opening laps of a grand prix, then she switched it off. 'He'll be asleep now,' she said.

'I should go,' said Clem.

She nodded.

He leaned across and kissed her mouth. She put a hand

against his chest as though she would push him away, but didn't. He drew himself closer, caressing her. He began to undo the buttons of her shirt.

'No,' she said, when he reached the third button.

They stood up. She smoothed the front of her shirt. 'Is this what you came for?'

'This?'

'To do this.'

'I came for you,' he said. 'Do you want me to leave?'

She put off the lights in the living room, left the light on in the passage and a small shaded side-light in the kitchen. 'Walk softly,' she said. Her room was towards the front door; the bathroom was on the other side of the passage. She went into the bathroom while Clem waited for her, sitting on the end of her bed. The walls of her room were lilac, the ceiling was white. He began to shake. He stood up and circled the room, pressing his shoulders and arms and looking at the photographs of Emile, the little vase of silk flowers on the dressing-table, the magazines spread on the carpet beside the bed. When she came in she was wearing a Japanese-style robe, blue and white. She had wiped off the little makeup she had had on. Her feet were bare.

'You're still in your clothes,' she said. He undressed, quickly, leaving his clothes on the floor. She stood in front of him, touched his face, his chest. Her hands were cool. She went to the dressing-table and lit a candle of honey-coloured wax, then put off the overhead light and loosened her robe. They lay beside each other on the bed. 'We must be quiet,' she said, 'very quiet.' She took his hand and pressed it between her thighs. He leaned across her, kissing her face, kissing her breasts, feeling her wetness on his fingers as he stroked her. She wanted him to suck hard at her nipples, and made a hushed but joyous sound when he did. They began to build a rhythm together. She was strong. As he went to mount her she pushed him back and straddled him, hanging over him, her breasts swinging between them, her nipples grazing his skin. In the honey-coloured light they stared at each other – a sex trance – as if each hoped to see some evidence of secret life, the soul like a white-bellied carp flick its tail and ripple the surface of the other's gaze. When they grew too vigorous, too noisy, she slowed them down, lapping against him, a fierce smile on her face. He licked the sweat from her neck. Her thighs shone. She clung to him, arched from him, clung to him again, then dug her hand between them and used her own long fingers to hurry on her pleasure, turning her face away and groaning in her throat as though at the recollection of some grievous memory.

For two or three minutes, hearts pounding, they held each other like castaways; then she peeled herself off him, picked up her robe from the floor and went out of the room.

'Leave the candle,' he said, when she came back. She climbed under the covers beside him. 'Did you know we were going to do this?' he asked.

'No,' she said. 'How could I have known? And you?'

'Not really.'

'But you hoped?'

'Yes.' He laughed quietly. 'I hoped.'

His sleep was dreamless, intense. When he woke, the candle was almost done, the flame swaying on its wick, the light over the ceiling like a reflection of water. Laurencie, her eyes wide open, was watching him from her pillow.

'What is it?' he whispered.

From the landing came the hum and clanking of the lift gear. A moment later a key scraped at the lock of the front door. The door was opened, softly shut. Laurencie raised a finger to her lips. Footsteps drew level with the bedroom door, paused for a second, then continued along the passage towards the living room.

'No one,' she whispered.

'No one?'

'A lodger,' she said: *un locataire*. 'Comes late, leaves early.'

The footsteps approached again. A tap ran in the bathroom, a man coughed, the toilet was flushed. Then once more the steps receded towards the rear of the apartment.

Was it not strange that she had failed to mention this before? Where did he sleep, this lodger? Was there a room beyond the living room, a door he had not noticed? He might have asked her but she had shut her eyes and was, apparently, already asleep. With a little flare of jealousy he thought of the young man with the muscles – what had she called him? Jean? Could *he* be the lodger? But why should he be? What reason was there to suppose such a thing? And to have a lodger was a sensible idea if she was only working half-weeks at the FIA, piano lessons to pay for, bicycles. He lay, listening hard, but heard only a soft wash of rain on the window, a car, streets away, reversing. Beneath the sheet he reached for one of her hands and folded it gently in one of his own. She muttered something, his name perhaps. He slept.

The next time he surfaced the candle was out, and for a moment, until he heard the slow to and fro of her breathing, he thought he was back in the quarryman's room at Colcombe and that the fuses had gone again. He slid to his side of the bed and swung his feet to the floor. Naked, he crossed the black room to the black door and into the blackness of the passage, a kind of swimming. When he pulled the cord in the bathroom he flinched at the sudden flood of light. The digital clock on the shelf above the bath said 4:47. He urinated, put down the toilet seat, left the bowl unflushed. He did not know where the passage lights were: he found his way to the kitchen with the light that spilled from the bathroom. The door to the kitchen was shut. He went in, filled a glass with mineral water from the fridge, drank it, then filled it again to take with him to the bedroom. He was almost out of the room, already anticipating being beside Laurencie again, shaping himself to her, when he paused, raised his face and sniffed the air. Cooking smells – the chicken, the oil. A whiff of tobacco. And something else, a scent that had been in the bathroom too but here was stronger.

He went into the passage, peered into the empty living room, then returned to the kitchen. No one, she had told him, no one he needed to think about, but he knew the scent now, had smelt it three days ago in the café by the church of St Boniface. Sweet rum; sweet rum and spices. He set the water on the table and turned to the curtain he had seen behind Emile's head as they had sat talking before supper. Did it move? Did its pleats shiver in some draught? Three quick steps took him to the sink and to the rack where he had stacked the supper dishes. He lifted the cleaver and the boning knife, hesitated, weighing them in the balance of his hands, then put down the cleaver and kept the knife. He crossed to the curtain and stood there, listening. When his blood had settled he gripped an edge of the material between thumb and finger and flicked it back along its rail. Inside, dim but discernible, was a shallow room, an alcove like a monk's cell, a single bed – made-up, unslept in – and a plain wooden chair, the only furniture. No face appeared, no fierce or terrified gaze rising to meet his own, but left on the seat of the chair was a half-devoured bar of chocolate, a book, and a pair of folded spectacles. He stooped and picked up the book, holding it out towards the lamp. It was a copy of the New Testament bound in creased and weathered pasteboard, an edition distributed by a French evangelist organisation with an address in Algiers, the ribbon marker stretched between two pages of the gospel according to John. He read a line – *He who does not dwell in me is thrown away like a withered branch* – then shut the book and reached for the spectacles, but as his fingers touched them he heard once more the soft opening and closing of the front door, and seconds later, the humming into life of the lift gear, the descent ending in a final muted click. He hurried to the kitchen window. All it showed to him was the stair-lights of the neighbouring block flickering beneath a sky of starless indigo. There was no view of the street from there, no glimpse of any figure, exposed, groping his way in the open.

He went back to the little room, to the bed so like his

father's on the island, or Silverman's 'dream of discipline' in Toronto. He sat on the blanket, the knife against the skin of his thigh, and turned the spectacles in his hands, examining them, the heavy frames, the unwiped lenses. Then, very cautiously, as though there might be some real danger in the contact, he raised them to his face and tried them on, blinking at the kitchen, the slewed table, the muddled play of shadow across the tiled floor. He had no idea, of course, what was wrong with the Bourg-mestre's vision – he had no good idea of what was wrong with his own – but after a minute or more of feeling the little muscles around his eyes slacken and tauten, his sight began to adjust. Things seemed clearer.

Part Four

3.01 *The totality of true thoughts is a picture of the world.*

Wittgenstein, *Tractatus Logico-philosophicus*

24

A last hymn ('Jerusalem') then the vicar with his vicar's voice, then the little organ playing the march. The doors opened: Frankie and Ray stepped into the shadow of the tower. Above them the gold hands of the blue-faced clock pointed to half past four. The photographer, a plump veteran with teeth the colour of onion skin, teetered on a chair and called shrilly that he couldn't see the people at the sides. 'You're all family now,' he shouted. 'Squeeze up, squeeze in.' He counted to three and fired the flash; fired it again. Everyone streamed down the churchyard steps. William Glass, in one of the suits he used to wear to work in Filton, slipped on a mush of damp leaves. Clem helped him up; Laura brushed off the back of his jacket. The Alfa with its yards of ribbon was parked on the road. The day was mild enough to have the hood down. Frankie started the car. Kenneth, primed, flung the first confetti, then a dozen others reached into bags or pockets and drew out fistfuls of blue and pink petals. As the car raced away the petals scattered from the back of it, a pink and blue cloud that fell on to the muddy road, on to verge and hedgerow.

Clem unlocked the doors of the old Volvo and let in Laura and his father. Fiacc's van was parked behind them. Clare waved to Clem through the windscreen; he waved back, climbed into the Volvo and spent ten minutes trying to coax the engine into life. They were the last to leave, the last to arrive at the house. By the time he found a space on the drive and Laura had rocked herself off the car's high leather seats, the hired four-piece in the marquee had launched into an upbeat cover of 'Non je ne regrette rien'. Inside the tent several couples were already dancing. These were mostly Frankie's friends, the men in jeans and white linen jackets, the women swirling in long, vibrantly coloured dresses. Whoopers and huggers, vodka drunks, heavy smokers, poets, social-security fraudsters. A slightly fragile-looking crowd descending into middle age with whatever defiance their narrowing means afforded them. Ray's crowd was no crowd at all. His mother was there and two other women of similar age. Also, a wall-eyed girl with a cold, and a young man with a heavy fringe, the badge on his lapel reading 'Destined for Greatness (but taking my time)'. The best man was Greek, though other than Ray, who treated him with considerable deference, no one seemed to know the first thing about him.

Down one side of the marquee were trestle tables with ranks of green bottles, Paris goblets, tins of beer. Two schoolgirls in white shirts – who had found these girls? – carried plates of mini Scotch eggs, smoked salmon on squares of brown bread, sausages on sticks. Clem found chairs for his father and Clare. Fiacc kept her distance, standing with a tumbler of mineral water at the far side of the dancers.

The speeches were short. Laura spoke sweetly about Frankie. About Ray, she said, she had had some doubts but she had been wrong. Ray was a good man and – she laughed – an incorrigible optimist. She asked people to drink a toast to Frankie's father, Ronny; a second toast for Frankie's aunt, her own dear sister, Nora. She dried her eyes with a bud of pink tissue. Frankie stood up to embrace her; everyone sighed and clapped. The best man spoke as though he had trained at some school of classical oratory. He stroked his beard, evoked the relevant gods, quoted Aesop, was charming and little understood. Ray thanked everyone. He said he was the living proof that wonderful things could happen to the most unpromising people. No one, he said, should give up on love: all hearts were visited in time. On the practical front they had, with Mrs Harwood's help, finally secured a mortgage for the flat in Poplar. They would be moving in before Christmas. Anyone who knew how to wield a paintbrush was welcome to visit. He took Frankie's hand and limped from the pallet stage on to the flattened grass. The band played 'Summertime' as though it were jive, but with Frankie in his arms Ray swayed to a tempo entirely his own.

Clem saw Jane Crawley by the entrance to the marquee. She was alone. He went over to her and said hello.

'Can I get you a drink?' he asked.

She shook her head. 'I can't stay. Will you tell Laura that I was here?'

'Of course.'

'Thank you.'

'Have you seen Clare?' he asked. 'At the surgery, I mean.'

'I saw her last week.'

'You think she's doing well?'

'Exceptionally well.'

'She couldn't have managed a party like this when we first came down.'

'No. She couldn't.'

'And you think it will go on?'

'What?'

'Her recovery.'

'If she's careful.'

'Looks after herself?'

'Yes.'

She smiled at him; he smiled back. He wondered if she had forgotten about his eyes or simply considered herself to be off-duty. He was not, of course, even a patient of hers, not officially. 'I've been away,' he said.

'Laura told me. Was it a success?'

'Nothing happened,' he said.

'You didn't find the man you were looking for?'

'Not in the end.'

'A pity.'

He asked again if she would have something to drink.

'I have to go,' she said. 'There's someone waiting for me.'

Clem walked her out of the marquee and watched as she slipped between the parked cars, turned at the gate, and disappeared. For some seconds he felt her absence very sharply, as though he had lost sight of the one person – the last? – who might help him. Then he entered the tent again, took a bottle of red wine from a trestle table, and went to where his father and Clare were sitting together holding hands like lovers.

He poured the wine. They drank to each other's health. Clare excused herself and left to find Fiacc. The band played a can-can. A line was formed and people kicked up their legs.

'She's not such an ogress,' said Clem's father.

'Who?' asked Clem.

'Finola Fiacc. Not quite the Amazon I'd expected.'

'No,' said Clem. 'And if Clare likes her . . .'

'They do seem very close, don't they?'

Clem glanced at the side of his father's face but saw that nothing had been intended, nothing wry or louche. For a moment he was tempted to say it baldly, your daughter's an invert, a tribade, a follower of Sappho, but the fact was he had no real evidence for it, nor did he wish for any. Clare, though not yet fully herself again, was something very close to it, and whatever helped her (besides Boswell's drugs), whatever category of the intimate, he welcomed it. When the music was calmer they danced together.

'You know,' she said, 'I was dreading this but now I'm actually enjoying myself.'

'That's good.'

'And Daddy seems to be surviving it.'

'I think so.'

'And Laura.'

'Yes.'

'I don't think you told me everything about your trip,' she said.

'Did you want everything?'

'I'd like to know if I'm supposed to feel guilty about it.'

'You're not.'

'Finola wanted to help you. Though I told her off for making such a piece of theatre out of it.'

He smiled. 'I would have heard about the arrest sooner or later.'

'So we're all right?'

'Yes.'

'Promise?'

He promised.

'I just want you to be happy, Clem,' she said.

Midnight was announced with a crash of cymbals. Frankie and Ray left the party. There was no honeymoon planned – they needed the money for Poplar – but it had been decided they would spend their first night in the privacy of the cottage. Clare and Fiacc had moved up to Laura's where the old rooms had all been dusted and aired and put to service again. Everyone gathered around the Alfa. There was a last long hug from Laura, a cheer from the guests, then the car swept down the drive, past the concrete boy (who wore tonight a wreath of ivy) and into the lane, the clattering of tins clearly audible for the two minutes it took them to arrive at the cottage. Another cheer, half satirical, then the circle broke and people wandered away, some to the house, some to the marquee, some into the garden where a score of candle-lanterns flickered daintily in the darkness.

The weekend after the wedding Clem was back in Somerset, this time to help shut up the cottage. Clare and Fiacc were going to Dundee. The mattresses, the pots and pans, the desk and the lamps, were carried to their old places and stored again in rooms and cupboards where they could continue the slow disappearing that the summer had briefly interrupted. The painting of the bread and cherries went back on to its hook on the landing; the garden tools were returned to the garage; the fridge was emptied and switched off; the mains switch under the stairs put to the off position; the fire grate swept; the windows closed. They checked drawers, carried out the cases, an almost forgotten mug, a black bin-bag. Laura came down to lock the cottage doors and to inspect the progress of the crack on the side of the building. In places she could slip the width of two fingers inside it. She said the sooner the place collapsed the happier she would be. It was, she complained, like waiting for the other shoe to drop.

Two days later, Frank Silverman called. There had been a message from him on the answerphone when Clem arrived home from Belgium, a call it had seemed then easier not to return. 'How is it,' said Silverman, 'we make such a hash of staying in touch with each other?' He had heard from Shelley-Anne that Clem was in Brussels. Belatedly ('I listen to strictly local news these days. I listen to the city gossiping about itself') he had discovered the reason for his being there. He had even, he claimed, considered flying over, and might have done it if he could have found someone else to collect from the restaurants, set up the kitchen, serve there and do the hundred and one other damn things that needed doing. He said he assumed Clem appreciated that. Clem said that he did. 'So,' said Silverman. 'Tell it from the beginning. All of it. Slowly.'

Where *was* the beginning? For lack of a better, Clem started with Fiacc driving down from Dundee with a cutting from the *Scotsman* in her coat pocket. Then Kirsty Schneider, the FIA, Laurencie Karamera, the meeting at the café. Several times Silverman made Clem loop back, be clearer, give details, state not just impressions but facts. He wanted to know who the young man was, how he fitted in. He wanted to know if Clem was sure, one hundred per cent sure, that the older man at Une Vue de Mars had indeed been Ruzindana.

'Any chance at all that you were hoodwinked? Why would he ask if you had been "blessed" with children? What the fuck did that mean?'

'Apparently his sons died at one of the camps.'

'Apparently?'

'It's what Laurencie Karamera said.'

'And how would she know?'

'I don't know that she did.'

'You don't?'

'I don't know exactly what she knew. How much.'

'Did you check out what she does at the FIA? Who does she lobby for? Someone's government? For all you know she works for the Belgian Sûreté. And why oh why didn't you take someone along to the café who could independently confirm Ruzindana's identity? Then you would have had a story.'

'I was told to come alone.'

'You went in there blind!'

'Blind?'

'And maybe fouled it up for someone else.'

'Someone who would have known what they were doing?'

'Yes! Jesus! I don't know what I'm getting so pissed about. It brings stuff back, I guess. I'm sorry.'

'Forget it,' said Clem. He mentioned the trip out to Tervuren, but not the trip back, and certainly not the night-moves that followed at the apartment. He did not want to hear any clever remarks about Laurencie Karamera falling for him a little too easily, a little too quickly, or how, by sleeping with her, he had fatally compromised his objectivity. As for the lodger – could he ever persuade Silverman that anyone had been there at all? The man in the café had been Sylvestre Ruzindana: he did not need any witness to confirm it. But the man in the apartment? He had thought he knew, so sure indeed that he had not even stayed to interrogate Laurencie (an omission he could not possibly confess to), afraid that it would force her to lie to him, that he would see fear or shame on her freshly woken face. Or triumph. Contempt. At first light, released from his trance of sitting, he had replaced the boning knife on the rack, retrieved his clothes from the bedroom, dressed, and walked to his hotel along shining carpets of hosed-down pavement, trying to work out why she had taken such a risk, and hoping that he himself was at least part of the answer.

Silverman made pondering noises, digesting information noises. He was not irritable any more. He mused and maundered and, from the tip of the satellite antenna twenty thousand miles over Clem's head, certain key words dropped like rainwater from a twig – Hope, Sincerity, Closure, Beauty . . . Then, in a kind of vocal spasm, the phrase, 'If people would only *embrace* each other!'

'How's Shelley-Anne?' asked Clem.

'Shelley-Anne?' Silverman quoted his wife's judgement that Clem had been strung-out when he called her. 'Pie-eyed was how she put it.' Clem admitted it. He could not, he said, remember what they had talked about but he remembered liking her.

'Me too,' said Silverman. 'I haven't given up on anything. There are still things I need to do up here. But later . . .'

'The people in the station? What became of them?'

'All of them out. All due to have their cases heard in the next couple of weeks. Prospect of positive decisions is strong. The boy's been getting some medical help, gratis. I'm teaching them a little English and showing them the wonders of my native land.'

'Niagara?'

'Yeah, we've done the Falls. They nearly died of pleasure. And this will make you laugh. I'm going to open an office here. Got my eye on a building in Cabbage Town. Thought I might call it the Maggie Peterson Centre. What do you think?'

Clem said he liked it.

'Not too grand?'

'Not at all.'

'We're getting some interest. We're even getting some funding.'

'I'm pleased.'

'We'll put this other stuff behind us now. OK? I admire what you tried to do out there, in darkest Belgium. But leave the rest to the tribunal.'

'I intend to.'

'It's finished, Clem.'

'I know.'

'Dust those cameras off!'

'I will.'

'There's still a lot that's worth doing. That's what I've been learning.'

'You're right.'

'It's over for us.'

'I know.'

'It's over.'

'It's over.'

'Yeah, it's over now.'

In October, Clare started again at the university. *I'll only be doing a few hours*, she explained in a letter she sent to Clem in the middle of the month. *It's really about keeping my hand in, staying in touch, feeling useful.* There were, she said, bad days still and bad nights, and she was never quite without the fear that the illness would close over her head again, but she thought she was managing, and managing was what counted. She wanted to thank him for his help. He had been a good brother and a good friend. He had been kind to her; she wouldn't forget it. What was he doing at Christmas? Had he made any plans? Finola – this as a hurried postscript – sent him her best.

Clem took to roaming again. Places he had walked in his shirtsleeves in May and June he walked now in his overcoat, sometimes with the sense that the streets he passed fell away behind him into heaps of mortar and dust as though he were some Hindu god of destruction. He was drinking more and eating less. At the end of the month he spent a week in bed with a viral complaint that started in his guts with three-a.m. retching and ended in his lungs, a cough like a fox's bark that he couldn't shake off.

Patsy Stellenbosch from the agency rang wanting to know if he was available for a job. He told her there were family commitments still, family problems. 'It's November,' she said. 'It's been a long time.' He suggested Toby

Rose. 'We'd rather have you,' she said. He said he was sorry. 'You call us,' she said, 'and tell us when you want to be a photographer again.'

Ray and Frankie moved to Poplar. They sent Clem a photocopied picture of their building, a pencilled arrow to distinguish their flat from the identical ones above and below. On the back of the picture was an invitation to the house-warming in December, the message ending with a jovial upper-case reminder for guests to bring their own food and drink.

His father phoned with the news that Simon Truelove had died. He had been ninety-four years old. As old as the century! He had fought at the battle of Amiens in the first war and served as a volunteer fireman throughout the second. He had stood as an independent in several national elections and, though never elected, never lost his deposit. 'A very considered life,' said his father. 'A considerable one too in its way. No regrets there, I think.'

By the end of the first week in December Clem was out of money. The bank, having allowed him a sizeable overdraft, changed its tactics from writing him polite but firm letters to calling him regularly at home. He sold the Leica ('A lovely piece,' said the man in the shop. 'A beautiful weight to it.'). He was paid fifteen hundred in cash. Five hundred he gave to the bank, the rest he put into a drawer in the kitchen. He started looking for somewhere much cheaper to live. After three days he found a place on the Harrow Road, thirty minutes' walk from his flat on the Grove. The neighbourhood reminded him of places he had photographed on assignment. A zone of workers' houses and small, half-empty shops, of plundered and burned-out cars; a place mostly missed by the Blitz and later put at the service of traffic, an arterial road much used by emergency vehicles. In the cafés, Portuguese men, owners of some residual Latin dignity, watched satellite television and sipped at little coffees. Clem's new landlord was Portuguese. His name was Leonardo. He looked at all the things that did not work in the flat as though, moments before, they had all worked perfectly. He took a screwdriver from his pocket and made what adjustments he could. He made a list with a stub of pencil. 'Don't worry about the pigeons,' he said. 'I'm going to poison them.'

Clem wrote a note to Frankie and Ray excusing himself from the house-warming. A few days later he sent a card to Clare (robin with a sprig of mistletoe in its beak) saying he would probably be out of the country at Christmas. His card from her (*Byzantine Madonna*, artist unknown) said she was sorry she wouldn't be seeing him but understood that work must come first. She thought she might go abroad herself. Ireland perhaps, or one of those Italian hill towns he had read to her about in Colcombe.

On the twenty-second of the month the Bourgmestre was arrested in Brussels. Clem heard it on the radio, the early-evening news. A spokeswoman for the Belgian government said that though it was, of course, a matter for the courts, she did not anticipate any difficulties with the extradition. Ruzindana would stay in custody until his hearing in the New Year. Belgium was committed to the principle of international justice, and those who stood accused of heinous crimes could not escape simply by crossing borders. For Ruzindana, his lawyer said it was a clear case of mistaken identity. His client was a victim of malicious accusations. He was innocent and in poor health and wished only to be with his family again.

Christmas Eve was cold and clear. Clem drank in the pub opposite the church. The old priest came in for his whisky and hot water, then crossed the road to take the midnight service. Clem reeled home, looked for more drink in the kitchen, found a quarter-bottle of dark rum and woke, Christmas dawn, lying on the carpet, a glass of rum untouched by his elbow. Over the holidays he packed up his flat. On 2 January he hired a van and made two trips to the Harrow Road, carrying the boxes up the stairs and leaving them in a pile on the floor of his new living room. The man who lived downstairs was called Mehmet. He helped Clem to carry his bookshelves, the parts of his desk, his mattress. Clem unpacked boxes until three in the morning, then lay on the unassembled bed listening to night buses, police cars, the all-night cooing of the pigeons. He heard Mehmet go out while it was still dark. He slept and came to at noon, lurching into consciousness as though the house were tipping sideways, crumbling into some dripping black seam below.

There were boxes in the kitchen too. He unpacked what he needed and pushed the rest into the corners. Beneath the kitchen window was an asphalt garage roof where pigeons gathered like commuters, their feathers puffed against the cold. Sometimes the birds huddled on his window-sill. One morning he tried to sketch them but the drawings looked childish and he threw them away.

In late January the weather became bitter: keeping the flat warm turned out to be impossible. Leonardo visited and tapped the failing boiler with the handle of his screwdriver. He told Clem about his daughter who had just qualified as a dental surgeon. Did Clem know what a dentist could earn? Clem congratulated him. Leonardo said the cold weather wouldn't last. Clem agreed. He started wearing his coat indoors, slept in his clothes. When it was too cold to stay inside he joined the men in the café watching television. He had an odd and contradictory sense of time, believing that he had almost slipped outside of it, but that also time was running out for him at a rate he would be wise to be very alarmed by. He wondered if he should call Kirsty Schneider and find out what had happened at the extradition hearing in Brussels, then realised he was no longer greatly interested in the tribunal's version of justice. The tribunal was there to say that men like Ruzindana were aberrations, cancerous cells that could, with the scalpel of the law, be cut out to leave the patient in perfect health. The tribunal would argue that someone like Ruzindana was meaningless, a freak of nature, a freak of culture.

In the kitchen, sitting on a stool inherited from a previous tenant, he started to write things down. He wrote on a lined pad. The paper piled up by his left elbow. He wrote about Nora and blindness, Clare and sanity. He wrote about Nora's death, the funeral cars oozing like black molasses through the narrow street outside the house. He wrote about Zara, about the little prostitute with the white slippers, about Frank Silverman and Shelley-Anne, Laurencie Karamera and Emile. He wrote about his photographs – the president's exhausted gaze, the Tamil girl balletic and heartbroken between her captors, the crowds in Karachi dispersed by monsoon rain. He wrote about Odette, little Odette Semugeshi in her blue pinafore, who might have healed them all. He hoped that if he wrote enough he would discover a piece of evidence to contradict what now suggested itself as the fitting conclusion, an outcome of logic, irresistible. He wrote for days, but under his nib the words squirmed. Language was not complaint: it had its own agendas and grew more interested in itself the more he used it, its truths all at curious angles to his own.

He bought another pad and wrote a story in which he took the voice of one of the men on Géricault's raft. He started at the moment they were cut adrift in the surf, everyone yelling uselessly as the raft was swept further and further out. Then the fear, the fighting, the onset of disease, the sick pushed into the sea at night. The tyranny of the strong, the tyranny of the weak. The vertigo of self-knowledge.

The character Clem chose for his narrator was the man who sat with covered head at the back of the raft, the philosopher with the young man's corpse across his knees. Soon his appetite will overcome his disgust and he will suck at the dead youth's bones, lash out at those who try to steal them from him. He does not scan the horizon any more: he cannot bear the thought of their being rescued. Found, they and their revolting craft would be a source of infection, a spiritual cholera, a blight on hope. He longs for a second storm, fiercer than the first. And when he hears the look-out's shout, a cry that must have seemed to climb a mile straight up into the empty sky, what then? He laughs? Flings himself into the maw of the next wave?

The story was only a few pages long, and though clearly there was something wrong with it, it satisfied him more than the other writing had. He copied it out, neatly, and put the pad away. Through the kitchen window the clouds were motionless and dirty grey. He left the flat. He wasn't sure of the time but guessed it was mid-afternoon. He was passing the cemetery before he realised he had forgotten his scarf and gloves. He pressed his hands into his pockets. London was a city made of iron. His feet rang on the paving-stones. Even his breath was a grey metal, beaten fine. At the junction with Kilburn Lane he turned right, paused by the canal, then crossed the railway bridge and came on to the Grove. At his old address he let himself into the house with a key he had kept. Mail was piled on the hall floor, most for people who would never return for it. There were several letters for him and a postcard with a photograph of a harbour on it. The letters were bills or circulars, except one, a small brown NHS envelope that contained, he supposed, the date of his appointment at the eye hospital. This and the postcard he put into a pocket of his coat. He shut the front door and went down to the road again. A light, indecisive snow had begun to fall. Outside the church, fresh flowers, roses on long stems, the blooms so red they looked as though the colour could be squeezed from them like a juice, had been threaded behind the neck and knees of the wooden Christ. Clem broke his step to admire them, then walked on beneath the Westway flyover and up the slope to the old police station beside Holland Park Avenue. Steps at the side of the station led to a small reception area. There was no one at the front desk. He waited. After a few minutes a woman sergeant came out.

Clem said he wanted to speak with someone from CID.

'What about?' she asked.

He said he had some information. She looked at him for a moment then told him to take a seat. There were three others waiting, and Clem had the impression they were people whose lives had brought them to that place before, perhaps many times. He unbuttoned his coat and took the postcard from his pocket. It was from Clare. The harbour was at Cork. Finola Fiacc's family lived in the nearby countryside and Clare had been staying with them. They were, she had written, *just as you probably imagine them*. His name was called. He stood up.

'I'm DC Kelly,' said the man. He led Clem to a door at the back of the reception area. He tapped a number into a keypad, opened the door and stood back to let Clem pass. They sat across a table from each other. Kelly was pale and dark-eyed. His hair was cropped close to his skull. There was something of the convalescent about him. He looked at Clem with the same assessing stare the sergeant had used. He asked Clem what his information was. Clem said he had come about the rape of the Spanish girl in June. The detective waited. 'What about it?' he asked.

'I did it,' said Clem.

'Did what?'

'The rape.'

'You're confessing to a rape?'

'Yes.'

The detective sucked in his cheeks. He opened a drawer in the table and took out a sheet of paper and a pen. He looked at his watch and made a note of the time. He asked for Clem's full name and address and wrote these down. 'So who was she, this Spanish girl?'

'I don't know her name,' said Clem.

'And the offence took place last June?'

'Yes.'

'Where?'

'On Portobello Road.'

'In a house?'

'On the street.'

'Right.'

There was a telephone on the wall. The detective made a short call, then, quite casually it seemed to Clem, arrested him. He asked if he wanted to contact a lawyer. Clem said he didn't. A young uniformed constable came in. Kelly stood up with the paper he had been writing on and left the room. Clem asked if he could smoke. The young police-man took a saucer from the desk drawer and put it on the table. Clem lit up. There was a window high on the opposite wall through which he could see the sky. Already it seemed to be half night. Kelly was gone for twenty minutes. Clem wondered if he would find some record of his assault on Paulus. When he came back he was carrying a file. He sat down, put the file on the table and opened it.

'Let's be clear,' he said. 'You're telling me that you raped this Spanish girl?'

'Yes,' said Clem. 'Shouldn't you be recording this?'

'Louisa de Castro.'

'That's her name?'

Kelly nodded. 'A nine-nine-nine call was made from a mobile phone at twenty-three fifty on the twenty-fifth of June. Her phone. A male reported that a woman had been assaulted. He gave an address on the Portobello Road but didn't give his name. Do you know who made that call?'

'No.'

'You're sure?'

'Yes.'

With the young constable on one side and Kelly on the other, they walked Clem across Reception and through a security door into the rear of the station. The female sergeant Clem had spoken to when he first arrived took him into custody. He emptied his pockets on to a table, signed a form, said again that he did not want a lawyer. Kelly left them. The sergeant and the constable took Clem down to a cell. It smelt strongly of bleach. He sat on the bed. The door was swung shut. He lay down. The man in the next cell was singing, a slurred lamenting that grew briefly raucous, then trailed off into silence. Clem wished they hadn't taken away his cigarettes and lighter. He shut his eyes, opened them again, squinted at the light shining from behind its mesh of protective wire in the cell roof.

After three hours the door was unlocked. Kelly came in with the file in his hand. Clem stood up.

'Louisa de Castro,' said the detective, 'has gone back to Spain.' He consulted the file. 'To a place called Burgos to be exact.'

Clem nodded. Burgos. For an instant, a whole and wholly imagined city appeared in front of him, with sombre churches and little squares in brilliant sunshine.

'In July,' said Kelly, 'she was at a language school. The Charles Dickens Institute or some such bollocks. Anyway, one hot night having had a bit too much of the sangria she fights with boyfriend Carlos, and being from a more vocal and expressive culture than our own it all gets very over-excited. Following?'

'Yes,' said Clem.

'There was no rape,' said Kelly. 'There was a very embarrassed Spanish teenager with an almighty hangover. But there was no rape.' He paused. 'Come here,' he said.

Clem stepped forward. Kelly stood him with his back to the cell wall, then leaned an elbow by the side of his face. 'You didn't rape Louisa de Castro,' he said quietly, 'because nobody raped her. You've been winding me up, Clement. Sending me on the proverbial. Which means I now have to decide whether to charge you with wasting police time, though if I charge you I'm going to waste even more time and frankly I don't have it to waste.' He moved away from Clem and for fifteen or twenty seconds frowned at a corner of the cell roof.

'Tears,' he said, looking back at his prisoner. 'Now who are those for? Not for Louisa de Castro. She doesn't need them. For you? For me?' He shook his head. 'I understand you better than you think, Clement. You're what I call a sins-of-the-world type. Obsessed with thoughts of moral chaos. Everyone guilty because everyone's the same. All of us with the mark of Cain on our brows. Confessing gives you some relief. Am I right? Pricks the boil? Yeah. It might amaze you, Clement, but I've thought about it too. I *see* things here, you see. Real rapists, real murderers. People who do appalling and disgusting things to other people. And when I go home at night I sometimes wonder about the man in the shaving mirror, if he's the same or different. Then I make the distinction. I sleep like a baby. I wake up and I go to work. I make myself useful. What is it you do for a living, Clement?'

'I take pictures.'

'A photographer?'

'Yes.'

'Any good?'

'I have been.'

The detective nodded. 'If I see you back here again it's going to be unpleasant. You keep looking for trouble you're going to find it. OK?' He turned and left the cell. The female sergeant escorted Clem back up the stairs. She gave him the bag containing his possessions, told him he was being de-arrested and handed him a card with the telephone number of Social Services on it. He signed for his things and followed the sergeant through Reception to the door of the station. It was still snowing. He could see the flakes silhouetted against the finely serrated haloes of the street-lamps. He buttoned his coat, turned up the collar. There was almost no one outside on such a night. He passed the Underground station, the fly-over, the church. As he drew level with the metal house, the substance abusers' old home, he stopped, suddenly unsure that he could go any further. He gripped the railings, then staggered up the little path and sat on the house-steps, his back to the steel door. After several attempts he managed to light a cigarette. The snow was heavier but softer, large flakes feathery against his cheeks. He sighed, shuddered. He began to cry again: warm, sticky, salty tears, running down the sides of his nose. He still could not have answered the detective's question, could not have said who he was crying for. Himself, he thought; himself alone. He wiped his eyes, inhaled, to the roots of his lungs, the metallic coldness of the night air. Something seemed to shiver out of him. He was very sober, very awake. He tilted back his head and let the snow fall on his closed eyes, on to his lips, into his mouth. His mind, which in recent months he had exhausted uselessly, began to feel like a spreading room in which at last some light, a clean snow-light, was rising. He was not a criminal. He was not a saint. He could not take refuge any more in the purity of extreme positions. And though the meaning of the massacre at N— remained confounding, a shape rendered against a brilliant and unremitting light-field impossible to stare at, he thought he had reached a point where he might be able to work from some slight but useful faith in himself, some small, stubborn belief in the others.

He rubbed a little warmth into his fingers, then took from his wallet the three transparencies – Odette, the Bourgmestre, the classroom wall – pressing them gently into the snow between his boots as though on to the white page of an album. Within a minute they were covered; in another minute completely buried. He stood up, beating the snow from his coat. The morning papers would speak of a blizzard, a white-out: dawn would show the whole of London beautifully unlike itself. Clem, with his eyes narrowed against the darting flakes, turned out of the gate, a tall figure crossing the girdered railway bridge, crossing the canal, then turning at the cemetery wall and bending into the fiercer gusts of snow there, his footfall inaudible under the sweep of the wind, his footsteps, like a blood trail or the winding spoor of something hunted, slowly filling in behind him.

AUTHOR'S NOTE

The massacre at N— is based on a well-documented atrocity in Rwanada in 1994. This novel, however, is not about the Rwandan genocide and was never intended to be so. Readers wanting to remind themselves of what took place in Rwanda might like to look at Fergal Keane's book *Season of Blood* or Philip Gourevitch's equally powerful *We wish to inform you that tomorrow we will be killed with our families.*

The John Berryman poem Frank Silverman begins to quote to Clem in Toronto is from 'Dream Song 1'. The lines Clem finds in Silverman's article about the massacre are from 'Dream Song 29' by the same poet.

The author gratefully acknowledges the support of the Villa Waldberta in Bavaria and of the Santa Maddalena Foundation in Tuscany where, in the course of consecutive summers, one stormy and one benign, much of this novel was written.